IF ONLY

(THE INN AT SUNSET)

CW00558050

SOPHIE LOVE

ISBN: 978-1-63291-966-3

CHAPTER ONE

The ring was more beautiful than Emily remembered. A twisting band of silver was interwoven with blue that reminded her of the ocean. A family of pearls nestled together. It was gorgeous, unique, and so utterly perfect.

A snowflake landed on Emily's hand, bringing her back to the moment. She glanced at Daniel, still down on one knee on the beach, black waves crashing behind him, stars twinkling above him, sand clinging to his pant legs. Tears glittered in his eyes and Emily felt her own eyes well up in response. She couldn't move, couldn't stand. The only thing she wanted to do was hold Daniel and never let go.

She wrapped her arms around his neck and pulled his body close to hers, kissing the exposed flesh on his neck over and over again and then winding her fingers into his hair.

"I'm so in love with you," she whispered.

"I love you more than words can say," Daniel replied, breathlessly. Then, with a small laugh, he added, "You're shivering."

Emily giggled too, feeling girlish, carefree. "That would be the snow," she said.

They finally pulled apart. Daniel grasped Emily's hand and pulled her to standing.

"Should we head back?" he asked.

Emily thought of the Thanksgiving party taking place in her B&B at this very moment. Practically the whole town was congregated there; surely her and Daniel's absence would have been noted by now. But she didn't want to go back. Not yet. She wanted to stay here with Daniel in this perfect moment for as long as possible.

Emily shook her head and rubbed the goose pimples on her arms. "Can't we stay here a bit longer?"

Daniel smiled tenderly. "Of course." He wrapped her in his arms. Together they rocked back and forth, as though dancing to music only they could hear.

"I can't wait to tell Chantelle," Daniel murmured after a while.

At the mention of Daniel's daughter, Emily felt a sudden surge of excitement. The little girl would be so happy for them. Suddenly, the idea of getting back to the B&B seemed much more appealing. Emily desperately wanted to see Chantelle's face when they broke

1

the news. It would be like a fairytale ending for the child who'd had such a terrible start in life.

"Come on, let's head back," Emily said, moving out of the embrace and taking both of Daniel's hands in hers.

"You sure?" he asked.

She nodded. Breaking the news of their engagement to Chantelle was now Emily's greatest desire. She was feeling suddenly confident and proud, and she wanted the whole world to know it. She wanted to stand on the widow's walk of her inn and shout the news across town so everybody could hear for miles around.

But as they strolled along the beach in the direction of the B&B, Emily felt her nerves begin to creep up on her. Making announcements wasn't exactly her favorite thing to do, and there would surely be no way to sneak in without people questioning their absence. That's not even to mention the ring. It was hardly inconspicuous. Anyone with eyes could see it sparkle from a mile away.

Emily couldn't help but imagine all of those faces gazing at her, some with supportive expressions but others with judgmental ones. Right now, their engagement belonged to her and Daniel and no one else. It was a private thing, a shared state of bliss. But as soon as they broke the news to others they would be inviting opinions into that sacred space.

Perhaps it wouldn't be like that at all, Emily thought as she strolled. Maybe the townsfolk would have been liberal with the mimosas in their absence and would all be so engrossed with their drinking, dancing, and merriment that they wouldn't even notice them return.

They reached the small path that led from the beach up to the street where they lived. Emily climbed up the steep bank first, Daniel following. As she emerged through the trees onto the sidewalk, she could see the lights of the inn glowing and hear the sounds of music and laughter floating through the air. Butterflies fluttered in her stomach.

"Ready?" Daniel asked as he drew up beside her.

Emily took a deep breath. She was nervous but also felt more confident than ever, like she could take on the world.

Hand in hand, they slowly walked along the drive, past the carriage house that was once Daniel's home, then up the porch steps and in through the front door of the Inn at Sunset Harbor. Immediately, warmth and brightness enveloped them. The comforting smells of Thanksgiving foods—turkey, cranberries,

2

corn, pumpkin pie—permeated the air. Emily instantly felt the love ebbing through the inn.

Just then, a laughing Serena burst out of the dining room and into the hallway. When she saw Daniel and Emily standing there, she smiled at them through her ruby red–painted lips. She was blushing a little, and Emily wondered if it had something to do with an evening of reciprocated flirting with Owen the piano player.

"Oh hey," Serena said, catching Emily's eye. "I was wondering where you guys had gone off to."

Emily and Daniel looked at each other coyly. Caught red-handed.

Emily found that she was suddenly tongue-tied, like a naughty child who must own up to stealing cookies from the jar. She looked at Daniel for help, but he looked worse than her, with a deer-in-the-headlights expression on his face.

Serena frowned. Then she narrowed her eyes suspiciously and a small smirk appeared on her lips. Clearly she could tell they'd been up to something.

"Hmm," she said, pacing up to them like a detective. "Snow in your hair. Sand on your jeans. My guess is you've been to the beach." She tapped her chin. "But why?" She paused for a moment, and then a look of realization flickered into her eyes. Gasping, she grabbed Emily's left hand, searching for confirmation for the thought that had hit her. At the sight of the ring, her eyes widened and her mouth dropped open.

"Oh. My. God! You're engaged!"

Emily felt the heat rising into her cheeks. It was the first time she'd heard someone say the word "engaged" in relation to her and it felt so bizarre. All those years of wishing for it and dreaming about it, and she was finally here, in that abstract state of "engagement."

She nodded quickly. Serena squealed and pulled them both into a clumsy embrace, elbows and arms flailing.

"Am I the first to know?" Serena asked when she let them go, the excitement in her tone growing.

"Yes," Daniel confirmed. "But can you get Chantelle? I want her to know before the rest of them."

"Of course!" Serena exclaimed.

With misted-over eyes, she took one last adoring look at Emily's ring before bounding away, a giddy spring in her step. Emily let out a noise that was somewhere between a nervous giggle and an embarrassed groan.

Daniel squeezed her hand reassuringly. It felt as though he was simultaneously congratulating her for having survived one person's reaction while boosting her in anticipation of the next reveal, the one that was far more important.

Emily took a deep breath. Her heart was racing a mile a minute. This was it. The big moment.

The volume of the party grew louder as the dining room door opened a crack. Then Chantelle's face appeared, peeping timidly around it. Emily heard Serena's voice from the other side, encouraging Chantelle into the hallway.

"Go on, it's nothing to worry about!"

Chantelle stepped fully out of the room and Serena closed the door after her, muffling the sound of the party-goers' merriment once more. Emily found the quietness suddenly stifling.

At one end of the corridor stood Chantelle, looking terrified. At the other end stood Emily and Daniel, their nerves just as palpable. Emily beckoned to the child and Chantelle scurried toward them.

"Am I in trouble?" she said, her little voice quivering. "Serena said you needed to speak to me."

"Goodness, no!" Emily cried. She reached for Chantelle and pulled her into a bear hug. "You're not in trouble at all!" She stroked Chantelle's soft, blond hair. "It was just that Daddy and I want to tell you something. Nothing bad."

Chantelle pulled out of the embrace and frowned up at Emily, her blue eyes betraying her skepticism. She was only seven years old but had already learned to be suspicious and distrustful of adults.

"Are you sending me back to Tennessee?" Chantelle said boldly, tipping her chin up with fake nonchalance.

"No!" Daniel exclaimed, shaking his head. If it hadn't been such a sad statement to make, it would have been comical. Seeking to end Chantelle's sense of doom as immediately as possible, Daniel crouched down so he was eye level with his daughter, took both her hands in his, and then, with a large breath, exclaimed, "Emily and I are getting married."

There was a moment of hesitation as Chantelle took in the news. Then the fear melted from her expression and her eyes widened with astonishment. A huge grin spread across her face.

"Really?" she squealed, gazing at them in wonder.

"Yes, really," Emily said.

She held out her hand so Chantelle could see the ring. Chantelle's eyes grew even wider as she stared as though in disbelief at the beautiful ring sparkling on Emily's finger. Chantelle held Emily's hand tightly.

"I thought…" she stammered. "I thought you were getting rid of me. But actually, it came true."

"What came true?" Emily asked curiously.

"My Thanksgiving wish," Chantelle said. She was still clutching Emily's hand, and her grip tightened. "I wished that you would get married so that we could be a family forever."

At the sound of Chantelle's earnest revelation, a lump formed in Emily's throat. She caught Daniel's eye. By the expression on his face she could tell that his heart was melting just as much as hers was.

In that moment, Emily felt more blessed than ever before in her life. Somehow the stars had aligned and sent her Daniel to be loved by and Chantelle to be humbled by. Everything felt right.

"Can I be the one to tell everyone?" Chantelle asked suddenly.

"You mean everyone in there?" Emily asked, pointing toward the dining room door from where the sounds of laughter and chatter emanated.

"Uh-huh. Is that okay, or did you want to make the announcement yourself?"

"Please go ahead!" Emily exclaimed, relieved that she wouldn't have to be the one to do it.

"Can I do it right now this second?" Chantelle asked, jumping up and down.

Emily grinned. Chantelle's reaction had made her more than ready for this moment. Seeing her excitement and joy had nullified Emily's nerves. As long as Chantelle was happy, then other people's reactions didn't matter as much!

"Right now this second," Emily repeated.

On hearing Emily's affirmation, Chantelle squealed and rushed off down the corridor. She was so quick, Daniel and Emily had to hop-skip to keep up with her. Then she burst into the dining room so abruptly that everyone turned around in surprise at the sudden intrusion. At the top of her lungs, Chantelle shouted:

"They're getting married! They're getting married!"

Standing at the threshold of the door, Emily and Daniel waited through the seconds of shock as people acknowledged Chantelle's shouting.

Then they watched the surprised expressions appear on the faces of their friends and neighbors: from Cynthia's exaggerated gasp, to the flutter of Vanessa's hand to her mouth.

People started to burst into huge grins. Yvonne and Kieran, Suzanna and Wesley, all the people they had grown to love and call friends began to clap.

"Congratulations!" Yvonne cried, the first to run up to Emily and embrace her.

Kieran was just behind. He shook Daniel's hand, then hugged Emily once Yvonne had let her go. Everyone took it in turns, coming up to Daniel and Emily with hugs and kisses, well wishes and exclamations of joy. Emily felt the love of her community surround her. She'd never felt so supported. What on earth had she been worrying about?

"We need to toast the happy couple," Derek Hansen announced in his strong, mayoral voice.

People began filling their glasses with champagne. A glass was thrust into Emily's hand. Beside her, Serena filled a champagne flute with cola so Chantelle could join in. Emily found her mind flitting all over the place, she was so overwhelmed with a sense of euphoria. It felt like she was in a dream.

Then everyone's glasses were high in the air, the light from the chandelier making a thousand spots of light dance across the walls, floor, and ceiling.

"To Emily and Daniel," Mayor Hansen called out. Then to Daniel, he added, "To finding one's soul mate," and to Emily, "And to following one's dream."

Everyone cheered and clinked glasses as Emily wiped the tears of joy from her eyes.

It was the best Thanksgiving she had ever had.

*

The party stretched on well into the night. It was filled with friendship and joy, and Emily was happier than she'd ever thought possible, not to mention thankful. But finally the party wound down, the guests trickled out into the crisp night, and a hush fell over the inn.

Even when she and Daniel had turned in for bed, Emily felt herself still buzzing with energy. Her head was swimming, and she tossed and turned, unable to shut it down.

"Can't sleep?" Daniel said, half his face concealed by the fluffy pillow it rested upon. Then he grinned. "Me neither."

Emily turned to face him. She ran her fingers across his bare, muscular chest. "I can't stop thinking about the future," she said. "I'm so excited."

Daniel reached out and stroked Emily's cheek. "I know something that might take your mind off things," he said. Then he pressed his lips to hers.

Emily sunk into the kiss, feeling all her thoughts melt away as her body was completely taken over with sensation. She pulled Daniel close to her, feeling his heart beating against her own. Daniel always ignited a fiery passion within her but what she felt now was beyond anything she'd ever felt before.

Just then, their bedroom door flew open. A shard of light from the corridor outside burst into the room like a spotlight. Emily and Daniel sprang apart.

Standing in the doorway was Chantelle.

"I can't sleep!" she declared, running in.

Emily laughed. "Well, that makes all of us, then," she said.

Chantelle leapt into the bed with Emily and Daniel, snuggling right in between them. Emily couldn't help but laugh. Chantelle was the only thing that could interrupt her and Daniel's lovemaking without frustrating her.

"When you and Daddy are married, will that mean you're my mommy forever?" Chantelle asked.

Emily nodded. But then she wondered. She and Daniel had been speaking to their friend Richard, who was a family attorney, about whether they could officially adopt Chantelle. Would being married strengthen their case against Chantelle's birth mother? Sheila was a drug user with no fixed abode, two things that already worked in their favor. Would their marriage help her adopt Chantelle?

She looked at Daniel and Chantelle, both now slipping into slumber. The sight overjoyed Emily. In that moment, she doubled her resolve to look into legal proceedings. The sooner the better. She wanted them to be a proper family more than anything she'd ever wanted in the world. With the ring sparkling on her finger, she felt closer than ever to making that dream a reality.

CHAPTER TWO

Emily woke the morning after Thanksgiving to a feeling of elation. She had never felt so happy. The beautiful winter sunshine was streaming in through the lace curtains, adding to her already amazed, excited state. After a brief second of doubt, Emily concluded that she wasn't dreaming; Daniel had indeed proposed, and they were really getting married.

Suddenly aware of all the things she had to do, she leapt out of bed. She had people to call! How had she forgotten to call Jayne and Amy to break the news? And what about her mom? She'd been so wrapped up in the moment, in her own joy and the celebration of her friends, it hadn't even crossed her mind.

She quickly showered and dressed, then ran down to the porch with her cell phone. Water from her still-wet hair dripped onto her shirt as she scrolled through her contacts. Her thumb hovered over her mom's number and began to tremble. She just couldn't find the courage to dial it. She knew her mom wouldn't give her the sort of response she wanted; she'd been suspicious about Chantelle and would assume that Daniel was only marrying Emily to turn her into a mother to his kid. So she decided to test the water with Jayne. Her best friend always told it to her straight, but it never came with the same air of disappointment her mom exuded.

She dialed Jayne's cell and listened to the ring tone. Then the call connected.

"Em!" Jayne cried. "You're on speaker."

Emily paused. "Why am I on speaker?"

"We're in the conference room. Me and Ames."

"Hi, Emily!" Amy called brightly. "Is this about the job offer?"

It took Emily a moment to work out what they were talking about. The candle business that Amy had started from her bedroom at college was, over a decade later, suddenly flourishing. She'd employed Jayne and had been trying so hard to get Emily into the fold. Neither could really understand why Emily would want to live in a small town rather than New York, why she'd want to run an inn instead of work in a swanky office with her two best friends, and they certainly couldn't work out why she'd want to take on another man's child (a man with a *beard* no less!) without any reassurance that he'd give her her own children one day.

"Actually no," Emily said. "It's about..." She faltered, suddenly losing her resolve. Then she checked herself. She had nothing to be ashamed of. Even if her life was going in a different trajectory to her best friends', it was still valid; her choices were still her own and they should be respected. "Daniel and I are getting married."

There was a moment of silence, followed by shrill screaming. Emily winced. She could imagine her friends with their perfectly manicured nails, their moisturized skin that smelled of rose and camellia, their shiny hair flailing as they jumped up and down in their seats.

Through the noise, Emily made out Jayne shouting, "Oh my god!" and Amy shouting, "Congratulations!"

She let out a sigh of relief. Her friends were on board. Another hurdle had been overcome.

The incomprehensible screeching finally died down.

"He hasn't knocked you up, has he?" Jayne asked, as inappropriate as ever.

"No!" Emily cried, laughing.

"Jayne, shut up," Amy scolded. "Tell us everything. How did he do it? What's the ring like?"

Emily recounted the story of the beach, of the declarations of love in the snow, of the gorgeous pearl ring. Her friends cooed at all the right moments. Emily could tell they were ecstatic for her.

"Are you taking his name?" Jayne probed further. "Or double barreling? Mitchell Morey is a bit of a mouthful. Or would it be Morey Mitchell? Emily Jane Morey Mitchell. Hmm. I don't know if I like it. Maybe you should stick with your own name, you know? It's the strong, empowered, feminist thing to do, after all."

Emily's mind whirled as Jayne spoke in her characteristically fast over-caffeinated way, barely pausing to give her time to answer any of the questions.

"We're going to be your bridesmaids, right?" Jayne finished, in her typically blunt, straight-talking way.

"I haven't thought about it yet," Emily admitted. Jayne and Amy may indeed be her oldest friends, but she had made so many more since moving to Sunset Harbor; Serena, Yvonne, Suzanna, Karen, Cynthia. And what about Chantelle? It was important to Emily that she played a pivotal role in the whole thing.

"Well, where's the venue, then?" Jayne asked, sounding a little grumpy that Emily was even considering other people as her bridesmaids.

"I don't know that yet either," Emily said.

It suddenly hit her how enormous the task ahead of her was. There was so much to organize. So much to pay for. She suddenly felt very overwhelmed by the whole thing.

9

"Do you think you'll have a big wedding or small one?" Amy asked. Her questions were less loaded than Jayne's but she still had an air of judgment about her. Emily wondered whether Amy was still upset about her own failed engagement to Fraser. Maybe she resented Emily for having a ring and fiancé when she herself had lost both.

"We haven't worked out any of the details yet," Emily said. "It's brand new."

"But you've been dreaming about this for years," Amy added.

Emily frowned. Marriage, yes. That had been something she'd wanted for a long time. But she'd never pictured the way her life would go. The love she had with Daniel was unique and unexpected. Their wedding ought to be the same. She needed to rethink everything to make it perfect for them, for this specific relationship, this life.

"Can you at least tell us the date?" Jayne asked. "Our calendar is packed."

Emily stammered. "I don't know."

"Just the month will do for now," Jayne pressed.

"I don't know that either."

Jayne sighed with exasperation. "What about the *year*?"

Emily grew frustrated. "I don't know!" she cried. "I haven't worked any of this out yet!"

Silence fell. Emily could just imagine the scene: her friends exchanging a glance, sitting in leather office chairs at a huge glass table, the sound of her outburst emanating from the phone in between them and echoing around the vast conference room. She cringed with embarrassment.

Jayne broke the silence. "Well, just make sure it doesn't turn into one of those engagements that goes on forever," she said in a matter-of-fact way. "You know what some men are like; it's like they didn't realize that once they proposed you'd be expecting an actual *wedding*. They do the whole overblown engagement thing and then once they've lured you in with a fancy ring they think they can rest on their laurels and never actually sign on the dotted line."

"It's not like that," Emily said tersely.

"Sure," Jayne said flippantly. "But to be certain, you should tie him down to an actual date. If it looks like he's going to drag the engagement out, run."

Emily squeezed her hand into a fist. She knew she shouldn't let Jayne—a commitment-phobe who'd never even had a proper long-term relationship—dictate the way she ought to feel about the situation, but her friend had a talent for putting doubt into her mind.

As ridiculous as they were, Emily could already tell she was going to ruminate on Jayne's words for days to come.

"I have an idea," Amy broke in, playing the diplomat. "Why don't we come up to toast you? Have a visit? Help you plan a few things?"

Despite her irritation with Jayne, Emily liked the idea of her friends coming to stay and getting involved with the wedding preparations. Once they were here, on her turf and in her domain, they'd be able to see the love she and Daniel shared with their own eyes. They'd see how happy she was and start being a little bit more supportive.

"That would be really great actually," Emily said.

They found a date that worked for everyone and Emily ended the call. But thanks to Jayne, her head was swimming and the flame of excitement inside of her dulled just a little. Her feelings were compounded by the fact she still needed to make the dreaded call to her mom, which would certainly go less well. She'd tried to invite her mom to Thanksgiving but the woman had acted like it was an insult. Nothing Emily did was ever good enough for Patricia Mitchell. If she'd felt grilled by Amy and Jayne, she would feel downright set upon by her mom.

And that was just *her* family! When she added Daniel's into the mix, her niggling fears intensified. Why did the rest of the world have to exist? Everything in Sunset Harbor felt perfect for Emily. But outside there were disapproving friends and problematic moms. There were absent fathers.

For the first time since the proposal, Emily thought of her dad, who'd been missing for twenty years. She'd recently discovered a stash of letters in the home that proved he was still alive. Then Trevor Mann, her next door neighbor, had confirmed seeing Roy at the house just a few years earlier. Her dad was alive, yet even with that knowledge nothing had changed. Emily still had no way of contacting him. The chances of him being there to walk her down the aisle were practically nonexistent.

Emily felt her emotions crowding in on her, threatening to extinguish the joy she'd been feeling. She looked down at the screen of her cell phone, where she'd selected her mom's number but hadn't yet plucked up the courage to dial it.

Before Emily had the chance to take the plunge and call her mom, she heard the sound of footsteps coming from the stairs behind her. She spun around and saw Daniel and Chantelle trotting down toward her. Daniel had dressed the little girl in one of her gorgeous vintage outfits—a rust-colored corduroy pinafore dress with a black-and-white floral print cardigan and matching tights. She looked adorable. He himself was in his usual scruffy jeans and shirt, his dark hair shaggy, his stubble framing his strong jawline.

"We wanted to go out for breakfast," Daniel said. "Do something special. A celebration breakfast."

Emily stashed her cell phone back in her pocket. "Great idea."

Saved by the bell. The call to her mom would have to wait. But Emily knew she wouldn't be able to put it off forever. Sooner or later she would be on the receiving end of the sharp tongue of Patricia Mitchell.

*

The smell of syrup permeated the warm air in Joe's Diner. The family slid into one of the red plastic booths, noticing the glances and whispers as they did so.

"Everyone already knows," Emily said in a hushed voice to Daniel.

He rolled his eyes. "Of course they do." He added, sarcastically, "In fact, I'm surprised it took so long. We broke the news a whole half day ago, after all, and I'm sure it only takes Cynthia Jones an hour or two to cycle through town and spread her latest bit of gossip."

Chantelle giggled.

At least the whispers and glances were cheery ones, Emily thought. Everyone seemed pleased for them. But Emily felt a little embarrassed to be the center of attention. It wasn't every day you walked into a waffle house and made every head turn. Her own mind was still swimming with questions following her call with Amy and Jayne and she wondered if now would be an appropriate time to broach some of them with Daniel.

Gray-haired Joe came over to the table, holding his pad in his wizened hands.

"I hear congratulations are in order," he said, smiling, clapping Daniel on the back. "When's the big day?"

Emily watched Daniel falter. He seemed just as bemused as she felt. Everyone wanted answers to questions they hadn't even asked themselves.

"Not sure yet," Daniel stammered. "We haven't ironed out any of the specifics."

They ordered their waffles and pancakes and once Joe had left in order to prepare their breakfasts for them, Emily got her nerve up to ask Daniel some questions.

"When do you think we should set a date for?" Emily asked.

Daniel looked at her with wide eyes. "Oh. I don't know. You want to do that already?"

Jayne's warning echoed in Emily's mind. "We don't need to fix the specific date but are we thinking of months or next year? Do you want a summer wedding? Or fall, since we are in Maine?"

She smiled but it felt strained. By the look on Daniel's face, she could tell he hadn't even thought that far ahead.

"I need to think about it," he said noncommittally.

"I want a summer wedding," Chantelle said. "By the harbor. With Daddy's boat."

"Think about what?" Emily said, ignoring Chantelle and focusing on Daniel. "There are only four options. Sunshine, blustery wind, snowfall, or warm breezes. Which one do you prefer?"

Daniel looked a little taken aback by Emily's somewhat snappy tone. Chantelle, too, seemed confused.

"I don't know," Daniel stammered. "There are pros and cons to all of them."

Emily felt her emotions swirling inside of her. Was Jayne right? Had Daniel proposed without even thinking about the fact that there was supposed to be a wedding at the end of it?

"Have you told anyone?" Emily probed further.

Creases of frustration appeared across Daniel's forehead. "It's been less than twenty-four hours," he stated plainly, hiding the irritation Emily knew she'd stoked in him. Between his teeth he added, "Can't we just enjoy the moment?"

Chantelle looked from Emily to Daniel with concern in her eyes. It wasn't often they bickered and the sight clearly alarmed her.

Seeing the little girl looking worried struck a chord inside Emily. Whatever concerns she herself may have, it wasn't fair to let Chantelle get caught up in them. This matter was for her and Daniel to resolve.

"You're right," Emily said, exhaling.

She reached out for Chantelle and took her hand for reassurance. Just then, Joe arrived with stacks of pancakes. Everyone began to eat silently.

Emily felt frustrated with herself for letting Jayne's and Amy's words ruin her high. It wasn't fair. Just yesterday she'd been on cloud nine.

"Will you let Bailey be the flower girl?" Chantelle asked. "And me be a bridesmaid?"

"We don't know yet," Emily explained, keeping her emotions in check.

"But I want to walk down the aisle with you," Chantelle added. "There will be an aisle, won't there? Are you getting married in a church?" The little girl rummaged in her backpack and pulled out a pink notepad and sparkly pen. "Let's write a list," she said.

Despite her underlying anguish, Emily couldn't help but feel cheered by the sight of Chantelle in organizer mode. She always looked so serious, so grown up and beyond her years.

"The first thing you need to arrange is the venue," Chantelle said in a very efficient voice that made Emily picture her running the inn one day.

"You're right," Emily said, looking at Daniel. "Let's think about the venue first then work from there." She felt determined not to let her high be ruined. "Let's not rush any decisions. "

For the first time since she'd pestered him for answers, Daniel seemed to relax. The frown lines on his forehead disappeared. Emily felt relieved.

Out the window of the diner, Emily could see that a tree was being raised in the center of town. In all the excitement she'd completely forgotten about the town Christmas tree; it was raised the day after Thanksgiving every year. She'd gone to watch it as a child whenever the family had been in Sunset Harbor for a winter vacation. She recalled that there was also an annual tree lighting that took place in the evening.

"We should go and see the tree being lit tonight," Emily said.

Chantelle looked up from her notepad, which was now filled with a long bullet point list written in her scrawling handwriting. "Can we?" She looked excited.

"Of course," Emily said. "But first we should get our own tree. If the town has one, the inn ought to have one as well. What do you think about that, Chantelle?"

Emily felt her own excitement grow as she realized that the inn would accommodate an enormous Christmas tree. As a child their father had only ever gotten a small one for the living room, since they were only ever vacationing in the house. But now that it was her home she could put an enormous ten-foot tree in the foyer. Maybe even fifteen-foot! She and Chantelle could decorate it together, using a stepladder to reach the top branches. The thought filled her with childish anticipation.

"Can we, Daddy?" Chantelle asked Daniel, who was sitting rather quietly as he munched on his pancakes. "Can we get a Christmas tree?"

Daniel nodded. "Sure."

"And then go to the tree lighting in town?"

"Uh-huh."

Emily frowned, wondering what Daniel was thinking, why the thought of such a delightful family outing wasn't filling him with joy like it did her and Chantelle. Daniel was as much a mystery to her as ever, even though she now had a ring on her finger and was more than ready to commit to him forever. She wondered if she'd ever really know what was going on in his head, or if even, when she became Mrs. Daniel Morey, she'd still be left wondering.

CHAPTER THREE

Dory's Christmas Tree Farm was a short drive away on the outskirts of Sunset Harbor. The family drove together in Daniel's rusty red pickup truck. There were still patches of Thanksgiving Day's snow on the banks, and as they drove past Emily touched the ring on her finger, remembering the snow that had fallen around her as Daniel proposed.

They pulled up into the makeshift parking lot and all hopped out of the truck. There were many families here; clearly everyone had the same idea. Parents milled around while their children ran excitedly about the place, threading through the lines of trees.

Instead of Dory, it was a young girl on the cusp of teenagehood who greeted them. She introduced herself as Grace, Dory's daughter, and she had the same wispy blond hair as Chantelle. She was wearing a fanny pack stuffed with dollar bills and a paper pad to write receipts.

"These are the trees ready for harvest," she said, smiling confidently, gesturing out to the field of pines. "They've all been growing for about seven to nine years." She grinned down at Chantelle. "So they're about your age, am I right?"

Chantelle nodded shyly.

"Once you find the tree you like," Grace continued, "cut it down and take it to the loading area. My dad will ride you and the tree back in the wagon to the baler, wrap it all up, and then you can pay me. We also sell hot chocolate and toasted chestnuts if you want something to keep you warm while you walk."

Emily bought them each a hot chocolate in a Styrofoam cup and a bag of chestnuts to share, and then they headed for the fields. Chantelle rushed ahead, more excited than Emily had ever seen her.

The smell of pine was powerful, awakening that Christmas feeling inside of Emily. She was excited by the prospect of her first Christmas with Daniel and Chantelle, with her family beside the hearth. It would be the first of many.

She and Daniel walked hand in hand, silently trailing behind Chantelle. Then Emily leaned into Daniel.

"How old do you think Grace is?" she asked.

"Eleven, twelve," Daniel guessed. "Why?"

"No reason," Emily replied. "She just reminds me of Chantelle. Made me think about what she'll be like as she gets older."

Up ahead, Chantelle ran along the paths between the trees, stopping to assess their height, the density of their branches, and the lushness of their color before moving on to the next one. Emily could easily imagine her as an older child, clipboard in hand, working her first job to earn pocket money.

But as she wondered about the future, Emily felt her mind being pulled back into the past. Chantelle, who reminded her so much of Charlotte, also reminded her of the loss of Charlotte, of the fact that her sister never got to grow up, that she never got to have a job during winter vacation. She had skipped through this very farm all those years ago, full of promise and potential, and then without warning her life had been snuffed out in the blink of an eye.

Emily looked ahead at Chantelle, and as she did so, the child morphed into Charlotte. Then Emily felt herself shrinking, until she was inhabiting a child-sized body. Her hands were suddenly swaddled with mittens. Snow began falling around her, clinging to the branches of the pine trees. Emily reached out with her small, mittened hand and shook one of the branches. A snow cloud puffed into the air, and the fine white powder dispersed. Up ahead, Charlotte was laughing, carefree and happy, her warm breath coiling through the air. She was wearing mittens too, and her favorite bright red boots looked stark against the backdrop of white.

Emily watched Charlotte stop beneath the tallest tree in the whole farm and gaze up with wonderment.

"I want this one!" the little girl cried.

Emily rushed toward her, kicking up snow in her haste. When she reached Charlotte's side, she too gazed up at the enormous tree. It was astounding, so tall she could hardly see the top.

The crunching of footsteps in the snow made Emily tear her gaze from the tree and turn to look over her shoulder. There, stomping through the snow in large strides, was her dad.

"You girls need to slow down," he panted as he drew up beside them. "I almost lost you."

"We found the tree!" Emily cried with excitement.

Charlotte joined in, jumping and pointing up.

"That's a bit big," Roy said.

He looked tired today. Depressed. There were dark circles beneath his eyes.

"It's not too big," Emily said. "The ceilings are very high."

Charlotte, as always, followed her sister's lead. "It's not too big! Please can we get it, Daddy?"

Roy Mitchell rubbed a hand over his face with exasperation. "Don't test my patience, Charlotte," he snapped. "Choose something smaller."

Emily saw Charlotte recoil. Neither of them liked to anger their father and neither could understand how they had. It seemed like the smallest of things annoyed him these days. He was always distracted by something or other, always looking over his shoulder at shadows only he could see.

But Emily's main concern was Charlotte. Always Charlotte. The little girl looked like she was on the brink of tears. Emily slipped her mittened hand into hers.

"This way," she cried brightly. "There are smaller trees over here!"

And just like that, Charlotte cheered up, comforted by her older sister. They ran off through the snow together, leaving their frowning, distracted father to chase after them.

Just then, Emily snapped back into the present day. The snow of the past was no longer falling on the present, the Christmas trees of decades earlier felled and replaced with these new, young trees. She was back to the here and now but it took her a moment to reorient herself with her surroundings, to see Chantelle standing before her rather than Charlotte.

During Emily's blackout, they'd manage to walk deep into the depths of the field. Here, the trees were so tall they cast shadows over everything, blocking out daylight. Emily shuddered, feeling colder now that the winter sun was hidden.

Up ahead, Chantelle was gazing at the tallest tree on the whole farm. It was at least fifteen feet tall.

"This is the one!" she cried, grinning from ear to ear.

Emily smiled. She wasn't going to be like her father, dashing a child's spirits. If Chantelle wanted the tallest tree on the farm, she was going to get it.

She walked up beside her and craned her head to see the top of the tree. Just like when she was a child, the tree seemed majestic to her.

"That's the one," Emily agreed.

Chantelle clapped in delight. Daniel looked somewhat disapproving of the elaborate choice, Emily thought, but he didn't challenge them. He leaned down and helped Chantelle make the first cut with the ax. Emily watched them, father and daughter smiling and laughing together, and felt warm joy spread through her.

Daniel passed the ax to Emily so she too could take a turn chopping, and then they went round in circles, taking it in turns, cooperating. When the tree fell they all cheered.

Grace's dad arrived with the wagon.

"Wow, this is quite a whopper you've chosen," he joked with Chantelle as she attempted to help lift the enormous tree into the wagon.

"It was the tallest one I could find!" Chantelle said, grinning.

The family climbed into the back of the wagon and snuggled up together. The wheels of the wagon turned and they began the slow journey back to the farm entrance.

"I lost you for a moment back there," Daniel said to Emily as they rode. "You had another flashback?"

Emily nodded. The memory had left her shaken. Seeing Charlotte's crestfallen expression, hearing the sharpness of her father's tone. Even then he was a man with a lot on his mind. She wondered if it had been something to do with Antonia, the woman he'd been having an affair with, or their mother, who was back at home in New York, or something else altogether. Though Emily was convinced now that her father was still alive out there, Roy was as much a mystery to her as ever.

"I keep remembering more and more things about my dad," Emily confessed. "Ever since I found those letters. I wish I knew what made him run away. I always thought that something sudden must have happened when I was a teenager, but I think he was troubled by something way before then. For as far back as my memories go, to be honest. Every time I flash back and see him I can see the trouble in his eyes."

Daniel held her close. It felt good to be comforted by him, to be close again. He'd seemed so distant back at Joe's Diner.

"Sorry if I was a bit quiet back there," Daniel said, as if reading her mind. "The holidays bring back memories for me too."

"They do?" Emily asked gently. "What kind of memories?"

It was so rare for Daniel to open up to her that she took every opportunity to encourage him.

"This might come as a bit of a surprise to you, but I'm actually Jewish," Daniel said. "My dad wasn't, though. He was Christian. We celebrated Christmas and Hanukkah while he was still at home, but when he left he took Christmas with him. Mom would only celebrate Hanukkah. Once me and my dad were back in touch, he would only celebrate Christmas at his house. It was odd. A pretty weird way of growing up, as I'm sure you can imagine."

"That sounds tough," Emily soothed, trying to hide her surprise that Daniel was in fact Jewish. She wondered what else she didn't know about him and was gripped with a sudden anguish over how they would raise the children, if there were to be any children. She would of course love to celebrate both but Daniel seemed to be holding traumatic memories about the holidays that might make it a little harder to approach.

They rode back to the entrance of the farm, where they paid the plucky and cheerful Grace while waiting for their tree to be put through the baling machine.

Emily was glad to be creating new, happy memories with her family. But at the back of her mind, she couldn't stop wondering about her father, about what was going on with him, what secrets he'd been keeping. But most of all, she wondered where he was now and if there was any way she would ever be able to trace him.

*

Back in the B&B, Emily and Daniel maneuvered the tree into position in the foyer. There were a few guests relaxing in the living room and they came out to watch with excitement as the enormous tree was raised.

Emily recalled the heap of boxes containing her dad's old ornaments stored in the attic and rushed off to fetch them. Then she and Chantelle sat together at the kitchen table, sorting through all the ornaments.

"This is so pretty," Chantelle said, holding up a glass reindeer.

Emily smiled to herself at the sight of it, recalling how she and Charlotte had pooled together their pocket money to buy it, and how they had then saved up every year to buy more, adding to their collection until they had enough to represent each of one of Santa's reindeers. Then Charlotte had marked each one so they'd be able to tell them apart.

Emily took the glass reindeer from Chantelle's hands and checked its hoof. There was a little scratch mark that looked like it might have been a D for Donner, though it could just as easily have been a B for Blitzen. She smiled to herself.

"There's a whole set in here," Emily said, looking at the tangle of fairy lights. "Somewhere."

They rummaged around until they'd found every single one of Santa's reindeer, including Rudolph with his red nose painted on by Charlotte with nail polish. Emily felt a tug of emotion as she recalled that they'd never gotten around to buying the Santa and sleigh ornaments—the last on their list and the most expensive— because Charlotte had died before they'd saved up enough money.

"Look at this!" Chantelle cried, breaking into Emily's thoughts by waving a grubby, felt polar bear in front of her face.

"Percy!" Emily cried, taking it from Chantelle's hands. "Percy the polar bear!" She laughed to herself, delighted she could pluck such an obscure memory from her mind. She had lost so many of them, and yet she could retrieve them still. It gave her hope for unraveling the mysteries of her past.

She and Chantelle sorted through all the decorations, selecting all the ones they wanted to use and carefully putting away the others. By the time they were finished and ready to add them to the tree, it had grown dark outside.

Daniel lit a fire in the fireplace and its soft orange glow spilled out into the foyer as the family began decorating the tree. One by one, Chantelle carefully placed each of her selected decorations onto the tree, with the kind of precision and care Emily had grown to recognize in the child. It was like she was savoring every moment, carefully storing a new set of memories to replace the terrible ones from her younger years.

Finally it was time to put the angel on the top. Chantelle had spent a long time choosing which decoration would be given the prime position and had eventually chosen a fabric, hand-knitted angel over a robin, a star, and a fat, cuddly snowman.

"Are you ready?" Daniel asked Chantelle as he stood at the bottom of the stepladder. "I'm going to have to carry you up so you can reach the top."

"I get to put the angel on the top?" Chantelle said, wide-eyed.

Emily laughed. "Of course! The youngest always gets to do it."

She watched Chantelle clamber onto Daniel's back, the angel clutched tightly in her hands so she wouldn't drop it. Then slowly, one step at a time, Daniel carried her to the top. Together they stretched out and Chantelle popped the decoration onto the tall tip of the tree.

The second the angel sat atop the tree, Emily had a sudden flashback. It came on so quickly she began to breathe rapidly, panicked by the abrupt shift from her bright, warm inn to the colder, darker one of thirty years prior.

Emily was looking up at Charlotte as she placed the angel they'd spent all day making onto the tree. Her dad was holding Charlotte aloft, who at this point in time was a chubby toddler, and he wobbled slightly from the numerous sherries he'd drunk that day. Emily remembered a sudden, overwhelming emotion of fear. Fear that her tipsy father would drop Charlotte onto the hard hearth. Emily was five years old and it was the first time she'd really understood the concept of death.

Emily returned to the present day with a gasp to find her hand pressed against the wall as she steadied herself. She was hyperventilating and Daniel was there beside her, his hand on her back.

"Emily?" he asked with concern. "What happened? Another memory?"

She nodded, finding herself unable to speak. The memory had been so vivid and so terrifying, despite her knowledge that no harm had befallen Charlotte that winter evening. She cherished most of her recovered memories but that one had felt sinister, ominous, like a sign of the dark things to come.

Daniel continued rubbing Emily's back as she made a concerted effort to slow her breathing back to normal. Chantelle looked up at her, worried, and it was the child's face that finally brought Emily out of the grips of her memories.

"I'm sorry, it's fine," she said, feeling a little embarrassed to have worried everyone so much.

She looked up at the angel, at the sequined dress she wore. It had taken her and Charlotte hours to glue all those individual sequins onto the fabric. Now, with the ebbing firelight coming from the living room, they sparkled like rainbows. Emily thought it almost looked as though they were winking at her. Not for the first time, she felt Charlotte's presence close by, communicating love, peace, and forgiveness. Emily tried to hold onto the feeling of her spirit, to take comfort from it.

"We should head off to the town square," Emily said, finally. "We don't want to miss the tree lighting."

"Are you sure you're okay?" Daniel asked, looking concerned.

Emily smiled. "I am. I promise."

But her assertions didn't seem to wash with Daniel. She could feel him watching her out of the corner of his eye the whole time they were wrapping up in their warm clothes. But he didn't question or challenge her further, and so the family got into the pickup truck and headed into town.

CHAPTER FOUR

Despite the biting cold, the whole of Sunset Harbor had congregated in the town square to watch the tree lighting. Even Colin Magnum, the man who was renting the carriage house for the month, was there, enjoying the festivities. Karen from the convenience store handed out freshly baked cinnamon rolls, while Cynthia Jones walked around with flasks of hot chocolate. Emily took the drinks and food gratefully, feeling the warmth seep into her stomach as she consumed them, and watched Chantelle playing happily with her friends.

Amongst the crowds, Emily spotted Trevor Mann. Once, the sight of him would have filled her with dread; they had been enemies the moment Trevor had decided to make it his life's mission to kick Emily out of the inn. But that had all changed over the last month when he'd discovered he had an inoperable brain tumor. Far from being Emily's enemy, Trevor was now her closest ally. He'd paid all of her back taxes—hundreds of thousands of dollars' worth—and now welcomed her into his home on a regular basis for coffee and cake. It pained Emily to see him suffering. Every time she saw him he seemed more frail, more in the grips of illness.

Emily approached him now. When he saw her, his face lit up.

"How are you?" Emily asked, embracing him. He felt thinner, his bones protruding sharply into her as they hugged.

"As well as can be expected," Trevor replied, lowering his gaze.

It shocked Emily to see him this way, to see him looking frail and defeated.

"Is there anything you need help with?" she asked, softly, keeping her voice hushed so as not to embarrass the man's pride.

Trevor shook his head, just as Emily expected him to. It wasn't in his nature to accept help. But it wasn't in her nature to accept no for an answer.

"Chantelle's been making snowflake chain decorations," she said. "They're just bits of glitter paper really but she's really proud and wants all the neighbors to have one. Okay if we come by and drop one off tomorrow?"

It was a sly trick, but Trevor fell for it.

"Well, I suppose we may as well have some tea and cake," he said. "If you're already coming around, that is."

Emily smiled to herself. There were ways through Trevor's armor, and she resolved then to visit her neighbor at the next available opportunity.

"Anyway, I was hoping to see you here," Trevor said, taking her hand in his. He was so cold, Emily noted, and his skin had a clammy feel. There was a sheen of sweat on his brow. "I have something for you," he continued.

"What's that?" Emily asked as he produced a piece of paper from his pocket.

"Blueprints," Trevor said. "Of your house. I was going through my attic, trying to get everything sorted for... well, you know what for." His voice grew quiet. "I'm not sure how they got mixed up in my things but I thought you might want them. They were drawn up by your father and his attorney, you see, and I know how much you want things regarding your father."

"I do," Emily stammered, taking the paper from his hands.

She gazed down at the faded pencil drawing. They were architect's plans. She gasped as she realized that the plans were for entire property, including the swimming pool in the outhouse, the one that Charlotte had drowned in. A lump formed in Emily's throat. She folded the paper quickly and shoved it into her bag.

"Thank you, Trevor," she said. "I'll look at that later."

They parted ways and Emily rejoined Daniel and Chantelle.

"What did Trevor want?" Daniel asked.

"Nothing," Emily said, shaking her head. She wasn't ready to talk about it yet; she was still reeling from the experience. The paper seemed to beckon to her in her bag. Could it be another piece of the puzzle that explained her father's disappearance?

Just then, the countdown for the lights began. Emily's mind swirled with memories of being here as a child, a preteen, a teenager. She seemed to pass through all those forgotten moments, year on year. Some contained Charlotte, alive and smiling, but many more did not; many were just her and her father, sinking more deeply into depression and distraction.

Then white lights burst from the tree and everyone began to whoop and cheer. Emily was pulled back into the present day, her heart racing.

"Are you okay?" Daniel asked, concerned. "You keep blacking out."

Emily nodded to reassure him, but she was trembling. Her mind seemed frantic. All these memories were suddenly resurfacing and she wondered if they'd been triggered by the discovery that her father was indeed alive. It was as if her mind had decided that she

24

could now reach back into the past and remember her father because she wouldn't be consumed with grief in doing so. Perhaps, if Emily were patient enough, she'd recover a memory that would help her in her quest to find him, something that would tell her exactly where he was hiding.

*

Exhausted from their evening of fun, Emily and Daniel tucked Chantelle into bed as soon as they arrived home. Chantelle asked for a story to be read to her and Emily obliged. But once the story was over, Chantelle seemed pensive.

"What's wrong?" Emily asked.

"I was thinking about my mom," Chantelle said.

"Oh." Emily felt her stomach tighten at the thought of Sheila, back in Tennessee. "What about her, sweetie?"

Chantelle looked at Emily with her wide, blue eyes. "Will you protect me from her?"

Emily's heart clenched. "Of course."

"Promise," Chantelle said in a desperate, pleading voice. "Promise me she won't come back."

Emily held her tight. She couldn't promise because she didn't know how the legal challenge to Sheila's guardianship would go.

"I will do everything I possibly can," Emily said, hoping her words would be enough to soothe the terrified child.

Chantelle lay back, her head on the pillow, blond hair splayed, and seemed to relax. A few moments later, she fell asleep.

Chantelle asking about her mom had awoken something in Emily. She and Patricia had spoken not that long ago when Emily had tried, and failed, to get her mother to join her in their Thanksgiving celebrations at the inn. Her mom refused to come and visit the house in Sunset Harbor; she viewed it as belonging to Roy, as a place she had been banished from. Even so, Emily thought, Patricia was still a part of her life. It was time to bite the bullet and tell her about the upcoming wedding.

Emily stood from Chantelle's bed, wrapped herself in a shawl, and went out onto the porch. She sat on the swinging seat, tucked her legs beneath her, and took one look up at the shining moon and stars. Something in their twinkling light gave her courage. She scrolled through the contacts in her cell and dialed her mom's number.

As always, Patricia answered the phone with a brusque, "Yes?"

"Mom," Emily said, inhaling, trying to hold onto her courage. "I have something to tell you."

There was little point in pretending to make polite conversation. Neither of them wanted that. May as well cut to the chase.

"Oh?" Patricia said flatly.

Emily had thrown a few curveballs her mom's way over the last year, from upping and leaving her home in New York, breaking up with Ben after seven years together, running off to Sunset Harbor, opening a B&B, and falling so madly in love with Daniel that she'd agreed to help raise his child. Her mom, unsurprisingly, disapproved of every single one of Emily's choices. The chances of her accepting the engagement were slim to none.

"Daniel asked me to marry him," Emily finally managed to say. "And I agreed."

There was a pause, one that Emily had predicted. Her mom used silence like a weapon, always providing Emily with enough time to worry about the thoughts that were crossing her mind.

"And you've been dating this man for how long?" Patricia finally said.

"Coming up to a year now," Emily replied.

"One year. When you have fifty or so to spend together."

Emily let out a huge sigh. "I thought you'd be happy I was finally settling down. You always loved rubbing it in my face how long you'd been married by my age." Emily could hear the tone of her voice and cringed. Why did her mom always bring out the belligerent child in her? Why did she care so much about getting her approval when Patricia herself seemed to care so little about her daughter?

"I suppose he needs a mother for that child of his," Patricia said.

Emily spoke between her teeth. "Her name is Chantelle. And that's not why he asked. He asked because he loves me. And I said yes because I love him. We want to spend forever together so you should just get used to it."

"We'll see," Patricia replied in a monotone way.

"I wish you could just be happy for me," Emily said, her voice beginning to waver. "You're going to be the mother of the bride, after all. People will expect to see you proud and cordial."

"Who says I'm coming?" Patricia snapped back.

The words stung Emily like a slap. "What do you mean? Of course you're coming, Mom, it's my wedding!"

"There's no of course about it," Patricia replied. "I'll RSVP to my wedding invitation when I receive it."

"Mom…" Emily stammered.

She couldn't believe what she was hearing. Would her mom really not come just to spite her? What would people think? Probably that Emily was an orphan, without her dad there, without her mom. And no sister. In many ways, she was an orphan. It was just her against the world.

"Fine," Emily said, suddenly hot-cheeked. "Do what you want. You always have." Then she ended the call without saying goodbye.

Emily didn't want to cry. In fact, she refused to. Not for her mom, it wasn't worth it. But for her dad, that was another matter altogether. She missed him desperately, and now that she was convinced he was still alive, she wanted to see him badly. But there was no way of reaching him. The woman he'd been cheating on her mom with had passed away several years ago, and anyway, she'd been as stumped as the rest of them about Roy's disappearance. All Emily knew was that while not having her mom at the wedding would be painful, not having her dad there would be devastating. In that moment, Emily doubled her resolve to track him down. Someone somewhere must know something.

Emily went back inside the inn. She was tired from the long day and climbed the stairs to bed. But when she reached her bedroom she saw that Daniel wasn't there. Her momentary panic was quelled when Daniel entered the room, cell phone in hand.

"Where have you been?" Emily asked.

"I just called my mom," Daniel replied. "To tell her about the wedding."

Emily almost laughed with surprise. That they'd both call their moms simultaneously like that was more than a coincidence; it was clearly a sign of their connection to one another.

"How did it go?" Emily asked, though she could tell by Daniel's expression that the answer wasn't going to be good.

"How do you think?" Daniel said, raising an eyebrow. "She played the Chantelle card again, saying she'll only come to the wedding if we promise to let her spend regular time with Chantelle. I wish she could see what a destructive force she can be and understand why I don't want her meddling with my kid. Not while she's still drinking too much. Chantelle needs to be around sober adults after what she went through with her own mom." He slumped onto the edge of the bed. "She just can't see my point. She doesn't get it. 'Everyone drinks,' that's what she always says. 'I'm no worse than anyone else.' Maybe she isn't, but it's not what Chantelle needs. If she cared about her granddaughter as much as she claims she does, she'd kick the habit for her sake."

Emily climbed onto the bed behind him and rubbed the tension from his shoulders. Daniel relaxed beneath her soft touch. She pressed a kiss onto his neck.

"I just called my mom too," she said.

Daniel turned to face her, surprised. "You did? How did that go?"

"Terribly," Emily said, and suddenly she couldn't help but laugh. There was something darkly comedic about the whole thing.

Seeing Emily dissolve into laughter made Daniel crack. Soon, they were both laughing hysterically, sharing their commiserations with one another, connected in that moment and rising above it together.

"I was thinking," Daniel said once his laughter had finally subsided. "Do you remember when Gus came to stay?"

"Yes of course," Emily replied. The elderly gentleman had been her first real guest at the inn. Thanks to his custom she'd been saved from the brink of bankruptcy. He was also one of the most delightful people she'd ever had the privilege to meet. "How could I ever forget Gus? But what about him?"

Daniel played with the sleeve of her top idly. "Remember how he went to that party out in Aubrey? The town hall?"

Emily nodded, frowning and wondering why Daniel was bringing it up.

"Have you ever been?" Daniel asked.

Emily grew even more curious. "To Aubrey? Or the town hall?" Then she laughed. "Actually, I've never been to either."

Daniel stalled, suddenly falling quiet. Emily waited patiently.

"The town hall does weddings," he said, finally getting to the point. "I wondered if we should, you know, make an appointment or whatever it's called? With the wedding planner? That is if you want to get married in Maine rather than New York."

To say she felt shocked was an understatement! Hearing Daniel suggest something to do with organizing the wedding without her having to pressure him into it was a huge relief to Emily.

"Yes, I want to get married in Maine," Emily stammered. "It feels more like a home to me than New York ever did. And I have more friends here. I don't want to make everyone travel all the way there for the sake of tradition."

"Cool," Daniel replied, looking away shyly.

"When were you thinking of going?" Emily asked.

"We could head over next weekend," Daniel suggested, still shy. "Take Chantelle. She'd love it."

Next weekend? Emily wanted to cry. *So soon?*

She felt her excitement grow. What had happened to her reluctant fiancé? What had caused such a sudden change of heart? Maybe Jayne's warning was completely unfounded after all. Daniel wanted a wedding just as much as she did. She'd been an idiot to doubt him.

But no sooner had Emily considered it than her thoughts flipped on their head. She wondered whether their horrible calls with their moms might have had something to do with Daniel's sudden interest. Had he been spurred on by Patricia's skepticism, wanting to prove himself as honorable and his intentions as honest? Or worse, was he just suggesting it to cheer Emily up, as a way of briefly calming her?

After agreeing to make an appointment for next Saturday, they climbed into bed. Daniel fell asleep quickly. But with concerns niggling in her mind, Emily struggled for a long time to find sleep that night.

CHAPTER FIVE

Serena walked into the B&B for her shift early Saturday morning, her arms laden with magazines.

"The tree looks great," she said, eyeing the enormous Christmas tree.

"What are those?" Emily asked from her place behind the foyer desk.

Serena walked over to the desk and dumped the magazines in front of Emily. They were wedding catalogues.

"Oh," Emily said, a little surprised. She'd been engaged for a whole week and hadn't yet looked at a single magazine.

"I thought you might need some inspiration," Serena said.

Emily thumbed through one of them, barely taking in the pictures. "Actually, Chantelle made this whole list of things for us to do. First on her list is the venue."

Serena laughed. "Yeah, she showed me. I love how involved she is. Have you got anywhere in mind?"

Emily smiled. "Actually, we have an appointment in an hour."

"You do?" Serena said, her eyes widening with excitement.

For the first time since the proposal, Emily felt a flutter of giddy excitement in her stomach at the thought of arranging the wedding, of walking down the aisle.

"It's in Aubrey," Emily continued. "It was Daniel's suggestion, that town hall that Gus and his friends couldn't stop gushing about."

Just then, she heard the sound of Daniel descending the staircase and looked behind her. He'd put on his best plaid shirt and even combed his hair back. Emily smiled to herself, pleased to know he would at least make a bit of effort. Serena wiggled her eyebrows, smirking her approval.

"Chantelle's just choosing what shoes to wear," Daniel said as he reached the bottom step.

Emily noticed his gaze fall on the glossy magazine in her hands. It was open on a spread of beautiful wedding gowns. Emily couldn't be certain, but she thought she saw a flicker of surprise in Daniel's eyes, and wondered what it meant. Had he not thought about a white wedding, about her in the typical dress and veil, him in a black suit? Had he just thought they'd get married in their usual jeans and shirts? She snapped the magazine shut with sudden irritation.

A moment later Chantelle appeared at the top of the stairs. She'd put on one of her fanciest dresses, white tights, and cute shiny T-bar shoes. She looked like a china doll. Emily couldn't help her delight at seeing how much this meant to Chantelle. At least someone was getting into the spirit of things.

Emily grabbed her purse and jacket, and, leaving the inn in Serena's capable hands, herded her family out the door and into the pickup truck.

"Are you excited to see the venue?" Emily asked Chantelle, looking in the rearview mirror at the girl in the backseat as Daniel pulled onto the main street.

"Yes!" Chantelle exclaimed. "And to try the food!"

Emily had forgotten all about the menu tasting. She wondered if she'd be able to try it; she was so nervous about her first meeting with an actual wedding organizer that it was making her nauseous.

After the twenty-minute drive to Aubrey, they arrived at the venue. Chantelle seemed the least nervous of them all. She bounded up the stone steps, exclaiming with delight at the hanging baskets and the stained glass windows. Emily thought the venue looked beautiful from the outside; it was old and very classical looking. There were large swaths of grass surrounding it also, with apple trees which would look lovely in the wedding photos.

They were welcomed at the door by a smartly dressed young woman called Laura. She led them inside.

Emily gasped as she observed the grandeur of the place. She could just picture it now, the ceremony, the guests, the dancing. For the first time she got a mental image of what it might look like to marry Daniel, to wear the beautiful dress and walk the aisle with their loved ones watching on. She felt her breath catch in her lungs.

"Would you like to take a seat?" Laura said, gesturing to where the tasting buffet was laid out.

Everyone sat, apart from Chantelle, who paced around the venue assessing its size and décor, everything from the carpets to the artwork.

"Don't mind her," Emily said to Laura with a grin. "She's our surveyor."

Emily and Daniel tasted the first set of entrees, which were presented in little bite-sized pieces. Emily couldn't help but feel very strange in this situation. She couldn't tell if it was Daniel's nerves or just her own, but it felt odd to be sitting next to him in this formal setting, taking mouthful after mouthful of different flavored dishes. It was like they didn't belong here, like they were very out of place. Emily could barely meet his eye as they worked their way through all the food choices.

Thankfully, Chantelle eased some of the pressure with her antics. She was in fine form, striding around like she owned the place, making affirmative statements about which foods she liked and didn't.

"I think you should have this for starter," she said decisively, pointing at the tomato and mozzarella bites, "then the fish for main, and for dessert…" She tapped her chin. This clearly took a bit more thought. "Go for the cheesecake."

Everyone laughed.

"But you've picked the three most expensive things on the menu!" Emily pointed out, giggling.

Laura seemed to take that as a cue to touch on the subject of money. "Have you decided on a food budget?" she asked.

"We haven't even decided on a wedding budget yet," Daniel joked, but Emily couldn't quite see the funny side. It felt a little too close to the bone. Why hadn't they decided that yet? Why hadn't they decided anything yet? Come to think of it, after deciding to make this appointment, they hadn't sat down again to discuss anything.

"Well, that's okay for now," Laura said, giving them a professionally blank smile. "It does take some time to sort all these things out. I don't suppose you have any idea about how many guests you'll be having? The venue can take two hundred."

"Oh, um…" Emily scratched her neck. If they didn't know whether their own mothers would come, how on earth were they supposed to know about the other guests! "We're still finalizing the numbers."

"No problem at all," Laura said, tipping her eyes back down to her ring binder, which contained glossy photos of food, flowers, and decorations, along with a list of prices and customizations.

Though she still had that robotically professionals smile on her face, Emily could read in her eyes a growing exasperation. She must be wondering how she was going to help them organize anything if they didn't know even the basics.

"Our suggested layout would be with the head table over there," Laura explained, gesturing toward the stage area at the back of the room. "That's usually for the wedding party, so bridesmaids, groomsmen, family. You can have a small table for just six, or a large table for up to sixteen. Do you have a rough idea of the numbers?"

Emily felt her chest constricting. This was a disaster. And Daniel seemed more nervous than her. In fact, he looked downright uncomfortable.

"It's a bit complicated," Emily explained. "With our families. Maybe we should move on and come back to that a bit later."

She couldn't bear the tension anymore. Laura looked flustered too, clearly realizing she wasn't dealing with the usual here.

"Yes of course." She quickly flipped through several pages in her binder. "So we have the large double doors over there. They can be left open if the weather is nice. Are you hoping for a spring or summer wedding, or are you more of an autumn/winter couple? We're completely booked for spring and summer next year so you'd have to wait, but we have autumn and winter spots available."

Emily watched Daniel's reaction to the news that their wedding could take place as early as next September. He went completely pale. The sight of him made Emily even more nervous.

Chantelle seemed to be picking up on the tension. Her goofy confidence was waning. She kept looking from Emily to Daniel, her enthusiasm fading with every passing moment.

"Maybe we should take your card for the time being," Emily said to Laura. "Rearrange when we know a few more details." She stood abruptly.

"Oh, oh, okay," Laura said, taken aback, dropping her binder in her haste to stand and shake Emily's hand.

Emily did so quickly. Then she rushed out of the venue, leaving Daniel behind to shake Laura's hand just as swiftly. She burst out of the doors and onto the steps, listening to the sound of Daniel's distant voice explaining to Laura that they'd be in touch.

Out in the cold, Emily held back her tears. She was shaken to the core. Not just from their lack of plans, or from Daniel's general quietness over the last few days, but from the micro-expressions he was making and what she inferred from them. Did Daniel actually want to marry her or was the proposal some impulsive moment he'd gotten swept up in? Was the reality of choosing a date in the not too distant future giving him cold feet? What if he took the cowardly approach of pushing the wedding back a few years, leaving her in a state of limbo, dragging out the engagement for as long as possible just as Jayne had warned?

"Emily," Daniel tried as he and Chantelle joined her.

She felt his fingertips brush her hand but she pulled away, not wanting his touch at this moment in time.

Daniel didn't try again. She heard him sigh. Then, silently, everyone piled back into the pickup truck.

The mood on the drive home couldn't have been more different from the mood on the way there. It was almost as if the air was permeated with anxiety. Chantelle's cute outfit suddenly seemed like a façade, like they'd dressed her up in order to trick Laura into viewing them like any other happy, uncomplicated family when they were in fact anything but. Their pasts—hers, Daniel's, even Chantelle's—complicated everything. And worse than that, their pasts complicated their very beings, their personalities, their abilities to deal with pressure and stress, their abilities to relate to one another.

For what felt like the hundredth time since he proposed, Emily wondered what was really going on inside Daniel's head.

CHAPTER SIX

When Emily had first told Daniel about her desire to adopt Chantelle, they'd contacted their friend Richard Goldsmith, who was a custody attorney from town. An informal chat had taken place in the inn over coffee and cake. But this time, their meeting was taking place in his office in town. This time it felt serious and very real.

Emily nervously smoothed down her skirt as she and Daniel entered the plush office, which looked like something out of a story book, set in an old red brick building covered with climbing ivy. Emily couldn't help her feelings of apprehension. What if Richard had bad news? What if she would never be able to become Chantelle's real, legal mother like the little girl seemed to desire as much as Emily herself?

The receptionist, a young woman with fiery ginger hair, welcomed them with a sweet, reassuring smile.

"Mr. Goldsmith will be with you shortly," she said, without them even needing to introduce themselves. "He's just been held up with another client."

Emily squirmed and chewed her lip. Client. It felt odd to think of herself in such a way. But that's what she was, and what she must be to achieve her goal. Taking legal custody of Chantelle wasn't just a matter of chatting with an acquaintance on her porch over coffee anymore. It would involve lawyers and courts, judges and legal documentation. This was real and she needed to get used to it.

Emily steeled herself. She could handle this. She had to; she loved Chantelle too much to fail, to wilt under the pressure. But there was another part of Emily that was still reeling from Saturday's failed trip to the wedding venue and the way Daniel had clammed up at the mere suggestion of selecting a season during which they would be wed. If he was changing his mind about this, he needed to be brave and tell her before things got serious, before contracts were signed and hearts were too much on the line to turn back. The words of her family and friends still repeated in Emily's mind, that Daniel was using her because he wanted someone to raise Chantelle for him, that Emily had made it too easy on him. She'd let him live rent free on the grounds of her property, she'd taken his child in without question, and had forgiven him so quickly for those long six weeks during which he'd prioritized his child over her. But what they didn't accept or understand was how all those things made her love him more: his resourcefulness and resilience during the years he'd lived in the carriage house, the care he'd shown the property during the decades it had stood empty, keeping it on life support in case Roy Mitchell returned, and the fact he'd stepped up for Chantelle without question, proving himself to be a real man, the sort that didn't shirk his responsibilities, that put his child's needs over his own.

The door to Richard's office suddenly swung open, making Emily jump out of the thoughts she'd been absorbed in. Richard stood in the doorway as he shook hands with a petite, blond woman sniffling into a tissue. She reminded Emily instantly of Sheila. A wave of guilt crashed over her.

Emily couldn't hear Richard's hushed words but she picked up on his reassuring tone. Then he bid goodbye to the woman and she shuffled past them, heading out the door in a flurry.

Once she was gone, Richard turned to Emily and Daniel. "Please, come in."

"Is she okay?" Emily asked as they followed him into his office.

She was concerned for the woman he'd just shown out, but also curious about the reason for her tears. Perhaps she was about to enter a court battle like them, only she was on the flip side of the coin, the side where she was having her legal guardianship revoked. Was it fair? Had she done anything to deserve it, drugs, abandonment? Did anyone ever deserve it?

But then she remembered Chantelle. No, it wasn't fair. But this wasn't about what was fair, it was about what was right.

"I'm afraid I can't discuss that," Richard said, putting an end to Emily's wild flight of fantasy. He settled into his large leather chair and adjusted the pant legs of his crisp gray suit. "I have to show the same level of confidentiality to all my clients. I'm sure you understand."

Emily's unease abruptly returned on hearing that word again. Client. It reminded her how serious this was. They were paying for this meeting, for Richard's expertise and his time. Everything had become suddenly very formal. Emily wondered whether she should have worn a suit.

Daniel seemed just as uncomfortable beside her. She could tell by the way he kept fidgeting and fiddling with the buttons on his shirt. They were both very much out of their comfort zone in Richard's plush office.

Richard removed his glasses and looked up from their file. "So there are two options to consider here. It partly comes down to semantics, but there are some crucial differences between the two courses of action we can take."

"Which are…?" Emily prompted.

"Guardianship or adoption," Richard concluded. "Guardianship, in its basic form, would simply establish a legal relationship between Chantelle and Emily but it wouldn't end Sheila's legal relationship with her child. On the other hand, with adoption, all of Sheila's rights and obligations over Chantelle would cease and Emily would henceforth be considered her mother. In other words, she would be a substitute for Sheila in every legal sense. Adoption is intended to create a permanent and stable home, so we would need Sheila to relinquish her rights over Chantelle, and to understand that this would be irrevocable."

Emily nodded, letting his words seep in. She thought of Chantelle in her room asking her to promise Sheila would never come back.

"Chantelle doesn't want a relationship with her mom," Emily explained.

"But a guardianship would be much easier to secure," Richard contested, folding his hands on the desk. "If Sheila isn't prepared to relinquish her rights over Chantelle, which from what you've told me of her thus far she would not want to do, we'll have to prove that Chantelle would not just be better off with you but that Sheila is unfit to care for her, and that allowing her any kind of contact with her mother would cause her harm."

"She's told me time and time again she wants me to be her real mom," Emily said. "That she never wants to see Sheila again."

Daniel looked uncomfortable. "I don't think it would be right to cut Sheila out entirely."

Richard listened to them quietly. "This isn't about visitation rights or anything like that. If you become Chantelle's legal mother, it would be up to you whether she ever sees Sheila again. Unless you're planning on taking out a restraining order on her. This is just about the legality, about who makes the decisions regarding her care."

It felt too clinical. How could a child's life and well-being be considered *just a legality*? This was her heart they were talking about. There was no way of separating out her emotions. It was impossible.

Emily touched Daniel's hand lightly.

"It needs to be full adoption," she explained. "Otherwise Sheila might take her away from us one day. Chantelle wakes up screaming in the night about that prospect. She's asked me over and over again to protect her from Sheila. She's asked if I can be her mom. I know she's only seven but that girl knows her own mind."

Daniel finally relented with a single, sad nod. Emily felt bad for him, but at the same time she was certain that this was the right thing to do for Chantelle's sake.

"We're going for adoption," Daniel confirmed.

Richard nodded. "Each state has a different process," he explained. "But here in Maine, we'd need to file a petition of relinquishment to Sheila. The courts would serve her with papers, then she'd be entitled to counseling, there'd be a mediation meeting in front of a family law magistrate with the aim of coming to a peaceful resolution. Finally, a court date would be set for a judge to make a decision. Of course, if Sheila gives consent, things will go more smoothly. If she fights the petition then things will take longer as there will need to be a summary hearing, a jeopardy hearing, a judicial review, and finally a permanency planning hearing."

"What costs are involved?" Daniel asked.

"Some," Richard explained. "But they're not as hefty as you'd expect. We're talking around two hundred dollars per meeting, so it will be less than a thousand dollars all in."

One thousand dollars. That's all it would take to make Chantelle their daughter. One thousand dollars, plus weeks and months of anguish.

"Daniel," Richard then said somewhat solemnly, "I must make it clear that your prior conviction won't do you any favors."

"Prior conviction?" Emily stammered.

"I told you," Daniel said in a hushed, embarrassed voice. "When I defended Sheila. From her ex-husband. You remember."

"You went to court over that?" Emily said. She hadn't realized it had been so serious. She'd assumed Daniel had just gotten a slap on the wrist by the local cops and sent on his way.

She shuffled uncomfortably in her seat, reeling.

Richard coughed and carried on. He didn't seem fazed. He'd probably seen it all in his office.

"What would really help for you, Daniel, is if you showed you were in paid employment."

"He is," Emily said. "He works for me."

"He's not on your payroll, though," Richard explained. "Cash-in-hand work doesn't look great. It needs to be consistent. A nine-to-five preferably."

"Okay," Daniel said, sounding resolved. "I'll do that if it will help."

38

Emily felt suddenly apprehensive. Daniel had always been available to her. Theirs was a fifty-fifty partnership. How would she cope with him out of the house all day? She'd be left to look after Chantelle alone. But the pressure for a full adoption was coming from her. If Daniel had his way, they'd take the less dramatic guardianship route. This was all her doing.

Richard folded up their file and returned his glasses to his nose. "Well, the next steps are for me to prepare the documentation, put the legal request forward to Sheila's attorney. Then I'll be in touch with more news. I must warn you, this will stir up bad blood in the short term. You ought to prepare for some drama."

Daniel squeezed Emily's arm for reassurance.

"We can handle it," Emily told Richard. "For Chantelle, we can handle anything."

CHAPTER SEVEN

With Richard Goldsmith's words still ringing in their ears, Emily and Daniel returned to the inn, hoping for some quiet time to reflect on their situation. Instead, they found that the inn was buzzing with activity.

The several guests who had arrived over the weekend were being served food in the dining room by Matthew, the young chef Emily had taken on full time to help Parker out now they'd started serving lunches and evening meals. Colin, who was still occupying the carriage house and now took most of his meals in the inn, was amongst them, his handsome face attracting stares from the women that he seemed impervious to.

Colin had kept mostly to himself since Thanksgiving. He always disappeared off to the carriage house as soon as he'd finished eating to immerse himself once again in his work. His dashing good looks were the talk of the town (amongst the female residents at least), and his quiet brooding just added to the mystery. Emily knew that he'd recently separated from his wife and wondered whether he'd thrown himself into his work (whatever that may be) in an attempt to take his mind off his troubles. His head was always buried in his laptop. Either that or he'd be scribbling furiously into a notepad, just as he was doing now at his dining table in the corner. Emily was intrigued about what his job may be but of course didn't want to be nosy and actually ask.

As Daniel and Emily walked through the corridor, Emily noticed a young woman in brightly patterned leggings standing at the empty reception desk waiting for service. Serena's shift was over and it was Lois, the new girl who'd only been with them a week or so, who was supposed to be covering reception duties. But she was nowhere to be seen. Emily looked at the rusty bronze antique till she'd purchased from Rico's sitting upon the heavy marble top. Theft wasn't exactly high on her list of concerns in a place like Sunset Harbor but you could never be too careful.

"I'm so sorry," Emily said to the waiting woman, rushing behind the desk in a hurry. "Can I help you?"

"I'm Tracey," the short woman said, beaming brightly and swishing her mousy chin-length hair. "The new yoga teacher."

"Oh!" Emily exclaimed, noticing for the first time the rolled up yoga mat beneath the woman's arm.

It had totally slipped Emily's mind that she'd arranged for yoga classes to be taught in the ballroom as a way of bringing in a tiny bit more income. She and Tracey had agreed on the telephone that twenty percent of the profits would go to the inn, but since Tracey's classes were only $10 and only Karen and Cynthia had thus far shown any interest, Emily wasn't expecting it to turn into much of a money spinner.

Still, on first meeting, Tracey seemed like she'd be a calming and reassuring presence in the inn. Emily was glad to know there'd be another person around the place since Daniel was soon going to be absent more often.

Emily led Tracey to the ballroom.

"It's so much more wonderful than I expected," Tracey gushed in her floaty voice as she gazed around her, taking in the polished floors and beautiful Tiffany glass windows. "This is a very relaxing environment," she continued. "Inspiring." She closed her eyes, took a deep breath, and then released it slowly. "Yes, this will do nicely. The room has a wonderful aura."

Emily managed to contain her smile. Then she left Tracey to set her yoga station up and rushed back to the still unmanned reception desk to grab the ringing phone.

"The Inn at Sunset Harbor," she said, distracted by the fact that Daniel was now nowhere to be seen.

She glanced all around, searching, then noticed him through the partly open door to the living room. He was hunched over a copy of the *Sunset Gazette*. His job hunting had already commenced, Emily realized, and though she admired him for getting right on it, she couldn't help but project her mind into a future where he was never available, and that caused her anguish.

"Sorry, what?" Emily said, realizing she hadn't listened to a word of the voice on the other end of the line. "Oh, no, I'm perfectly happy with my current Wi-Fi provider."

She hung up, her gaze still focused on Daniel and the intensity of his job hunting. Just then Lois emerged, coming down the staircase in a fluster.

"There you are," Emily said.

"I'm so sorry," Lois stammered. "I was helping Marnie fold the bedding."

Marnie was the new housekeeper. Emily loved the fact that her staff were becoming good friends, that they were helping one another out, and in her mind she immediately forgave Lois for straying from her duties.

"That's okay," Emily told the young woman. "Just remember it's important to keep the desk attended whenever possible."

With Lois finally located, Emily clocked off and went into the living room to see Daniel. He was sitting at the table in the bay window, chewing the end of his pen, the newspaper spread out in front of him and covered in red circles.

"Looks like you've had some luck there," Emily said, coming up behind him and wrapping her arms around his shoulders.

"Yeah, I've found a couple of things," Daniel said distractedly. "Handyman jobs mostly. But they're all just the same kind of casual work I do here. Nothing permanent."

Emily thought he sounded a little despondent.

"You can't expect to find the perfect job the first time you open a newspaper," she said. "I'm sure you'll find something soon." She kissed the crown of his head and looked up at the clock. "We need to go and pick Chantelle up from school."

Daniel looked up from the paper, shocked. "It's that time already?" He looked back down at the newspaper and then up at Emily with a slightly pained expression. "I've got a ton of calls to make. Is it okay if I stay here and plow on with the job hunt?"

"Sure," Emily said, faltering.

Daniel had never missed a drop-off or collection of Chantelle. The school run was one of the times he seemed most energized, most like the father he was learning to become. Was this the beginning of him taking Emily for granted? Her feelings were so conflicted. This whole adoption thing was her doing. She couldn't have it both ways. Perhaps Daniel was treating her like Chantelle's mother because that's what she was asking to be?

She went out to her car and realized there was no car seat for Chantelle. Had she really not driven in her own car since Chantelle had arrived? They'd so easily fallen into the habit of taking Daniel's pickup truck everywhere, traveling everywhere as a family.

After grabbing the car seat from the truck and fixing it into her own car, Emily felt a sudden surge of reminiscent independence. This was the car that had transported her to her new life in Maine, after all.

She turned the key in the ignition and took a moment to listen to the thrum of the engine as it turned over, still spluttering and struggling just as it had done all those months ago. Then, with a confident exhalation, Emily headed along the drive and out onto West Street.

As she passed Trevor's house she wondered what was going on behind his closed curtains. Remembering her resolve to visit him more often, she decided to do so this afternoon. Maybe Chantelle would want to accompany her. The child had such a caring side and she knew her presence would really help lift Trevor's spirits. And anyway, Daniel was too preoccupied to entertain Chantelle after school, so she may as well tag along with Emily.

Emily turned onto the coastal path, following the roads of Sunset Harbor toward Chantelle's school. As she drove, she tried to sift through all her thoughts, to organize the jumble of events into something coherent. Adoption, Trevor, her father, Daniel, the wedding; it wasn't like she was short on things to ruminate over.

So absorbed in her thoughts was Emily that the drive to school went by in a flash. Before she knew it, she'd reached the busy parking lot, where the familiar cars of her new parent friends crawled into spaces. Being in her own unfamiliar car gained her glances from the other parents, and reminded Emily that this was her first solo trip collecting Chantelle. But she always found the school gates to be a place of support, so she swallowed her flutter of nerves as she parked and headed to the school gates with her head held high.

Emily wasn't sure whether people were talking about her or whether she was just paranoid, but she felt great relief when she spotted her friend Yvonne. She was alone as well, stood with her back resting against the fence, completely engrossed in her cell phone. Emily made a beeline for her.

Yvonne looked up and, blushing, shoved her phone into her pocket.

"These games are so addictive," she laughed, reaching for Emily and embracing her.

Emily felt instantly more comfortable standing beside Yvonne. Yvonne never seemed to care what other people thought of her and it was something Emily admired in her friend. She wished she could be as confident.

"No Kieran today?" Emily asked.

"His flying schedule at the moment is crazy," Yvonne explained with a shake of the head. "He's doing the ten-day transatlantic route, back and forth between Hawaii and Japan. Then he's straight off to Paris to vacation with his other kids. I won't see him for three weeks!"

Emily couldn't help but project her own feelings onto Yvonne's situation. Like her, Yvonne had responsibilities beyond her own family, namely Kieran's children from his prior marriage. Yvonne was also juggling that fine line between being accommodating and being a doormat. Emily wondered if that would be her soon, picking Chantelle up alone with Daniel never to be seen, torn from the family by a job their legal situation demanded he take. The thought troubled her.

Just then the school doors opened and Bailey and Chantelle came running out, bounding down the steps. When Chantelle had first started here she'd been timid, following the firecracker that was Bailey, always in her shadow. Now she held her own. She was confident, animated. Since moving to Sunset Harbor the child had really come to life. Seeing her smile was just the antidote Emily needed for her worries. Everything was worth it for Chantelle.

Chantelle rushed up to Emily excitedly and threw her arms around her. Emily bundled her up in her arms, noting the incongruity of the situation. Just a few hours earlier she'd been discussing court cases and legal battles, but for the girl it had just been another carefree day at school, chatting with friends, painting pictures and reading books. The contrast between her role as a comforting mom and a hard-nosed appellant was somewhat jarring.

"Right, we're off to ballet practice," Yvonne said, kissing Emily goodbye.

The little girls also bid their farewells, and then Emily and Chantelle headed hand in hand to the parking lot.

When Chantelle saw Emily's beat up car instead of Daniel's pickup truck she frowned.

"Where's Daddy?" she asked in her sweet, innocent voice.

"He's just doing some work at the inn," Emily explained as calmly as she could, though the question triggered a flutter in her chest. "I was wondering if you wanted to go and see Trevor?" she said quickly, changing the subject before Chantelle could probe further into Daniel's absence.

"Okay," Chantelle said as she climbed into her car seat and buckled up. "But we'll have to stop by a store so we can bring him some fruit."

Emily hadn't explained the graveness of Trevor's situation to Chantelle. She'd just told her that he was very unwell. Fruit wouldn't take away Trevor's brain tumor but Emily didn't have the heart to tell Chantelle that.

"Great idea," she said with a smile.

She got into her own seat, whereby she turned the car on and drove them to the grocery store. Chantelle chose some shiny red apples, a bunch of grapes, and several bananas. She also added hot chocolate packets to the basket, microwavable popcorn, and some sparkly stickers, the sort of things that made her happy when she was sick. Satisfied that their care package was complete, they headed off in the car again and pulled up in front of Trevor's house.

Emily went ahead and rang his doorbell. When he answered the door, he looked terrible.

"Oh, Trevor," Emily gasped, her heart clenching with sorrow. The grocery bag filled with fruit and snacks seemed suddenly juvenile.

"Emily," Trevor replied, smiling thinly. "I'm glad to see you. Chantelle, you're here too."

Chantelle handed him the paper bag. "For you," she said, grinning.

Trevor took the bag and peered over the top at the sparkly stickers. Though he smiled, Emily could see the emotion in his eyes. He was holding something back.

"Chantelle, why don't you run home now? Go and see Daddy," Emily suggested, suddenly concerned for Trevor. "Mogsy and Rain need a walk. And Owen's coming over for your singing lessons so have a snack," she added. "Remind Daddy, okay?"

But the little girl was already halfway across the lawn, skipping and looking carefree. "Okay!" she called back.

Once Emily had watched Chantelle safely enter the house, she turned her full attention to Trevor.

"Trevor, is everything okay?" she asked tenderly. "Is there anything I can do for you?"

Silently, Trevor gestured for Emily to come inside. She stepped over the threshold into his house, the antiseptic smell now familiar to her. They went and sat together in his living room, which was decorated sparsely, almost clinically. Trevor had no photographs up on the mantel or shelves. He said he preferred his living space to be uncluttered, but Emily wondered whether it was because he actually had no one left to put pictures up of. The thought pained Emily.

They settled into his comfortable, crisp white sofa.

"I had another appointment today," Trevor explained in his calm, dignified way.

"And?" Emily asked, encouraging him to continue.

Trevor did not meet her eye as he spoke.

"My prognosis has been reduced. They've given me three to six months."

Emily pressed a hand to her gaping mouth with shock. Three months? It was so little! She quickly calculated it in her head and realized there was a chance that Trevor might only just make it a little past the new year. She couldn't comprehend it.

"I'm... I'm so sorry," Emily said breathlessly.

Trevor just shook his head. "Apologies won't keep me alive," he said, sighing.

Emily felt mute, dumb, useless. There was nothing to be done. Trevor's death was imminent. No amount of popcorn or stickers could stop it.

"Let me fix you some dinner," Emily said.

She could tell he hadn't been eating properly because of the amount of weight he'd lost recently. Again, it didn't feel like enough, but it was something.

"Emily, you don't need to do that," Trevor protested.

But Emily insisted. She knew it was only his pride that made him refuse her offer of help.

"I'm not going to allow you to neglect yourself," came her rebuke.

Finally Trevor relented.

They went into the kitchen, which was as immaculately clean as ever. Emily made them coffee first, then began cooking dinner.

"You can always take your meals at the inn," she told him as she chopped peppers.

"I couldn't."

"Why ever not?" Emily replied. "It's not like you'd be the only person in Sunset Harbor to do so!" She laughed, thinking of how she'd started collecting all the waifs and strays of the town, how they'd begun congregating at the inn like it were some kind of meeting place. The thought warmed her.

"I'm not an invalid," Trevor said with dry sarcasm, smoothing his moustache. "Not quite yet anyway."

Emily just shrugged and turned back to her chopping. "Well, Parker will be cooking an extra dish each day anyway so you may as well..." She looked over her shoulder and grinned mischievously.

"Fine," Trevor relented. "But only because I hate the thought of it going to waste."

Once the food was cooked, Emily served it up to Trevor and then sat at the table with him so he had company while he ate. She caught a glance at the clock and realized Owen would soon be arriving for Chantelle's singing lesson. She wondered whether she ought to be heading home, whether Daniel had remembered to give Chantelle her snack. But then she found her focus drawn back to Trevor, away from the mess of her life. Having some distance from the inn gave her a brief respite from wedding woes and adoption anxiety. For the first time in a long time she felt a sense of peace. To think she'd find that in Trevor Mann's company! She vowed to spend as much time as she could spare with Trevor, to be a good neighbor, a good person, to make sure his last few months on this earth were not spent alone.

It was dark by the time she left Trevor's house. The lights were on in the carriage house, and as she passed she could just make out Colin through the windows as he paced back and forth holding a paper before him, gesticulating wildly and talking to himself. Emily wondered if perhaps he was a Shakespearean actor. Or a madman. Either way it wasn't her business.

Lolly and Lola the chickens had tucked themselves away in their coop for the night and were out of sight as Emily made her way up the back path. As she opened the back door, Rain and Mogsy rushed for her, leaping up for pats and licks. She wondered if Daniel had remembered to walk them in her absence.

She entered the kitchen and found Parker and Matthew washing dishes.

"Is dinner over already?" she asked, shocked by how much time had passed.

"The last guests finished at nine p.m.," Parker said. "Everyone's either out in town or up in their rooms already."

Emily couldn't believe it was so late. She'd gotten completely lost in her visit with Trevor and hadn't realized how much time had passed.

From the living room she could hear the sound of Chantelle singing, accompanied by Owen on the piano. He must have been here for two hours already! It was almost Chantelle's bedtime!

She rushed into the living room.

"I'm sorry I'm so late," she said, bustling in.

It was only then that she noticed Serena sitting on the sofa. For a brief moment Emily felt confused—Serena didn't have a shift tonight. But then she noticed the way her friend was gazing adoringly at Owen on the piano and she smiled to herself, happy to know that affection was growing between them. Perhaps they would begin dating soon, if Owen ever got the guts up to ask Serena out.

"You must have been playing for hours!" Emily said with a gasp.

"Yes, but I don't mind," Owen replied, smiling, his fingers not stopping for a second. "Playing this beautiful instrument is an honor, really. And hearing Chantelle sing, of course. She's really improving. I didn't know such a thing could be possible."

Chantelle beamed. Emily was glad to see her confidence growing. She'd been so terrified to sing in front of an audience, yet here she was now looking more than comfortable with Serena watching on.

"That's wonderful," Emily said. "But I'm afraid we'll have to call it a night now. Chantelle has school in the morning. It's time for bed."

Owen's haunting piano playing stopped abruptly. He went to stand.

"Not you," Emily smirked. "You can stay as long as you like!"

As she led Chantelle out of the room, she winked at Serena. Her friend blushed, clearly embarrassed by just how transparent she was making her feelings.

"Where's your dad?" Emily asked Chantelle as she led her upstairs.

She'd been expecting to see Daniel in the living room during Chantelle's singing lesson, but once again he'd made himself invisible. She worried that their meeting with Richard had something to do with it, that perhaps he was having second thoughts.

But then she noticed the look on Chantelle's face—a naughty kind of smirk—and she could tell the little girl knew something that she wasn't letting on. Her stomach sunk at the thought she was about to be the brunt of a prank.

"Chantelle," Emily said in a somewhat warning tone. "Tell me where your dad is and what he's up to."

Chantelle shook her head. "Not telling you. But you'll find out soon."

They reached the landing and Emily braced herself, expecting Daniel to leap out and scare her, or a face full of silly string. Instead, the only thing that Emily noticed that was out of place was the dancing light of candles coming through the crack under her bedroom door, and the perfumey smell that permeated the air.

"What is that?" she said, confused.

Chantelle giggled. Just then, the bedroom door flew open and there stood Daniel. Not dressed as a ghoul or with a plate filled with whipped cream, but in his pajamas.

"This way," he said, gesturing for Emily to enter the room.

She frowned, bemused. "But Chantelle needs a story before bed and—"

Chantelle cut her off by giving her a little shove. "Serena's going to put me to bed. It's all settled. Don't worry."

Emily shook her head, confused. "It's all settled? What's all settled?"

"Your date!" Chantelle announced.

48

Just then, Serena appeared behind her, having crept up the stairs silently.

"You were in on this?" Emily laughed.

Serena just held a finger to her lips. She whisked Chantelle away into her room, leaving Emily standing alone in the corridor, with Daniel before her.

He held out his hand, palm up. Emily smiled and placed her hand in his.

He led her silently through the master bedroom and into their en suite. There, Emily saw that he was running a bubble bath. Lined around the outside were scented candles. There was a bowl of fresh strawberries and two glasses of champagne.

"What's all this?" Emily asked, touched.

"I thought we needed a bit of time just the two of us," Daniel said. "To relax and not think about any of the heavy stuff."

Emily kissed him deeply. "Thank you, it's perfect," she said.

As Emily undressed and sunk into the hot, bubbly water, she felt all her worries over the last few days melt away. All that existed for her in that moment was Daniel. And she couldn't have been happier.

CHAPTER EIGHT

Several days passed in a blur of telephone calls with Richard Goldsmith, tending to Trevor, wedding discussions, and business with guests at the inn. Though Emily was thankful that business was picking up, she also found herself becoming increasingly swamped and overwhelmed.

It came as a surprise (and great relief) when Emily found herself in the living room one evening, with Chantelle drawing by the window and Daniel lighting a fire, the dogs stretched out on the rug. It felt comforting and familiar.

It was only in this state of calm that Emily even remembered the architect's plans that Trevor had given her the day after Thanksgiving. She'd been so shocked by the sight of them that she had put them to one side, not quite ready to deal with any emotional fall-out they might cause. But now she decided to take a look, to feel that connection with her father, to allow more forgotten memories to emerge.

She spread the plans out onto the coffee table, the paper feeling like waxy baking parchment beneath her fingers. She looked down at the plans, drawn in faint pencil lines with angular precision, each different floor of the house separated out so they appeared side by side, connected by a jagged line that represented a staircase. There was the widow's walk and the secret flight of stairs running from the third floor to the roof. And there was the ballroom, closed off and hidden down its strange corridor. Emily could see now, looking at the plans, that the ballroom had once been an entirely different structure and that it was that small, strange corridor that connected it to the main house. She wondered whether her dad had decided to conjoin them via the narrow, low-ceilinged corridor as some kind of personal joke, or if it was symptomatic of his secretive mind.

Just then, something on the plans caught Emily's eye. She'd just located the living room (the very space in which they now sat) on the plans when she noticed there was another corridor, not a small spindly one like the one that led to the ballroom, but an enormous one as wide as the room, connecting an outbuilding to the living room.

Almost as if she'd been burned by flame, Emily leapt up, surprised, and looked about her with confusion.

"What's wrong?" Daniel asked, turning his head from the now blazing fire in the hearth.

Chantelle looked up from her drawing and studied Emily's face. But Emily was too bemused to speak. She ran up to the far wall and placed her fingers against the wallpaper. Most of the inn had been renovated when she moved in, but not the wallpaper in this room. It had been in too good condition for Emily to justify replacing it, since it was the original and it felt criminal to strip it out for no reason. Now she realized that that decision had kept another one of her father's secrets from her for many more months.

"Emily, what are you doing?" Daniel asked, frowning, coming up to her side.

"Look at the plans!" Emily gasped. "On the table. There's another room back here."

Daniel's eyes widened with surprise. He did as she commanded, running to the coffee table, searching the diagram until he'd located the source of Emily's surprise.

By now, Chantelle had jumped from her seat to join in. She seemed thrilled. A secret room was the stuff of fairytales for a child of her age.

Emily ran her fingers all the way along the wall, searching for a seam or a fissure that might indicate where the door was hidden.

"It's behind the shelves!" Daniel said, looking up from the plans at the table. "I'd always wondered about that extra extension at the side of the house. I'd just assumed it was an outer foundation wall or something, there are so many oddities with this house after all. I did wonder about it, though. Now it all makes sense."

The shelves he'd indicated were currently stuffed with books and ornamental display plates. Emily hastily began taking them down, bundling the books into Chantelle's arms so she could place them in piles on the table and floor. Daniel helped, removing the more fragile items that Emily couldn't trust her trembling fingers not to drop.

Once they were clear of items, it was time to remove the large wooden shelves. They were made from repossessed railways sleepers, each weighing what felt like a ton. After some groaning and straining, they stood staring at a now empty alcove.

Emily knocked against the wall and heard the dull echo that indicated its hollowness. Chantelle gasped with surprise. She knocked too, almost leaping back in shock at the repeated hollow sound. Emily felt her excitement grow. Chantelle was practically buzzing with anticipation. Beside her, Daniel's eyes sparkled.

"How do we get in?" Chantelle cried, bouncing up and down.

"Sledgehammer?" Daniel suggested.

"Absolutely not!" Emily replied. "Think of the wallpaper."

She ran her fingers over the textured print.

"I wonder if this does anything," she heard Chantelle's small voice say.

Emily looked down. The child was crouched in the corner, peering at something. To Emily's astonishment she realized it was a small lever, tucked out of sight in the lowermost corner.

She shook her head with shock, a million feelings vying inside of her. Her father's strange habit of hiding things from view had come to its extreme conclusion. This was no longer a dusty vault in the corner of a wine cellar; it was an entire room that had been boarded up behind a false, plasterboard wall. According to the architect's drawings there was a whole room on the other side, double the one they were standing in again. Emily just had to pull the secret lever to open it up. She couldn't even begin to imagine what she would find behind it! Her father's secret spy's lair? Concealed stairs to his underground bunker where he'd been living in hiding for the last twenty years? Her mind swam with thoughts, each one more fantastical than the last.

"Go on," Daniel prompted her.

Taking a deep breath to steel herself, Emily took hold of the lever and pulled. There was a low, growling noise, the sound of a long disused mechanism coming back to life. Then, with a click, the wall sprang back an inch. Emily pushed the small opening and felt the wall resist her pressure. She pressed again, harder this time, and the wall began arcing open, creaking like a trapdoor to a basement, revealing pitch blackness on the other side.

Flabbergasted, overwhelmed, Emily stood staring at the gaping void, at the blackness that might contain everything or nothing. Daniel and Chantelle rushed off to grab some flashlights. On their return, everyone stepped together into Roy Mitchell's most recently unearthed secret.

Emily directed the beam of her flashlight all around, gasping in surprise at the sight that greeted her. In the ten-foot extension to the living room was a huge mahogany bar, complete with tables and chairs, bar stools, and optics on the wall.

"What on earth?" Emily exclaimed, walking inside.

The room was gorgeous, and the bar was clearly very valuable, with an antique marble top and mahogany wood paneling below and behind it. Emily gasped with surprise as she realized it was also fully stocked with liquor. It was like a movie set.

Daniel and Chantelle were both looking around her with shocked expressions. Emily felt exactly the same. How had this stayed hidden for all those years?

"I think this was a speakeasy," Emily cried. "Look, some of these posters are from Prohibition!"

She squealed with excitement. She'd stepped into a museum, with the same musty smell of dust, hidden in a real room inside her real house.

"We need to restore it," Daniel exclaimed. "It would be an amazing addition to the inn."

Emily looked back out at the warm, firelit living room just through the other side of the alcove. The whole wall must have been a fake all along, put up in order to hide the liquor.

"We could have a New Year's Eve party here!" Daniel added. He was clearly getting excited about the prospect.

Emily explored the space. There were hints that the room hadn't been forgotten about, signs that someone (and she presumed it to be her father) had been in here not too long ago. On the labels of some of the bottles of liquor, Emily saw they had dates from just a few years prior, and that they'd been nestled behind the older antique bottles to be kept hidden.

Just like the date on the letters from just two years ago, seeing the liquor bottles from only a few years hence was further confirmation to Emily that her father had been here. She added it to her list of revelations—which also included Trevor's sighting of Roy in a beat-up car—that confirmed her father was not only alive but that he had very recently returned to the house.

She wondered if her dad had used this secret room as a drinking den, as a place he could escape to in order to indulge in the shameful habit that had contributed to the breakup of his marriage and the death of his youngest daughter.

While Emily's mind was wrapped up in thoughts, Daniel was still on a roll, considering all the possibilities of the new room.

"I could restore it like I did with the carriage house," he exclaimed. "Work behind the bar."

"You're supposed to be finding a proper job, remember," Emily said.

Just then, Serena walked in through the living room door, her arms laden with freshly laundered towels.

"Sorry to interrupt, it's just that one of the guests…" she began. Then she paused and her mouth gaped open as she took in the sight of the new room, the expanse that had opened up in the living room. "What the…"

"Isn't it great?" Daniel exclaimed, gesturing his arms wide. He already seemed to be feeling some kind of ownership over the bar.

Serena rushed forward, grinning from ear to ear. "This is amazing! Are you going to restore it?" she asked. "You have to!" She grabbed Emily's hand. "Can you imagine how awesome the parties would be if we had a bar in here?"

Emily nodded but it was all a bit too much to take in.

"My friend Alec is looking for bar work," Serena continued. "I bet you he'd work for tips. You know what us students are like."

"And I'll fill in if need be," Daniel added. "May as well while I'm applying and waiting for interviews. I could call George in the morning to look into restoring the room. Take the rest of this fake wall away."

He knocked on the plasterboard and the sound of its hollowness resonated.

"Okay," Emily agreed, smiling finally. "It's a good idea. Let's do it."

Everyone cheered.

Emily grabbed one of the dusty, vintage bottles of whiskey and poured a drink for herself, Daniel, and Serena.

"Sorry, kiddo," she said to Chantelle. "I don't think there's anything here for you."

"How about this?" Chantelle asked, producing a dusty glass bottle of root beer from the back of a cupboard.

"Perfect," Emily said, though she wasn't sure whether such an old soda would taste good. It would certainly be flat by now!

Now that everyone had a glass, they clinked them together and, somewhat hesitantly, took sips of their decades old beverages.

Serena raised her eyebrows. "Wow. That's actually really good."

Daniel nodded. "Amazing quality," he said, peering at the bottle. "And eighty years old! That's pretty vintage!" He seemed more enthused than he had for days.

Emily sipped her own drink, enjoying the sharpness that slid down her throat. It felt like another gift from her father, another thing he'd kept hidden and stored for her when the time was right to unveil it.

Just then, Chantelle made a disgusted noise. "This is horrible!"

Everyone laughed.

"I'd better get back to work," Serena said, looking a little ruddy-cheeked after the unexpected whiskey shot.

Excited by the restoration work, Daniel hopped onto his laptop and began looking into what would need to be done, firing off text message exchanges with his friend George, who had so artfully restored the Tiffany glass for them. Chantelle, ever the organizer, made a list of things she thought should be in the new room, including arcade games and a popcorn machine.

While everyone's creative juices flowed, Emily spent some time in the strange new room. In here, she could feel her father more than in any other room in the house. His study was where she'd first felt connected to him, then she'd felt him in the basement where clues of his secret life had been distributed throughout the labyrinth of wine cellars and the peppering of vaults. What if there was something more in here?

She rushed around, looking for one of her father's hidden vaults. There were none behind the bar, none hidden in trap doors in the floor. Then Emily remembered the Prohibition poster on the wall. Could he have hidden a vault behind it?

Carefully, Emily removed the picture frame from the wall and placed it gently on the floor. And there it was. The door of a vault.

She stared at it, breathing raggedly. Like all the other safes in the house, she knew this one would contain more secrets, more pieces of the puzzle of her father's life.

Then Emily was even more surprised to discover that this safe was not locked. The door was partially open, just a crack. She reached forward, hooking her fingertips into the crack, and pulled the metal door toward her.

Straightaway she saw that there was a stack of papers inside. Her father had a habit of locking all his important documentation away, dispersed throughout the house as though he were paranoid someone would get their hands on them. She felt a sudden deflation at the thought that they would just be random papers, documents and deeds, files from his job, shopping lists.

She began rummaging through them, her emotions a mixture of apprehension and excitement. With each random piece of paper she looked through her hopes faded more and more. But then she noticed something that made her heart flutter. It was a printout of an email exchange regarding the purchase of a car from an auto dealer. The sale had fallen through by the looks of things.

But that wasn't why Emily was interested. What had caught her attention was the email address of the recipient: e-jcm@rm.net. Could it be a code? E-J for Emily Jane, her full name. C for Charlotte and M for Mitchell. Then RM for Roy Mitchell. Could it be a coincidence or was this email address her father's?

Her heart began hammering a mile a minute. Clutching the piece of paper in her hands, Emily ran out of the speakeasy.

"Are you okay?" Daniel asked as she rushed by.

But Emily found she couldn't speak. She just paused and looked at him mutely, the paper in her hands. Finally she managed to stammer, "I have an email to send."

Then she hurried upstairs to the computer. Fingers shaking with excitement, she opened up her emails and composed a new message.

Dad?

Are you there?

It's me, Emily.

What can I possibly say after all these years? First of all, I need you to know that I'm not angry with you. I was for a long time, but I'm a woman now, not a child, and I harbor no ill will toward you. Looking at the world through an adult's perspective means I understand that life can be messy and complicated, that sometimes we make decisions we regret, and then feel unable to admit our mistakes. I don't know why you left but I need you to know that you can come home now. Please don't stay in hiding just because you're scared to face me, scared to apologize, scared to admit you made the wrong decision all those years ago when you ran away. I forgive you. And moreover, I miss you. It's time to come home, Dad. It's time to be a family again.

So much has changed in the years since you left. I live in your house now, the house in Sunset Harbor. I have met a wonderful man, Daniel. I have no children of my own, but Daniel is a father, and by default I have become a mother to his beautiful daughter, Chantelle. She is so much like Charlotte, Dad. You will love her.

Daniel and I are getting married. It would mean the world to me to have you walk me down the aisle. After years spent wondering whether you were dead, then discovering over this past year of unearthing your clues that you are not, the idea of you walking beside me down the aisle has become more pertinent, more compelling. It would be a dream come true if you came back even if it was just for one day. I need you, Dad, now more than ever.

I've found myself here, ironically, in the place where I lost you. And I've found your clues, unearthed your secrets. There's nothing left to fear, to be ashamed of. I know how Charlotte died, I know that you blamed yourself. I've pieced together the reasons for your guilt—your affair, your alcoholism—and I need you to know that none of that matters. Too much time has slipped away. Please let us spend what we have left together as a family.

I forgive you for everything. The question now is can you forgive yourself?

My love, always and forever,

Emily Jane.

She sent the email as quickly as her fingers would allow, then sat back, panting, almost delirious with excitement.

Time passed, second by second, Emily feeling each one keenly. As more and more time sifted away from her, she felt her hope begin to wane. What if she'd misinterpreted the email address, had chosen to see a pattern in a random collection of letters? No, it couldn't be. It was too much of a coincidence. Which left two options. Firstly that the email address was defunct or never checked by her father. Secondly (and more likely), that he didn't want to reply.

Emily prayed that direct contact from her would be enough for him to finally break his silence, to reveal himself. But twenty minutes passed without her prayers being answered.

As she stared at her empty inbox, Emily was struck with a familiar sensation, like heavy armor falling onto her shoulders, one that kept her safe but at the expense of her emotions. Her dad was still absent, still missing from her life. She was getting closer but she was still so far. It was all up to him, to Roy, just as it always had been. He was in the driver's seat and as long as her father chose to stay hidden, he could maintain that distance between them forever.

Feeling crushed, Emily folded down her laptop. But that didn't stop her from pocketing her phone, carrying it with her religiously and checking every five minutes to see if a new email had arrived in her inbox.

CHAPTER NINE

Despite the bad reception at the inn, Emily kept her phone in her pocket every minute of every day that came, waiting and hoping for an email from her dad to arrive. But none did.

Even when the family bundled into the truck and headed off to Chantelle's Christmas performance one crisp, black evening, Emily kept checking her cell.

"You're glued to that thing," Daniel quipped, unaware.

Emily hadn't wanted to tell him, worried that he'd slip into his logical and practical mindset and tell her the email address she'd found couldn't possibly belong to her father, that she was just dreaming. As long as only she knew about the email, the only person who could disappoint her was her father himself.

"Sorry," Emily muttered, staring at the blank screen. "Just work stuff."

Daniel, gazing out through the windshield as he gripped the steering wheel, made a grunting noise. Emily took it to mean he didn't want any mention of work since he himself had failed to find any.

Emily went to stash her phone back into her pocket but just before she did, a notification lit up the screen. Not an incoming email, but a weather report.

"It's going to snow tonight," she said, peering up at the sky through the windshield. The stars were obscured by clouds.

They arrived at the school and headed into the hall. Yvonne had saved them seats in the front row and she waved when she saw them both. Emily noticed she was still alone and wondered whether her friend got lonely during the day.

As they headed toward Yvonne, Emily felt her phone vibrate in her pocket. She grabbed it quickly but it was just a text from Jayne expressing excitement for their upcoming visit. Frustrated and sad, Emily decided to power down her phone. She couldn't be jumpy throughout Chantelle's performance. The child deserved her full attention.

Emily and Daniel took their seats, waving to Suzanna and Wesley as they arrived and sat nearer the back of the hall. Then the lights dimmed and some twinkling piano music began to play.

Chantelle had kept most of the details of this performance a secret from Emily and Daniel so they weren't entirely sure what to expect, though they knew her singing would be on show. What they didn't realize was that she would also be dancing! They watched with delight as she pranced across the stage with Bailey, both dressed in sparkly white leotards.

"Did you know about this?" Emily whispered to Yvonne.

Yvonne grinned wickedly. "I helped them choose the outfits. They're snowflakes."

"I can see that!" Emily laughed.

The girls danced in time to the twinkly piano music, twirling and fluttering to mimic the movements of snowflakes. Emily couldn't stop the tears from beginning to well in her eyes. They always did when it came to Chantelle and her achievements.

Then Bailey fluttered away, leaving Chantelle center stage. Emily gripped Daniel's hand, knowing that a solo was coming.

The lights dimmed, the spotlight fell on Chantelle, and the little girl began to sing. Accompanied only by Ms. Glass on the piano, Chantelle's voice rang like crystal throughout the whole hall. Owen was right, she *had* improved. Even the parents in the audience who'd heard her before and knew what to expect were taken aback. It wasn't just that she could sing so well, it was the emotion she sang with, and the way she performed, so beyond her years.

Emily's pride swelled. And as she looked about her, she could see the pride on other parents' faces too. Chantelle was flourishing thanks to Sunset Harbor, to the whole community, and it couldn't be more proud of her.

*

Snow began to fall on the drive home from the recital. Daniel grumbled the whole way home, complaining about how it wasn't sensible of the school to organize a play in the evening because now Chantelle would be too hyper for bed.

"Can I play in the snow when we get home?" Chantelle asked, bouncing up and down in the backseat.

"Of course," Emily told her.

Daniel sighed and glared at her. Emily tried to reassure herself that his grumpiness was to do with him not having a job and all the stress around the adoption. But as a natural worrier, Emily couldn't help but ruminate on whether it might be wedding related, whether Daniel was changing his mind.

The family arrived back home and Emily quickly helped Chantelle change into something more appropriate than her sparkly costume for playing in the snow. As they went back downstairs ready to play, Daniel called Emily over.

"You go on out, I'll be a minute," Emily told Chantelle.

The girl rushed off and out the door, and Emily went to the reception desk where Daniel was beaming widely, his hand still holding onto the telephone he'd clearly just put down. The sight of his smile almost shocked Emily. She'd gotten so used to him being sullen and moody.

"Why are you grinning like that?" Emily asked suspiciously.

"I've got a job," Daniel announced boldly. His hand was still on the phone. He'd clearly just taken the call.

"You do?" Emily gasped.

She ran up to him and threw her arms around his neck. Daniel whipped her off her feet and spun her in circles.

"Where?" Emily asked the second he'd set her down on the floor. "With who?"

"Jack Cooper's," Daniel said. "You know, the carpenters in town. They're the ones who create bespoke pieces of furniture from locally sourced wood."

"Daniel!" Emily squealed. "This is amazing news!"

Noticing that Lois was peering out from behind the door to the kitchen, Emily took Daniel by the elbow and led him into the living room so they could celebrate away from prying eyes. Out the window, they could see Chantelle running around with Mogsy and Rain, playing joyfully in the thickening snow.

"So when do you start?" Emily asked as she went over to the drinks cabinet and rummaged through the liquor bottles. She poured him a celebratory whiskey and ginger ale, which he accepted gratefully, beaming from ear to ear at his success.

"That's the thing," Daniel said. "My first day is tomorrow!"

"Oh," Emily said, feeling her mood deflate.

So soon? She'd barely had time to mentally prepare herself. Of course she was relieved that Daniel had found the job, that he would have the secure and steady income the adoption documents demanded, but she was also nervous for the future, for the fact that she would be alone in the B&B more often, and that Daniel would have something to preoccupy him other than her and Chantelle. She gripped her glass.

"What's wrong?" Daniel asked, sensing the shift in the atmosphere.

"Nothing," Emily said. She swilled the amber liquid. Ice cubes tinkled against the edges. "I'm happy for you. And proud. I'm just anxious about the change. About you being away and me being responsible for Chantelle. You know what I'm like. If there's something to worry about I'll find it." She smiled weakly.

Daniel closed the distance between them and kissed her lightly.

"It will be fine," he said, soothingly. "There's no need to be anxious. You'll do great."

She nodded. Timidly, she added, "When will we find the time to plan the wedding?"

She wasn't sure, but it seemed as though Daniel bristled at the mention of the wedding. He walked back over to the couch, his back turned to her.

"Did I say something wrong?" Emily asked.

Daniel sighed heavily. "Sometimes you talk about the wedding as though it's this big task you have to organize, like there's nothing fun about it at all."

Emily frowned, not certain she understood what he was saying. "Well, it is a big task," she refuted. "And it does need to be organized at some point."

"I know, I know," Daniel grumbled. "But we've just had so much other stuff to sort out with Chantelle and the adoption. And it's not like you've been particularly switched on. You're always busy. I thought me getting a job would make you happy, but it's just like you've ticked the box and moved straight onto the next thing. I don't want our wedding to be some kind of irritating event you have to organize."

Emily had no idea where Daniel's attitude was coming from. "If anyone's treating it with irritation, it's you," she said. "Every time I bring up wedding logistics you bristle."

"There you go again," Daniel snapped. "Logistics? You should hear yourself. No wonder I bristle when you're so clinical about it."

Emily felt her anger grow. After weeks of anxiety Daniel was throwing it back in her face and blaming her?

"Maybe I'm acting that way because I feel like I'm scaring you off," she said, hotly. "Every time I mention it you seem really reluctant to talk about it. Sometimes it's like pulling teeth." She broke her gaze from him, instead dropping it to the amber liquid swilling in her glass. "I mean, do you want to back out?"

The moment she'd said it she wished she hadn't. She didn't want to know the answer. In this case ignorance was bliss.

But Daniel was beside her in a second, his arms latching around her middle.

"Of course not," he implored. He put his glass down then took hers from her hands so they were both free to embrace fully. "I'm sorry if I gave you that impression. I'm just a little overwhelmed. I've got no real income to pay for this wedding and I can't help but worry about money."

Emily sank into his chest, relieved. Before she had a chance to tell him not to worry, Chantelle ran into the room. Her cheeks and nose were red from the cold and she was grinning. Not wanting the child to see them arguing, Emily decided to drop the topic. At least Daniel was still committed.

"Hey, kiddo," she said to Chantelle, wiping the fine wisps of hair from her eyes. "I suppose a southern belle like you has never been sledding before, have you?"

Chantelle shook her head.

"Would you like to?" Emily added. "On the weekend?"

Chantelle squealed with excitement and ran to embrace Emily and Daniel.

Though their tiff hadn't exactly put all of Emily's doubts to rest, at least she and Daniel had finally aired some of their grievances. And in this tight, warm embrace, Emily reminded herself what was important. Daniel. Chantelle. Their life. Their family. All the other stuff—the engagement, the wedding—was superfluous as long as they had each other.

CHAPTER TEN

The next morning they awoke to a white world. The snow must not have let up at all during the night, because there was now a thick blanket of it outside, beautiful and sparkling. Emily loved the snow, not just because it was fun and pretty, but because of the way it brought people together and made them smile.

Emily quickly showered and dressed in her warmest clothes. She checked on Chantelle and found that she was already awake.

"Did you look out your window yet?" Emily asked, grinning.

Chantelle shook her head. She went to the curtain, pulled it back, and let out an exclamation.

"Oh!"

Emily smiled to herself, overjoyed to see Chantelle's reaction. She helped Chantelle dress and then they headed downstairs for breakfast. As Emily entered the kitchen, the phone rang. It was the receptionist at Chantelle's school saying it would be closed today.

"Guess what!" Emily said as she put the phone down. "No school today!"

"My first ever snow day!" Chantelle exclaimed with sheer delight.

Elated, Emily made fresh coffee, scrambled eggs, bacon, toast, hash browns, and homemade fruit smoothies. Daniel came down to eat with them, surprised by the feast laid out on the table.

"What's this in honor of?" he asked.

"Snow day!" Chantelle cried.

"Let's go sledding today," Emily suggested. "I wonder if the other parents will want to come, since we're all unexpectedly free."

"I won't be able to," Daniel grumbled. "I'm working today, remember?"

"Surely Jack won't be expecting you in today?" Emily said. "It's not exactly driving weather!"

Daniel shook his head. "It's my first day. I don't want to look unreliable or make excuses."

Emily understood but she couldn't help but worry about Daniel driving in this weather. Plus she wanted him to join in the fun with them. It didn't seem fair for him to miss Chantelle's first ever experience sledding.

"Can you take pictures for me?" Daniel asked.

Emily could hear the hint of sadness in his voice. She felt bad, wondering whether this was the start of things to come, of Daniel missing out on key moments of fatherhood.

"Of course," she said, echoing his melancholy tone.

She remembered then that her cell phone was still switched off in the pocket of her jeans. She hadn't turned it back on again after the performance, distracted by their argument last night and then the snow this morning. She didn't want to get up any hope but couldn't help the little spark that maybe her dad would have emailed her.

She didn't want anything to ruin her mood today and knew that her empty inbox would certainly do that. So she used the phone instead to arrange to meet up with Chantelle's school friends for sledding and decided to take her old digital camera with her.

"Be careful," Emily warned Daniel as they waved goodbye to him in the pickup truck. "And good luck." She kissed him tenderly.

Then she and Chantelle trudged off through the snow toward the park, where there was a small hill that would become their sledding track.

When they arrived, everyone was already there dressed in their warmest winter outfits. Yvonne and Bailey, Toby with Wesley and Suzanna, Ryan and his dad Elgar, Levi with his parents Holly and Logan and their young daughter Minnie, and Gabriella with her mom, Allison.

"Race you to the top!" Emily called out to Chantelle.

The little girl raced up the hill, kicking soft white snow up behind her, laughing as she ran. Emily gave chase, her speed hampered by carrying the sled. When she caught up to Chantelle at the top she was panting.

"It's a long way down," Chantelle said, glancing back down the slope.

"Are you scared?" Emily asked.

"No way!" Chantelle cried. "I'm excited!"

Emily laughed. Of course the fearless child wouldn't bat so much as an eyelid at the sight of an enormous slope.

"Come on then," Emily said, gesturing to the sled. "You get on the front and I'll sit behind. You'll go extra fast with my added weight."

Chantelle was so excited she could hardly sit still. Emily wedged herself behind Chantelle, then pulled out the camera.

"Let's take a picture for Daddy. Say cheese!"

Emily snapped a selfie of her and Chantelle on the sled. Then she held onto the little girl and pushed them over the precipice. She felt her stomach flip as they began their descent.

The ride down was exhilarating. Emily could hardly catch her breath as they whooshed down the slope, the white world whizzing by. The slope was extra icy from the number of kids who'd already raced down which meant they built up a tremendous speed.

"Wheeee!" Chantelle squealed.

They reached the bottom of the slope and skidded to a halt, tumbling over the side and into the snow. They lay there laughing until Emily's sides ached.

"Well?" Emily asked Chantelle, rolling on her side. "How was it?"

"Amazing!" Chantelle cried.

Then she was on her feet again, yanking Emily's hand. Snowflakes clung to her hair. Her eyes were bright.

"Let's go again!" she cried.

"Why don't you ride with Bailey this time?" Emily suggested. She needed a little longer to catch her breath. "That way I get some more photos for Daddy."

Chantelle nodded and ran off in search of her ginger-haired friend. Then Emily watched, grinning, as the two girls ran to the top of the hill and goaded one another on to go down alone.

As Chantelle flew down the hill for the second time, Emily snapped away, taking photo after photo for Daniel. She felt sad for him that he was missing out on such a joyful experience with his daughter and hoped the pictures would make him feel better about not having been there.

"So Emily," Allison said, coming up to her side as their children dragged their sleds up to the top of the slope again. "How far have you gotten with your wedding preparations?"

Emily squirmed. After her and Daniel's tiff she wanted to avoid the topic.

"Nowhere," she confessed. "No plans yet."

Levi's mom, Holly, overheard. "If you're having a summer wedding there's an amazing park and gazebo over in Ogunquit," she said. "Overlooking the beach. Fantastic spot. Logan and I had it on our shortlist of venues."

Shortlist? Emily didn't even have a long list!

"My sister has a cake business," Elgar joined in. "I could get you a discount. It's all vegan, FYI."

"The company who made our invitations was amazing," Holly added. "I can dig out their details for you, unless you've already sent them?"

Emily shook her head. Far from having sent invitations, they hadn't even agreed on who'd be coming. Or the date. Or the venue. All essential pieces of information that needed to be on the invites!

"Remind me where you honeymooned?" Yvonne asked Holly.

"We backpacked around Europe," Holly said, grinning. "Remember, that was before those two came along." She laughed and nodded at Levi at the top of the hill helping his little sister into the sled, Logan standing at the bottom with his arms wide beckoning them down. They looked like the perfect family.

"That's adventurous," Yvonne said. "Kieran and I went to Barbados. Lying around in the sunshine is more our style."

Everyone laughed. Everyone except Emily. Her head was swimming. Once again she had no answers. Nothing had been arranged. Barely anything had been discussed. She had no idea if Daniel would want a lazy honeymoon in the sun, or an adventurous one backpacking around Europe. Would he want to ride his bike through the mountains of Italy or row a boat in the lakes of Slovenia? Would he want to go skydiving or snowboarding? Or would he want to be pampered in a luxury spa? Or detox in a yoga retreat? She literally had no clue!

As her mind was running through these thoughts, Emily suddenly noticed a figure approaching them that was very familiar. Daniel?

Seeing him emerge through the snow sent a jolt of pleasure through her chest. She ran up to him.

"What are you doing here?" she said.

Daniel was beaming with what she recognized as accomplishment. "Jack gave me the rest of the day off since the workshop was freezing cold."

He slid his hand in hers and they strolled slowly toward the rest of the group, swinging their hands between them as they walked.

"How did it go?" Emily asked,

Daniel grinned. "It was amazing. It was like how I redid the kitchen in the carriage house times a million."

Emily felt happy for Daniel but anguish still rolled in her stomach. She was proud of his achievements, but she herself felt tender, almost bruised, by the questions her friends had asked about the wedding and her complete inability to answer them.

"How's it going here?" Daniel asked. "Did you take any photos for me?"

Emily handed him the camera and he scrolled through, gushing over the pictures of Chantelle in the snow. He laughed with abandon at her funny expressions.

They reached the others and everyone exchanged greetings. At the top of the hill, it was Chantelle's turn to go down. She hadn't noticed Daniel yet. He watched proudly as his fearless daughter leapt onto the sled and began the descent. Half way down the hill she noticed that he was there and the grin that burst across her face warmed Emily's heavy heart. But it wasn't quite enough to alleviate her anguish.

"Daddy!" Chantelle cried, landing at the bottom of the hill in a heap of snow. She jumped up immediately and rushed into his arms. "Will you sled with me?"

"Of course," Daniel replied.

He handed the camera back to Emily and rushed off up the hill with Chantelle. Emily took a picture of them waving at the top, and another as they settled onto the sled together. Then she took a series of funny action shots as they whooshed down the hill together, looking like two peas in a pod.

"That was fast," Daniel exclaimed, standing up and shaking the snow from his hair.

"Let's go again," Chantelle cried.

"Sure!" Daniel agreed, and the two ran off again.

Emily watched, smiling, though feeling somewhat melancholy.

Slowly, her friends began to head off home, too cold to stay outside, taking their weary children with them. True to her nature, Chantelle wasn't deterred by the chill at all and they soon found themselves alone in the park, the last ones standing.

"Shall we go out for dinner tonight?" Daniel suggested as the sky began to fade behind him. "We are celebrating, after all."

"We are?" Emily asked, distracted.

"My first day of work," Daniel said.

He seemed elated, like he was on a high. In fact, he seemed as happy as Emily had felt earlier that morning. But her friends' innocent, excited questions had put her in a bad mood.

"I'd prefer to eat at home," she said. "I don't want to drive in this weather."

"It's fine," Daniel contested. "Trust me. I got to work and back no problem."

"Well, it wasn't dark then," Emily snapped. "And we have a fridge full of food at home. I thought we were supposed to be saving money for the wedding, not burning through what little we have on frivolous meals out."

Her tone was sharp enough to alarm Chantelle. The little girl looked up at her with a frightened expression.

Daniel frowned. "What's wrong now?" he asked.

Emily just shook her head. She was too tender to speak about it, too overwhelmed. The day had started out with so much promise, but as they strolled back to the B&B, cold and tired from overexertion, Emily felt herself deflate. A fatigue seemed to be enveloping her, not just a physical exhaustion, but an emotional one as well. There was just too much going on for her mind to process and she was taking it out on Daniel and Chantelle.

As soon as they got back home, Emily took herself quietly upstairs, stating that she needed some alone time. She undressed and took a long, hot shower, trying to banish the cold that seemed to have permeated her very bones. Then she dressed in her warmest pajamas and crawled under the duvet, pulling it right up over her head. Exhausted to her core, she let herself fall into a deep, deep sleep.

CHAPTER ELEVEN

It came as a welcome relief to Emily when Jayne and Amy arrived for their long weekend visit. She'd started to feel so bogged down by the drama of her life that she'd been craving something to bring her back to reality, and her New York City friends would be just that. The only downside to their arrival was that Amy had always been suspicious of Daniel, and Jayne had always been far too vocal about how attractive he was. Subjecting him to scrutiny and ogling was not something Emily was looking forward to.

Thankfully, Daniel was at Jack Cooper's workshop and safely out of the way when Emily heard the thrumming engine of Amy's car coming up the drive. She rushed out onto the porch, wrapping a woolen sweater around her shoulders as her friend's brand new, sparkling white Chrysler 300 roared up the driveway. Business must be going well then, Emily concluded.

Jayne was hopping out of the car before Amy had even killed the engine.

"Em!" she cried, rushing for her friend and hugging her tightly. The sensation of her new breast implants against Emily's chest was somewhat alarming.

"You're looking... different," Emily said when Jayne finally let her go.

"Oh, you mean these?" Jayne said, grabbing her chest. "First thing I bought with my work bonus. Not sure if I'm keeping them, though. They're heavy."

Emily raised an eyebrow. "I'm not sure you can just put them in and take them out again."

Jayne shrugged. Just then, Amy got out of the car, flinging her unnecessary shades onto her seat before slamming the door. She strode up to Emily, looking more professional than ever, and air kissed her.

"You've got new wheels," Emily noted.

Amy wiggled her eyebrows. "Who knew scented candles could be such a sweet little earner? Sure you don't want to get a slice of the pie?"

Emily rolled her eyes. "Not that again. I've told you a million times I'm happy here. I'm happy with my life in Sunset Harbor."

"And having a ring on your finger," Amy added. "So, show us then!"

Feeling a little embarrassed, Emily presented her left hand to her friends.

"Oh Emily, it's gorgeous," Amy gasped.

"Where are the diamonds?" Jayne said flatly.

Amy slapped her arm and Jayne narrowed her eyes.

"No diamonds," Emily explained. "Daniel and I like unique things, antiques. The pearls represent the ocean."

Amy's hand fluttered to her chest as she pulled a touched expression. Jayne, on the other hand, grimaced.

"But is it still worth something?" she asked. "Like, if he were to break your heart you'd still be able to pawn it and get something for your trouble?"

Now it was Emily's turn to smack Jayne's arm. Amy's broken engagement wasn't too far in the past yet for the pain to have lessened and Jayne of all people should have been aware of that.

If Amy felt stung, she didn't show it on her face. She seemed to have grown a steely exterior since Emily had last seen her, though Emily couldn't help but wonder whether it was just for show. The last time Amy had been here she'd been a sobbing mess, a heartbroken, deceived woman. She ought not to feel embarrassed in front of Emily; she had nothing to be ashamed of.

"Come on, let's get inside, shall we?" Emily said. "You must have woken up super early to get here at this time."

"We're used to early starts now, aren't we, Jayne?" Amy laughed as they all began to walk back to the house. "Trading overseas means keeping to international times. We've had conference calls at three a.m., five a.m., pretty much all the a.m.'s you can think of."

Jayne nodded her head with mock solemnity, making Amy laugh. Emily couldn't help but feel a little left out. Her two best friends were achieving so much together, living a dream come true. She had to remind herself that they didn't have Sunset Harbor, that they didn't have Daniel or Chantelle.

"Where's the kid?" Jayne asked as they entered the inn, passing Lois at the front desk and heading into the kitchen, which was quiet now the lunch shift was over.

"Chantelle," Emily prompted. "She's at school at the moment, then she's going for a playdate after. You should see her, guys. I mean she was doing pretty well last time you were here but now she's just soaring. The progress she's made."

Jayne made a disgusted noise. "You sound like her mom!" she said.

Emily frowned. "I am her mom."

Silence fell and hung awkwardly in the air. Everyone hopped onto kitchen stools, as if for something to do.

"Let's talk wedding," Amy said, trying to change the topic. "You know I'm literally over the moon for you. Honestly, that whole Fraser thing is old news. It's all about you now."

"Thanks," Emily said quietly, uncomfortable to be the center of attention. When Amy was the bride-to-be she'd lapped up the attention. Emily couldn't picture herself being in the spotlight like that. Being with her friends gave Emily the confidence to finally admit it. "I'm actually getting a bit overwhelmed about the whole thing."

"Babe," Amy said, grabbing her hand across the breakfast bar. "We have totally got this covered. Honestly, you could leave the whole thing to us and you know you would end up with the perfect wedding. We know you inside and out."

Emily felt comforted by Amy's assurance, though she wasn't quite so certain that they did know her inside and out anymore.

Amy must have sensed her hesitation.

"Look, I know I haven't always been that supportive over this whole thing." She gestured widely, as though to encompass the whole B&B. "But I've got your back now, okay? I mean, you saw how awesome my wedding was going to be." She laughed, and it really did seem as though Fraser was old news. "Remember how I wanted to be a wedding planner once? Before the candle business took over?"

"Yeah, vaguely," Emily laughed, casting her mind back to high school Amy, to the creative girl who'd had dreams that were derailed when her college dorm room business took over.

Amy's hand was still on hers—bejeweled now, Emily noted, with silver rings and bracelets, all expensive looking—and she squeezed.

"I want to help you plan," she said.

"Oh," Emily replied, shocked. "You do?"

Amy nodded brightly. "Yes! For free. Can I?"

Emily thought of Chantelle's bullet point list, the huge number of tasks they needed to work through. If Amy could take some of that burden off her shoulders that would be amazing. Just the thought seemed to lift some of the weight from her.

Seeing that Emily was faltering, Amy added, "Fraser and I argued a lot over wedding things. It was stressful. I don't want you and Daniel going through that."

"We have been bickering," Emily admitted.

"Well, there you go," Jayne said, butting into the conversation she'd been otherwise locked out of and clearly craving the sound of her own voice once more. "All settled. Amy organizes the wedding. I take over as acting director at the candle business…"

Amy sighed. "We'll talk about that later," she said to Jayne with a laugh. "This trip is all about Emily."

For the first time, Emily felt like a burst of life had been breathed into the stalled wedding preparations. Suddenly rejuvenated, Emily remembered the speakeasy.

"I have something amazing to show you guys," she said, hopping down from the breakfast bar. "Come with me."

Her friends exchanged a look as they followed her out of the kitchen, along the corridor, into the living room, and through the alcove into the newly uncovered bar-come-speakeasy.

"This is incredible!" Jayne cried. "I mean it stinks of dust but that can be resolved."

She reached into her purse and pulled out a small glass bottle of perfume and began spraying it around her. The pungent smell made Emily cough.

Everyone settled onto the red velvet stools and Emily poured them each a drink of vintage liquor.

"So when's Daniel home?" Amy asked, her elbow propped on the bar. "I have a ton of questions to ask him."

Emily checked her watch and saw that it was approaching five p.m. She squirmed. "Nowish. But he's got a new job doing carpentry in town and has to work late sometimes."

Jayne raised an eyebrow. "Has to? Or chooses to?"

Amy and Emily both glared at her.

"Joke," she said with a shrug.

"Why don't we call him?" Amy said.

Emily shook her head. "Not at work. It's a new job. He doesn't want to give a bad impression."

"Okay, well, I'm not letting him off the hook," Amy replied. "I will be grilling him later."

As if on cue, Emily heard the distant sound of Daniel's pickup truck coming up the gravel drive. He must have made the effort to come home early in order to see her friends. Emily smiled to herself, touched by the gesture.

"That will be him now," she informed her friends.

A moment later, Daniel poked his head around the wall partition that still separated the speakeasy from the living room.

"Hey, guys," he said, shyly.

It always surprised Emily to see Daniel turn timid. It reminded her of how aloof he'd seemed to her when they'd first met, an aloofness she'd learned was actually him being guarded.

"Come in," Amy said, as though this were her house. "Take a seat."

Daniel wasn't about to argue with Amy's sternness. He hurried in and sat down. Thanks to the dim lighting and the antiquated setting, Emily felt as though she were witnessing a mafia interrogation. Daniel certainly looked about as terrified as if it really were one!

Amy wasted no time. "Now, don't think too hard about your answers," she said. "We're going to do a quick fire round. Okay?"

Daniel's eyes widened. He looked at Emily as though appealing for help. She just shrugged.

"How big of a wedding do you want?" Amy asked.

"Small," Daniel said. "Intimate."

"How many people do you want in your groom's party?"

Daniel faltered. "None. Just a best man."

"And who will be your best man?"

"George, I guess," Daniel said, shrugging. "Or Jack?"

Emily frowned. "Your *boss*?"

Daniel looked alarmed. "Is that a bad idea?"

"Shh," Amy told Emily, stopping her before she could answer. "Don't say a word. This is quick fire, remember. There are no wrong answers."

"Okay, but—" Emily began. She couldn't finish. Amy had covered her mouth with her hand. Emily gave up with a sigh.

"Maybe I could get in touch with some of my old friends," Daniel said. "There were some guys in Tennessee I was close to when I was younger."

At the mention of Tennessee, Emily wished she hadn't interrupted. Tennessee was Sheila's domain. Surely any friends Daniel still had from there would have known her. And he was a different man back then, he'd told her as much. That was when he was in his bad-boy phase, when he'd gotten his conviction. She was wary of that Daniel.

"Do you still have their numbers?" Amy asked.

Daniel nodded, something that also surprised Emily. Daniel wasn't much of a talker. She couldn't imagine him chatting on the phone with anyone.

"Great," Amy said, breezily. "Give them a call so we can get a feel for numbers. It will really help with the rest of the preparations, you know the venue, et cetera."

Daniel just kept on nodding. Amy was clearly someone he didn't feel comfortable standing up to. But thanks to her grilling session, they'd made more progress with the wedding preparations in three minutes than Emily had managed in three weeks!

"You can get those calls done tomorrow morning," Amy concluded, clapping her hands. "While we're in town looking at wedding dresses."

Now it was Emily's turn to look petrified. "Wedding dresses?" she squeaked.

At the same time, Jayne clapped loudly and exclaimed, "Wedding dresses!"

"Of course!" Amy exclaimed. "You need to try on as many as you possibly can so that you know exactly what you like and exactly what you don't. This is the one time in your life when you will get to wear a tailor-made gown. You have to make sure it's perfect."

Emily squirmed.

"I've got a whole itinerary," Amy said, producing a notebook from her purse.

"You do?"

"Of course." Amy grinned. "I came prepared."

Daniel stood then.

"Where are you going?" Emily asked, her voice an octave higher than usual.

Daniel smirked. "Sounds like it's your turn for a quick fire round," he said, laughing. "I think I'll leave you ladies to it."

"You're not off the hook yet!" Amy called to his retreating figure. "I expect you to have called at least five people by midday tomorrow!"

No longer in sight, Emily heard Daniel call out, "Got it!"

With trepidation, Emily turned back to Amy, ready to face the wrath of the inquisitor.

*

Bright and early the next day, Emily found herself herded down the main street.

"What's first on the itinerary?" Jayne asked, clutching an oversized latte in one hand.

"We're start small and non-intimidating," Amy explained. "Invitations."

She steered Emily into her carefully researched and selected stationery store. As they browsed the shelves, Emily realized there was more to invitations than she'd ever anticipated. There was color, paper thickness, shape quality, envelope size. So much for non-intimidating! And the whole thing wasn't helped by Jayne's contributions.

"Pastel pink is so in at the moment," she explained. "At least it is for hair. I'm not sure if that translates to wedding invites."

"Ignore her," Amy laughed. "I'm the expert."

After much deliberating, they left the store with a selection of different papers to take home and consider in more depth.

"Next we're going to try some cakes," Amy explained, gently shoving Emily down the street. "I found a highly rated place just round the corner."

Jayne took a gulp of her latte. "I'm surprised there's so many good-quality shops in such a small town."

Emily rolled her eyes. Jayne's compliments were always veiled criticisms.

"I know, it's very lucky," Amy explained. "The dress store is in the next town over, and there's a cake store there too but my research concluded that the baker in Sunset Harbor was actually better. It's one of those quaint family-run places and people prefer the more personal, homey touch. And they supply the cake stands as well so that will all be taken care of."

Emily couldn't help but drag her heels. "You know, my friend's sister bakes cakes so I'll probably just use her. Or my friend Karen. She makes all the cakes and bread for the town…"

Amy looked horrified. "Emily, this is your *wedding*, not some insignificant party you're just throwing together. You should feel absolutely no obligation to get your cake from some random acquaintance or Karen at the convenience store. You deserve the best cake you can get!" She gesticulated with her notebook.

Jayne took a slurp of latte. "The best cake you can get in *Maine*," she corrected. "I mean the actual best cake you can get would mean shipping it in from Milan…"

Amy shot her a glance. Then she turned back to Emily, who felt like she was shrinking under the weight of all these decisions.

"Look," Amy said, gently. "You need to trust me. And relax. We're just going to try some cake. That's all. Nothing needs to be decided today. It's just three old friends having a good time and eating cake."

Emily tried to take Amy's advice and relax but it was almost impossible. As Amy took Emily by the shoulders and steered her down the street, she couldn't help but feel anxious.

They finally reached the bakery, which was right on the outskirts of town. The store smelled delicious. They were greeted by a portly, maternal woman named Pauline.

75

"You must be the bride-to-be!" Pauline gushed, squeezing Emily at the tops of her arms and plonking her into a seat at a long table where a row of sample-sized cakes were laid out.

Emily wondered why everyone felt entitled to touch her now she was a bride-to-be. She'd been steered through town by Amy, pushed in all directions. It was becoming somewhat invasive. And she hadn't even started trying on dresses!

Amy and Jayne sat at the table beside her. Pauline seemed genuinely enthusiastic about Emily's wedding, which made her feel bad because everyone seemed more excited than she was herself.

"So we have chocolate mud pie here," Pauline said, gesturing to one end of the table. "Then we move onto Victoria sponge, red velvet, pineapple upside down, cookies and cream cake, and finally, my personal favorite, double toffee banana walnut whip."

She grinned with triumph. Emily felt a lump forming in her throat. With an overwhelming sense of trepidation, she took her first sample, all under Pauline's eagle eye. With each bite-sized sample piece she ate, it became harder and harder to swallow. Nausea swilled in her stomach.

"We do different sizes," Pauling explained as they ate. "You can get the mini package which is up to one hundred pieces, then there's the medium package, which is a three-tier standard wedding cake, or you can go for monstrous." She gestured to a display cake in the window which stood at least three feet tall and consisted of ten different layers. It was indeed monstrous.

Emily found herself tongue-tied. She struggled to swallow her mouthful of double toffee banana walnut whip cake.

"I think she might have had enough sugar for one day," Amy said, filling the uncomfortable silence Emily's lack of response had caused.

They finished up and bid farewell to Pauline, then piled into Amy's fancy new car to begin the drive to the wedding dress store. The bumpy ride made all the cake samples swill in Emily's stomach, mixing with her anxiety about trying on dresses.

"Here it is," Amy grinned as she pulled up outside. She looked very proud of herself.

The store was exquisite looking, with a charcoal gray sign with silver lettering that said *La Belle*. It was a world away from Pauline's bakery. It was the sort of place you'd see in a magazine.

Emily got out of the car, feeling her anxiety grow even further. She felt scruffy, not to mention bloated. Why had Amy planned the dress wearing *after* the cake eating?

They'd hardly all gotten inside when Emily's emotions burst out of her. Tears began to flow down her cheeks.

"Oh no," Amy said, scooping an arm around her friend's shoulders and leading her to a chair to sit down. She looked up at the approaching store clerk, her stern look communicating that they needed some privacy. The clerk scurried away. "Have I pushed it too much?" she asked.

Emily shook her head. "It's not that. It's just the stress of it all. I mean, I don't know how we're going to afford a wedding. Daniel's only just started working and it's manual labor, it hardly pays well. The inn's doing okay—we have a decent amount of money coming in from the carriage house at the moment—but it's so changeable and unpredictable right now. And the more guests I get the more staff I need." She was aware that she was wailing now. "And Lois is useless!" She let it all pour out.

Jayne was crouching in front of her, gripping her hands in her lap. "Do you want me to fire her for you?"

Emily couldn't help but laugh. It was one of those snotty, messy laughs. She must have looked a state.

"No," she said with a sigh. "Lois isn't the problem. I mean, yeah, she is useless, but I'm just taking it out on her. It's everything else, really." She looked over at Amy in the chair next to her. "I mean I have no idea how you got Daniel to talk last night! I haven't been able to get him to commit to so much as a date."

She noticed Jayne's face, how hard her friend was trying to stop herself from saying "told you so."

"It's okay," Amy said, rubbing Emily's shoulder. "That stuff is just superfluous. Focus on the important stuff, on you and Daniel. On your love and how you want to spend forever together. If you get wrapped up in the wedding then you'll lose sight of the bigger picture. That's how I almost ended up making the biggest mistake of my life."

Emily snuffled up her tears. It was amazing how her friends were able to draw so many emotions out of her. In front of them she was completely comfortable, able to let it all out, all her ugly parts, all her fears. Then with them, she could be put back together, patched up. She realized then how much she'd missed them, how much her decision to be with Daniel had been a sacrifice. But she knew that it was the right decision, that the sacrifice was worth making.

Feeling so close to her friends gave Emily a sudden burst of courage.

"I need to tell you guys something," Emily said.

"You're pregnant," Jayne stated. "I knew it. Didn't I tell you, Ames, that Emily was pregnant?"

Emily shook her head emphatically. "I'm not pregnant!"

Jayne seemed to deflate. "Oh," she pouted.

"Sorry to disappoint," Emily added with a smirk. But then she turned serious again. She looked from Amy to Jayne. "It's my dad. I found a way of contacting him."

Amy gasped loudly and grabbed her mouth with her hand. Jayne didn't even try to hide her shock. Her eyes practically popped out of her head.

"That's... that's quite some news," she stammered.

"When did this all happen?" Amy asked. Her tone had softened considerably.

"The other day," Emily explained. "It was in the bar, actually. I found one of his safes and it was full of paper. I thought it was just a pile of junk but then, amongst it all, there was this printed out page of emails. The email address was all of our initials strung together."

"So you emailed him?" Amy asked, her voice notching up a semitone.

Emily nodded. Before her friends even had a chance to ask her the outcome she explained, "He hasn't gotten in touch."

Amy's and Jayne's disappointment was palpable. It felt like someone had let all the air out of the room.

"I'm sorry, hon," Amy said. She squeezed her arm around Emily even tighter than before.

All at once, Emily's tears began to fall again. This time in torrents. This time all her pain and anguish and that sense of rejection came gushing out of her.

"I'm this close to having my dad walk me down the aisle," Emily said, holding up her fingers an inch apart. "After all those years trying to accept he wouldn't be there and then I find a way of reaching him and... and it's still futile. I hoped that having some direct contact with me would be enough to make him realize he didn't need to keep hiding." She sighed deeply. "But no. It wasn't enough. *I* wasn't enough."

"Don't say that," Amy implored. "What happened with your dad was not your fault. Don't ever think that. You are loved and wanted. By me and Jayne, Daniel, Chantelle. Your dad."

Emily sucked up her tears. "Not by my mom."

Amy didn't miss a beat. "I know it might seem like that sometimes, but your mom does love you."

"She said she might not come to the wedding," Emily confessed.

"She will," Amy insisted. "She's just kicking up a fuss. Being Patricia about it all. She's hurt you left New York, that's all. She thinks you've chosen your dad over her and that has to sting a bit."

"Well, she needs to get over it," Emily bit back. "Her only living child is getting married. She should be happy for me!"

Amy squeezed again. "She'll come. I promise."

Emily nodded, but she couldn't be so certain. Right now, everything felt very precarious. And even with the comfort and assurance of her best friends, Emily couldn't lift herself out of the gloom that had descended upon her.

CHAPTER TWELVE

Early Monday morning, Emily walked Amy and Jayne out of the inn and to Amy's white Chrysler. It had been a somewhat emotional visit, but also cathartic for Emily.

"We'll talk on Saturday," Amy reminded Emily as she climbed into the driver's seat. "Then we can go over those cake options. Make a decision once you've had a chance to think things through."

She spoke in the soft, persuasive way of a parent, like she wasn't going to let Emily off the hook. Emily appreciated that someone was taking the lead on the whole wedding organization.

Just then, Daniel came down the porch steps and headed out to his pickup truck.

"See you ladies next time," he said, waving, barely masking his relief that the two of them were leaving. Then he blew a kiss to Emily.

Amy reached out the car window and lightly touched Emily's hand. "Don't let him dictate this, hon. Please. You have every right to ask questions and tie him down to some answers."

Jayne leaned across Amy and poked her head out the window. "Or just don't ask," she said. "Tell him how it's going to be."

Amy shook her head and turned on her car. "And ignore Jayne. Always." She winked.

Emily stepped back from the car and waved as it began backing out of the driveway. She was going to miss having those two goofballs around, even if it had been a blur of a weekend crammed with wedding talk, wedding talk, and more wedding talk.

As Amy's car disappeared around the corner, Emily noticed Colin Magnum walking up the drive from the carriage house. The breakfast shift was beginning for the guests, which meant it was time for Emily to wake Chantelle and get her ready for school.

She went inside, immediately feeling lonely without Amy and Jayne. It was like the inn had fallen back into a quiet slumber without them. But the absence she felt was also because of Daniel. This was going to become her new routine now, getting Chantelle ready for school by herself, spending the days alone in the inn with no one to speak to. She wished Serena had more shifts rather than Lois, then instantly felt guilty.

Emily trotted up the stairs, bidding good morning to the guests coming down for their breakfast, and went into Chantelle's room. She woke the little girl up with a kiss on the cheek, then helped her choose an outfit for the day ahead.

Emily didn't like to make a habit of eating breakfast with the guests, preferring instead to make sure they had some privacy during their stay, so she and Chantelle ate breakfast in the busy kitchen. It was steamy and loud as Matthew and Parker rushed about making food for everyone, so they hardly got a chance to speak to one another, compounding Emily's solitude.

When they were done eating, they headed to the car. At last she and Chantelle could have a chat. But no, the little girl pulled out her favorite book and read the whole journey there! Yvonne wasn't even at the school gates and Ms. Glass was in too much of a hurry to even exchange pleasantries.

Emily sighed sadly and returned home.

During her quiet, lonely lunch, Emily found herself staring at her blank phone with its empty inbox, wondering about her father. Had he received her message or had it just been wishful thinking on her part that the email address she'd found belonged to him? If he had received her message, had he read it and chosen not to respond, or had he discarded it because it came from an unfamiliar address? What if it had disappeared into a spam folder?

She was so absorbed in her thoughts that she didn't even notice Tracey the yoga teacher bounding up the driveway in her loud, patterned leggings, with her purple yoga mat tucked under her arm.

"Emily?" Tracey cooed as she trotted up the steps. "You okay? I've been calling your name for ages!"

Emily had become so accustomed to the lack of company it took her by surprise that someone would be wanting to talk to her. She snapped to attention. "Sorry, I was miles away. Do you have a class today?"

"I do indeed." Tracey beamed. "It's my recently rebranded Gentle Yoga for the Mature Lady class." She winked. "You know, the one Cynthia and Karen come to."

Emily laughed. "Yes, of course, your Monday class. I'm not very switched on at the moment."

Tracey's expression turned to one of sympathy. She exuded calmness, comfort, and Emily couldn't help herself from revealing the brewing sadness inside of her with her eyes.

"*Are* you okay?" Tracey pressed. "Because if you need to talk, please know that I'm here for you."

"Thanks." Emily smiled, touched. "I'll walk inside with you."

She stood, collecting her empty lunch plate, and then she and Tracey walked into the inn.

"I can't believe you found a secret room," Tracey said as they passed the living room. "It's like something from a movie! Are you going to restore it?"

Emily nodded. "Daniel wanted to be the one to do it, of course. And I wouldn't have it any other way. So he's working at Jack Cooper's during the day, and he's going to start working on the bar in the evenings and weekends." She felt herself swell with pride and admiration. Daniel worked so hard, not just for the family but for this home, for this place they both loved so much.

"Tell me where I can find my own Daniel," Tracey joked.

Just then, Karen and Cynthia arrived and the three women headed to the ballroom for the carefully named "Mature Ladies" class.

Alone once more, Emily decided to continue her exploration of the bar. She'd been inspired by her conversation with Tracey and realized it was about time she cleared out all of her dad's old papers. She'd been avoiding it since the discovery of the email address, which had managed to consume most of her thoughts ever since.

She went into the room and made a beeline for the vault she'd discovered. She emptied out the pile of dusty papers and stacked them onto the surface of the bar. Propping herself onto a barstool, she began sorting through all the bits of random paper. Typical of her father, most of the bits of the paper were junk—receipts and bus tickets, that sort of thing, items the average person would know to throw away. But her dad was one of life's hoarders and held onto everything, either psychologically unable to throw things out, or so paranoid about his paperwork being read he'd lock it up rather than risk it being retrieved from the garbage can. Emily wondered why her dad had left all this stuff in his house if he was so worried about being spied on, then checked herself. Her dad had never *really* gone. Not properly. He'd been back, had kept an eye on the house over all those years. He'd kept everything in vaults, hidden, locked away, dispersed. It might not have occurred to him to throw these things out because he knew Patricia would never come back to the house and so that left only her, Emily, at risk of discovering it. Or...

Perhaps he left this stuff specifically so I would find it, Emily thought.

She brushed the thought away. It didn't ring true. Her dad hadn't thought about her when he'd run away, so why would he have thought to leave these clues for her? No, it was far more likely that it hadn't occurred to him that his daughter may one day return.

Or perhaps there was a third option—that her dad had never expected to be away so long. Whatever had driven him into hiding all those years ago was not supposed to keep him away indefinitely. Could it be her father was always planning on returning but that like many people in life he'd ended up losing year after year after year, letting the absence drag on then, feeling less and less able to resolve it, until one day it had just become his new way of being and he'd forgotten there'd ever been a plan to return?

A million thoughts swirled in her mind as she looked through her dad's correspondence, some old, some more recent.

After what felt like hours had passed, Emily decided she was going to email her father again. What harm would it do? He probably wasn't going to read it anyway.

She took out her cell and began composing the message.

Hi Dad,

Me again. I found the hidden bar. What a gem! You really did keep some pretty amazing secrets, didn't you? Ballrooms. Bars. Antiques. Paintings. A mistress. I wonder what else you were hiding...

I've been reading through your letters from Toni, I found them in one of the safes in the basement. And I've been reading all the letters hidden in the secret bar room. I know you were here, that you've been visiting the house over the last twenty years. I have so many questions for you, but I know they'll never be answered.

So I may as well tell you about my weekend. What harm can it do? I went out shopping with Amy and Jayne (remember them?). We were looking for things for the wedding. I got overwhelmed by it all and ended up in floods of tears. I guess I'm freaking out about the commitment. After all those years of wishing Ben would commit and now I'm the one getting cold feet with Daniel! Ridiculous. But kind of expected, wouldn't you say? You and Mom were hardly the models of wedded bliss...

She stopped there, her fingers hovering over the keys. Emotion made her throat thick. She had so much more to say, but suddenly none of the energy left with which to say it. She thought about going back and editing what had turned into something of a stream of consciousness, then decided against it. Roy Mitchell would not read the words she'd written so what did it matter? She deliberated for only a moment before she hit send.

There were no windows in the bar, so when Emily emerged back into the main house, blinking in the dazzling light, she discovered it had started snowing again. She decided to walk to

Chantelle's school to pick her up, anxious about driving in the snow, but also because walking always helped clear her head.

The air was crisp and everything seemed quieter than normal as Emily walked along the sidewalk with the ocean to one side of her. An icy sensation bit at her cheeks and fingers. It was bitterly cold, reminding her of the terrible weather she'd encountered when she first arrived at Sunset Harbor, when she'd practically frozen to death in the drafty old house. How far she'd come since then. How much she'd achieved. How much she'd gained.

She touched the ring on her left hand with her fingertips, feeling how cold the pearls had become.

Then she drew up to the school. She must have been walking languorously because the parking lot was already half emptied, and the kids who'd not yet been collected were playing on the lawn as snow began to settle. Ms. Glass supervised them, handing them over to their parents. She waved to Emily as she saw her approach.

"Sorry I'm late," Emily said to Ms. Glass. Chantelle came over and Emily rested both of her hands on her shoulders. "Did you have a good day today?"

Chantelle nodded. She handed Emily a painting of a Christmas scene, in her signature silver sparkles. Emily smiled as she slid it into her purse.

"She's doing excellently," Ms. Glass said. "Honestly, you and Daniel are doing a great job."

Emily smiled, proud of herself, but the mention of Daniel's name made his absence all the more obvious. She turned to Chantelle.

"Shall we take a stroll along the beach? The water at the harbor is starting to freeze over and it will look beautiful."

Returning back home for several Daniel-less hours seemed suddenly unappealing to Emily. Why not make the most of the snow while they could?

Chantelle nodded and they walked together hand in hand. Emily was sorry not to have bumped into Yvonne today. She could have used some moral support, a friendly face to help bolster her during her loneliness.

The icy harbor was beautiful, glistening. Emily stared out at the water feeling lonely, despite Chantelle's company. It was then she realized the child was completely silent.

"What's up, chicken?" she asked.

Chantelle shook her head.

"You know you can tell me anything," Emily pressed. "No secrets."

Chantelle chewed her lip. "It's Christmas soon," she said finally.

"And that makes you sad?" Emily asked.

Chantelle shrugged. "My mom will be alone."

Emily felt a clenching sensation in her chest. "Do you want to send her a card? A present? Because it's absolutely fine if you do." She hoped that Chantelle wasn't harboring any guilt about wanting to comfort her lonely mother.

Chantelle stared into the distance. "Maybe," she admitted. "But I don't think she'll send me anything."

Emily sighed sadly. "She might not. But Daddy and I will make sure you have a really fun Christmas. Do you know what presents you might want?"

"I don't need presents," Chantelle explained. "I have everything I need."

Her words made Emily even sadder. "It doesn't have to be about need. It can just be something you *want*. For fun. A toy. Clothes. Some crafts."

But Chantelle said nothing. Emily realized that at seven years old Chantelle had learned something that many adults never learned—that things were not equivalent to happiness, that joy came from comfort, love, and security, not clothes or possessions.

No matter what Chantelle thought, Emily was determined to get her the best gift ever. The girl deserved so much. She deserved the best Christmas a child could hope for. And Emily was going to make sure she got it.

CHAPTER THIRTEEN

Emily waltzed through the wintry streets, numerous shopping bags swinging from her arms. Her Christmas shopping had started successfully enough, but somehow she still had a ton of people left to cross off her list. And since she'd already exhausted the stores in Bangor, Augusta, and Portland with her overenthusiastic gift buying, she'd had to drive all the way down to Kittery to procure some last-minute gifts.

She reached her car and dumped the bags in the trunk. As she attempted to squish the door down she felt the heat rising into her cheeks. She'd gone a little overboard this year. But, Emily reasoned, it was her first Christmas with Chantelle; she'd needed to get presents for her school friends, teachers, and all the parent friends Emily herself had made. Then there were all the inn's staff, whom Emily had needed to get gifts for, and it hadn't felt right not to add Owen to the list since he was part of the inn family, or Tracey, for precisely the same reason.

Then there was the business side of gift giving. Karen had sent her homemade figgy puddings, Raj had sent a winter-themed bouquet, and the wine suppliers had sent a complimentary bottle of port. Emily felt compelled to return the favors.

Emily decided to take one last stroll down the main street in Kittery. As she went, she stumbled upon a cute stone building and wondered whether it would make a suitable venue for the wedding. She made a note to mention it to Daniel later. They hadn't spoken about it at all since Amy's interrogation and a conversation felt well overdue.

A little farther down the street, Emily found a delightful music store, the perfect place to find a gift for Owen. But as she perused the shelves, a sudden worry struck Emily. Was Owen spending Christmas alone? He'd told her recently that his parents lived abroad, that they rarely got to see one another. She couldn't bear the thought of him spending Christmas alone.

On her cell, she dialed Owen's number and the shy pianist answered.

"I hope you don't mind me asking…" Emily said after they'd exchanged pleasantries.

"Is it to do with the singing lessons?" Owen interrupted with a panicked voice. "I can come more often if you'd like. Or do you want them less often? I can do shorter sessions if she's getting tired after an hour? Oh no. Does Chantelle want to stop them altogether?"

"No, no!" Emily said quickly. "It's not about Chantelle. It's about Christmas."

"Christmas?" Owen sounded confused.

"Daniel and I are doing a large dinner as we have a few guests staying over the festive period. We'd love you to come. Some other folk from town will be there. Rico, for example."

"Rico?" Owen asked. "Does that mean—"

"Serena can't come," Emily said with a smirk. "If that's what you were wondering."

"Nope, just curious," Owen said quickly in an attempt to hide his blatant interest. Then after a pause, he added, "I would love to come. If you're happy to have me."

"It would be wonderful."

"Thank you, Emily. I really appreciate it."

Emily was relieved. Though her and Daniel's parents would be absent for Christmas dinner, they certainly weren't going to be alone. There would be a skeleton staff staying at the inn for the week to take care of the ten-person-strong Canadian family who'd booked over the holidays, and then there would be the handful of Sunset Harbor folks who had nowhere else to go.

There was one person Emily hadn't been able to convince to come to the celebrations, however, and that was Trevor Mann. It made her so sad to think of him alone on Christmas, especially since it would most certainly be his last. Selecting the right gift for someone with a terminal illness felt like an impossible task as well. She didn't want to get anything that might suggest Trevor was an invalid and it seemed crass to buy things with longevity. Then an idea struck her.

She called Raj Patel.

"Is your store still open?" she asked when the florist answered. "You haven't closed for the holidays yet?"

"We're still open," Raj confirmed.

Emily sighed with relief. "Do you have any fruit trees I could buy?"

It was the perfect idea, Emily thought. Trees would live forever. They'd become Trevor's legacy.

Raj chuckled, clearly amused by such an odd request. "I have a peach tree, a cherry tree, an apple tree, and a lemon tree. But you do know the ground is far too hard to plant at the moment?"

"Oh," Emily said, deflating. "It was supposed to be a gift for Trevor."

"For Trevor?" Raj sounded confused. "Why are you getting gifts for him?"

Emily quickly realized her error. No one else knew about Trevor's demise, and even though Sunita was Raj's wife she'd be upholding patient confidentiality.

She let out a nervous giggle. "I just want to block his view of my garden."

"Okay…" Raj said, sounding more bemused than ever. "Well, if you have a greenhouse to store them in they'll keep fine until the ground softens in spring."

Spring. It seemed a long way away for someone who had just a few months to live. But Trevor did have an old greenhouse around the back of his property, Emily recalled. At least he'd be able to enjoy watching the trees grow, even if he didn't live long enough to plant them.

"I'll take them," Emily said, feeling a stab of grief.

Emily drove back to Sunset Harbor and parked beside Raj's garden center. He met her at the doors, and then they walked through the store together to where the four fruit trees stood. They were only a few feet tall each, bare, with no leaves, their roots taped up in garbage bags. Not much to look at.

Since Emily's car was too stuffed with gifts to fit the trees inside the only option was to tie them to the roof. As Emily drove carefully through the streets of Sunset Harbor, she was relieved everyone was inside preparing their own Christmas celebrations, although she did earn herself a bemused wave from Birk at the gas station as she crawled past.

After parking at the inn, Emily carried the fruit trees into one of her outbuildings to keep them out of sight. Then she quickly checked to make sure she hadn't gotten any soil on her clothes before hurrying to Trevor's house.

After she spent a minute knocking on his door, Trevor answered. He looked worse than ever. He was wearing his pajamas, something he wouldn't have dreamed of doing a month ago.

"Emily," he said, shuffling away from the door to allow her inside.

Emily tried her hardest not to look concerned or overly alarmed. But as he led her toward the kitchen, Trevor seemed more frail than ever. Emily couldn't help but glance into the rooms as they passed and, for the first time since she'd known him, his immaculately clean home was looking messy. She would have to send Marnie over later that evening to fix the place up.

Emily made some tea and she and Trevor sat together at the kitchen table.

"I'm just here to try and twist your arm over Christmas dinner," Emily said. "We really want you there."

Trevor sipped his tea slowly. "I don't want to burden you."

"It wouldn't be a burden," Emily implored. "We're already making dinner for thirty people! And since our own families aren't coming, I know Chantelle would love you to be there. You're the closest thing she has to a grandpa."

Trevor seemed touched by Emily's words. But at the same time, he was unshakable.

"I'm going to have to decline your generous offer," he said.

Emily couldn't help but feel like he'd given up, like he'd already resigned himself to death. She wanted to shake some sense into him. If this was to be his last Christmas he should darn well enjoy it! But at the same time, it was entirely up to Trevor how he decided to spend his remaining days of life. Her only hope was that he wasn't trying to save face, that it wasn't his pride holding him back. There really wasn't enough time for that kind of nonsense.

"If you're worried about what people will say…" Emily began.

But Trevor patted her hand, stopping her mid-sentence.

"Emily, I know what you're doing and I appreciate it, I really do. After how terribly I treated you, it really is a testament to your character that you'd go so far as to offer me charity on Christmas Day of all days. But I would like to spend the day alone. I hope you can respect that."

Emily swallowed the hard lump in her throat. The thought of anyone alone at Christmas upset her deeply. It made her think of her dad spending Christmas after Christmas on his own, and her mom in her tony New York City apartment refusing to spend Christmas with her daughter because she didn't approve of her life choices. To Emily, being alone was the worst thing to want in the world.

They drank the rest of their tea in silence. Emily washed the cups so Trevor didn't have to exert any more energy doing so. She ignored the voice in her head telling her to tuck Trevor up in bed.

"I can see myself out," she told him as he stood from the kitchen table.

Trevor nodded. He'd passed the stage of arguing with her over certain matters. Though decorum told him he should see his guest to the door, his illness prevented him. Instead, he walked her as far as the foot of the stairs.

"I'll come around with your gifts soon," Emily told him.

Trevor just smiled, cupped her hands in his, and kissed her on the cheeks. "I have no need for gifts now, my dear," he said. Then he dropped her hands.

Emily walked the rest of the hallway, opened the door, and stepped out of the house. The moment the door closed behind her, she let her tears fall.

CHAPTER FOURTEEN

Emily tiptoed across the driveway, trying not to make the gravel crunch beneath her boots. She was carrying a bucket filled with bottles of cleaning fluid and several colorful sponges. Following quietly behind her was Chantelle with some garbage bags and Daniel carrying a ladder. It may have been Christmas Eve and barely 5 a.m. but the whole family was awake for this mission.

Daniel hadn't been particularly thrilled about Emily's choice of gift for Trevor. But when he'd seen how excited Chantelle was about the idea of secretly fixing up Trevor's greenhouse he'd agreed to join in.

Just then, Emily noticed Colin Magnum leaving the carriage house, his suitcase in tow.

"I hope we didn't wake you," Emily said. She side-eyed the suitcase in Colin's hands. "Are you going somewhere?"

Colin smiled cordially. "Yes, actually. I'm leaving a little earlier than planned." Then his eyebrows rose upward. "My wife suggested we spend Christmas together."

He sounded as surprised as Emily felt.

"You reconciled?" she exclaimed.

Colin nodded. "I shan't be needing these any longer."

He handed the keys to the carriage house to Emily. She felt a small pang of sadness to know he would be leaving them. Colin had been in Sunset Harbor so long now he'd started to feel like part of the furniture.

"We'll miss you at Christmas dinner," Emily added, as she stashed the keys away in her pocket. "And in general. It's been a pleasure having you."

He glanced at the bucket in Emily's hands. "Yes, it's been a wonderfully odd month." Then he smiled with mischief. "I left your Christmas gift with Lois at reception. I hope you like it."

Colin loaded up his car and got inside. As Emily waved him off she realized she would never get an answer to the mysterious project he'd been working on for the last month.

Emily rejoined Daniel and Chantelle, and the three of them crept through the hole in the hedges that separated the inn from Trevor's property and went to the greenhouse out back. The place was a mess, filled with broken pots, grubby garden furniture, and dead plants. It was clear the greenhouse hadn't been used for many years, but it was warm and Emily could picture how beautiful it would look all spruced up and with the fruit trees inside.

They got to work, clearing out all the broken ceramic pots and throwing them in garbage bags. Chantelle swept away all the cobwebs while Daniel cleaned the grubby windows with a rag. Then they filled their buckets with warm soapy water and scrubbed down the cast iron picnic bench until it was gleaming. Finally, they carried the fruit trees into their new positions in Trevor's greenhouse.

Standing back to admire their handiwork, Emily had to admit it didn't look like much at the moment, but once winter gave way to spring they would start to flourish. With sunshine streaming through the glass it would look beautiful in here. Emily hoped as the years passed they would grow strong and fruitful as a lasting testament to Trevor.

"We'll need a nap if we want any chance of staying awake tonight," Daniel said.

"What's tonight?" Emily asked.

"Don't tell me you've forgotten," Daniel said with a shake of the head. "The Christmas Eve soiree at the inn!"

Emily gasped with shock. How had she let it slip her mind? She had been so focused on making sure Trevor had the most exciting surprise for Christmas that she'd forgotten about the rest of her responsibilities. Tonight Chantelle would be singing at church with the town's choir for the very first time!

The family headed back home, freezing cold and covered in dirt. Chantelle's denim overalls had huge brown patches on the knees and she had somehow managed to get mud all over her face.

The inn felt toasty warm as they entered. As soon as they were inside, Lois excitedly beckoned them to the reception desk. There was a glossy magazine spread open before her.

"Colin handed this to me," Lois explained, turning the magazine 180 degrees so they could see. "He said to tell you Merry Christmas."

Emily glanced at the picture on the double page spread. It looked strikingly familiar.

"That's our inn!" she gasped.

Lois grinned and nodded her head.

Hands trembling a little, Emily scanned the travel piece, reading Colin's glowing review of the inn. *Superbly succulent dishes. Exquisitely designed. A seafront location in a quaint, welcoming town.*

"So that's what he'd been was up to?" Emily said, laughing. "Writing a piece in a fancy travel magazine about the inn?"

Filled with Christmas cheer, everyone got to work preparing for the evening's soiree. They had a lot to organize and there wasn't a second to waste. Chantelle was bathed. Decorations were hung. Wine was mulled.

When Emily went into the living room to check everything was ready, she saw that three stockings had been hung in a row on the mantel. They weren't completely evenly spaced, almost as if a gap had deliberately been left on the end for one more. Her mind wandered as she imagined a fourth stocking occupying the space for the potential child she and Daniel might one day create together. Had Daniel been unconsciously thinking the same as he'd hung them?

Just then, Daniel walked in.

"You hung these up already?" Emily asked him.

"As is traditional," Daniel mocked. "They're Chantelle's creations."

"I can tell," Emily said, recognizing the child's handiwork in each of their names sewn onto the stockings. "I hope she's rested in time for the performance. I can't believe I made her wake up so early. I think we'll chalk that one up as a parenting fail."

Daniel kissed her on the forehead. "Considering you succeed at pretty much one hundred percent of your parenting decisions usually, I think we can let that one slide."

Emily smiled, filled with love and contentment. The pang for a child with Daniel grew even stronger, taking Emily by surprise. Though she'd always imagined children in her future, she now felt that desire more keenly than ever before. It was an almost painful longing.

"I saw a nice venue in Kittery," Emily said, suddenly remembering the quaint town and its ivy-covered stone folly. "For the wedding. Perhaps we should make an appointment?"

Daniel gave her a look. "Emily, I got up at the crack of dawn to renovate a greenhouse for you, I've decorated your inn for Christmas, and now I have about a thousand meat pies to bake for your Christmas soiree. Can we please give wedding venue talk a miss for just one day?"

Surprised by his tone, Emily nodded. She'd hardly mentioned weddings to him since Amy's interrogation! His dismissive tone brought with it Emily's insecurities.

She followed Daniel into the kitchen but meat pies were the last thing on her mind.

*

The evening fast approached and Emily had only one thing left to organize for the event: herself! As she hurried down the hall she could hear the sound of Chantelle practicing her hymn in the living room. Owen had been kind enough to come over early to help settle any of her last-minute jitters. The whole hallway was decorated with fairy lights that sent a kaleidoscope of color around Emily as she sprinted up the stairs and into her room.

As she searched her wardrobe for a dress to wear, Emily tried to sort through her scrambled emotions. First and foremost, she was upset about Trevor spending Christmas alone, her grief compounded by the knowledge it would be his last. Then she was feeling rushed off her feet thanks to the festive period. That strange and sudden urge she'd experienced for a child wasn't helping matters. And the icing on her scrambled-emotion-cake was, of course, Daniel dashing her feelings and dragging up her insecurities.

Emily went over to the vanity mirror to fix up her makeup and straighten her hair. But as she looked at her face in the mirror, she saw it begin to transform. She knew immediately that she was slipping back into her past, into her memories.

She grasped the edge of the table as though doing so could stop the memories in their tracks, although past experience had told her such a thing was not possible. There was no way of controlling when she was dragged back into the past, when the pressures of the present day would send her spiraling into her own mind.

Emily found herself suddenly sitting beneath a sad, small Christmas tree. It was still early morning so the fire hadn't been lit yet. Her father was in his armchair, sipping on his second eggnog of the day. Charlotte was still in her pajamas, her hair unbrushed. A pile of ripped gift wrap surrounded them. But despite the gifts of toys and books they'd already opened, they both wanted to play with the same singing mermaid doll.

"I'm older!" Emily shouted. "I should get to press the button first!"

"No!" Charlotte wailed. "I want to press it first!"

"Just take turns," Roy said with a heavy, weary sigh.

Emily turned her head over her shoulder to face her father. "I just want to press the button first. Then I'll let Charlotte try."

"Does it really matter who presses it first?" Roy exclaimed. "You'll both be able to hear the damn thing sing!"

Emily gripped the mermaid doll tightly in her arms and turned her back on her little sister. Charlotte began to cry. She kept reaching for the toy, but Emily turned her back on her sister over and over again so she could never quite reach it, which made Charlotte more and more irate.

"Emily Jane!" Roy roared.

But Emily was feeling stubborn. She didn't care that she was riling Charlotte. In fact, she was glad of it. Charlotte could be such a baby.

Suddenly, Charlotte snatched the mermaid doll from Emily's arms. In a second the younger girl was on her feet, running for the door. Emily swiveled on the spot and threw herself across the floor, reaching out for Charlotte, and, in doing so, knocked over the side table that her father's eggnog was sat on. The drink went flying, spraying the sweet, milky liquid all over the rug. The glass smashed against the floorboards.

Emily suddenly snapped back to the present day to find thirty-five-year-old Emily staring back at her in the mirror once more.

What a waste, she thought. If only she'd known that Charlotte would be gone so soon she'd never have wasted those precious moments with her. Despite the decades that had passed, Emily felt guilty over their argument. She wished she could go back in time and hand the mermaid to Charlotte, to let the little girl be the first to press the button and make her sing. Because it didn't matter really who pressed the button first; what mattered was the time they had together, that short time.

The sound of thunderous footsteps brought Emily fully back to the present day. Then suddenly light was streaming into her room and Chantelle was standing in the doorway.

"Daddy told me to tell you that the ebbnog is ready," she said, frowning with confusion. "Eddnog? Eddmog? I can't remember. Something like that."

Emily smiled and stood from the stool of the vanity mirror where she'd been perched for who knew how long. She took Chantelle's hand and they went downstairs together. She could hear a hum of voices coming from the living room and realized the party had started without her.

Feeling a little bad, Emily entered the dining room to see many of her friends, staff, and guests milling around. The warmth they generated radiated through her.

Daniel excused himself from his conversation and walked up to her.

"There you are," he said, handing her a glass of eggnog. "I thought I'd lost you."

Emily took the drink and stared down at the yellowy liquid inside.

"Memories," she explained. She gave him a sheepish look. "I got a little lost."

He didn't press any further. "Well, drink up. There's only an hour before we have to leave."

Just then, Karen sashayed through the crowds toward Emily.

"My darling," she said, kissing Emily on each cheek. "The place looks fabulous! I love the lights. So classy." She took a large glug of her eggnog, her pink cheeks revealing this certainly wasn't her first of the evening. Then she whispered conspiratorially, "I see you weren't able to tempt the dragon from his nest."

"Dragon?" Emily asked, confused.

"Trevor, of course!" Karen cried, and she began to laugh. "I can see the light on in his top window, the one that means he's spying on you!"

Emily swallowed the lump in her throat. She wanted to tell Karen to be more kind, but knew she couldn't. Trevor entrusted her with his secret. The least she could do was keep it.

Just then, Emily felt a bump from behind and almost spilled her drink. She turned to see Cynthia spinning around, holding hands with a terrified-looking Matthew.

"He's half your age!" Emily exclaimed. "Put the poor man down."

But Cynthia just grinned and twirled the helpless young man away.

Though glad to see her friends enjoying themselves, Emily wished she herself had fewer worries on her mind. Spotting Richard Goldsmith across the room didn't help matters, since it reminded her of all the adoption stress. And watching her married friends dance and joke together made her more anxious about the wedding plans, or lack of them. And even when Emily was able to relax and lose herself in the moment, she'd find her attention drawn to the rug, to the stain in the corner from a glass of eggnog she'd kicked over all those years ago…

Emily felt relieved when the time came to leave for the church service. Everyone was too inebriated to drive so they bundled into cabs or shared rides.

Snuggled in the back of a cab beside Emily, Chantelle seemed nervous. Singing with the town choir was a big moment for her, even if it was only for one song. They'd been so kind to allow her to join in with their Christmas show to help build her confidence with performing. Just think, only a month ago she'd been scared to sing in front of anyone; now she had two school performances under her belt and was about to sing to the entire town! Emily couldn't be more proud of the little girl.

The procession of cars streamed up to the church and parked in the lot. Everyone got out and entered the church, where they were welcomed by Father Duncan.

"I see you've brought quite a troop with you," he said as he shook Emily's hand.

She nodded. "Everyone has a place at my inn," she explained. Then she thought of Trevor, alone at home, watching them from the top window, and a knot of pain twisted in her stomach.

Father Duncan seemed to sense that she was troubled. "Is there anything you'd like to discuss?" he asked.

Emily shook her head.

Father Duncan took her hand and placed a small candle into it. "If you don't feel able to speak to me, there is always someone you can confide in."

Thanking him, Emily took the candle over to the steps where many other candles were lined up, their flames dancing in the gentle breeze. She lit the small white candle and whispered a prayer for Trevor, then placed it down.

It was then that she noticed a beautiful silver menorah set in one of the windows of the church. She'd always known that Sunset Harbor was a loving and accepting community. This was the perfect representation of it.

She watched Daniel lead Chantelle up to the menorah and explain what he was doing. He used the middle candle to light the other eight before placing it back in its central position. Ever the student, Chantelle watched with keen interest, soaking up another piece of her history. She listened with intent as Daniel said a blessing, then she placed the dollar he'd given her in the dish.

Just then, the choir master came over and collected Chantelle, ushering her to a position in the wings so she was ready to take to the stage when called. Daniel saw her off and then came and joined Emily in the pew.

"That was beautiful," Emily said when Daniel sat. "Watching you two share in lighting the menorah."

"We should get one for the inn," Daniel said. "Do it properly."

Emily was intrigued. Daniel had only recently told her he was Jewish; now he seemed to be getting into the Chanukah spirit.

"It's been years since I've taken part in any kind of Jewish tradition," he continued. "But seeing the menorah there brought it all back to me. I want Chantelle to enjoy those moments like I did

97

as a kid. I want to pass that on to her. Maybe teach her a couple of hymns. Eat some donuts."

"Okay, you have to be kidding now," Emily said, laughing.

"I swear," Daniel said. "They're called sufganoit."

Emily smiled. It made her so happy to hear Daniel get in touch with his past. He'd shared few stories with her, kept so much to himself. Anything he ever did divulge was usually the dark stuff, about his father leaving and his mother's problems with alcohol. But as he recounted his fond moments of tradition, he seemed to come alive with brightness. The idea of bringing such joy to Chantelle was very appealing.

"You should teach me how to make them one day," Emily said.

Just then, Father Duncan took to the pulpit to deliver his sermon. Everyone settled into the pews to listen to his words of love and compassion.

Just as it came up to midnight, the choir stood, ready to begin their hymns. Emily gripped Daniel's arm as Chantelle emerged from the side like an apparition, holding a candle ahead of her, walking slowly with the choir. Then her bell-like voice rang out, echoing through the hall. The whole audience held their breath with awe as she sang her solo in her beautiful soprano voice.

Listening to Chantelle sing this evening moved Emily more than ever before. The crowd around them, too, seemed even more stunned than usual.

Then the rest of the choir joined in with Chantelle, their voices merging in perfect harmony. Everyone relaxed into the pews as the choir and Chantelle sang them into Christmas.

CHAPTER FIFTEEN

"Wake up, wake up, wake up! It's Christmas!"

Emily startled awake to Chantelle's excited cries. The little girl jumped onto the bed, hopping up and down on her knees.

"Shhh," Emily said, laughing. "You'll wake the guests!"

She glanced at her clock to see it wasn't yet 5 a.m. Daniel was still asleep. Or at least pretending to be.

Emily fell back against the pillow with a groan. Two early starts in a row!

"Chantelle!" she murmured sleepily. "Couldn't you have waited until it was at least light outside?"

But Chantelle wasn't taking no for an answer. She bounced again on her knees, and this time it was enough to wake Daniel from his usual comatose sleep.

"What's all this shouting about?" he said, one bleary eye open against the white pillow.

"It's CHRISTMAS!" Chantelle screamed.

"Really?" Daniel joked. "I'd never have guessed."

Clearly realizing that her dad wasn't going to be easily roused, Chantelle grabbed Emily's hand and started pulling on it. Emily had no choice but to get out of bed and follow the young girl downstairs.

"Can I put some coffee on first?" Emily asked with a yawn.

Chantelle folded her arms. "Grown-ups," she said, rolling her eyes.

Emily laughed and quickly went into the kitchen to feed the dogs and brew some coffee. By the time the pot was gurgling, permeating the air with its fragrant aroma, Daniel had made it downstairs. He came up behind Emily and rested his hands on her hips, then kissed her neck.

"Merry Christmas," he murmured.

Emily spun and wrapped her arms around him. "Merry Christmas."

Emily felt overwhelmed with joy. This was their first Christmas together, and they were spending it engaged, with a beautiful child and a wonderful home. Never in a million years would she have expected her life to go this way.

She kissed Daniel deeply, passionately. Then she heard a small cough coming from the doorway. They broke apart to see Chantelle standing there, arms folded.

"I said you could get some coffee, not stand there kissing!" she exclaimed. "Come *on!* We have presents to open!"

Daniel and Emily exchanged an amused glance, then followed Chantelle to the living room to look inside their stockings.

"I'd better make a fire," Daniel said, rubbing his hands together from the cold.

"Good idea," Emily agreed. "And I'll make some cinnamon hot cocoa."

Chantelle's eyes gleamed at the thought.

Once coffee and cocoa had been consumed, and the fire was alight and making them toasty warm, it was finally time to exchange gifts.

Chantelle rushed out of the room then came back with her arms laden with gifts. They were wrapped in pages of magazines and bits of tissue paper, with bows on the top and sparkly stickers stuck all over them.

"You got us presents?" Daniel asked, choking up.

"When did you do all this?" Emily added with surprise.

Chantelle tapped her nose but Emily guessed that Yvonne had had something to do with it. If she could hide sparkly white cat suits from them she could certainly hide this! She smiled to herself, grateful to have made such a wonderful friend.

"These are for Mogsy and Rain," Chantelle said, putting two gifts aside. "And I got one for Lola and Lolly to share, which I hope they won't mind."

Emily felt tears spring into her eyes. Chantelle was such a sweet, gentle child. She'd even gotten gifts for the chickens!

Then Chantelle handed them each a gift. Emily's was wrapped in pages from a glossy Barbie magazine. Daniel's looked like pages from a local phone book. Emily couldn't help but laugh at Chantelle's attempts to theme the gift wrap.

Lost for words, she began to unwrap her gift. To her utter delight, it was an antique broach, a slightly gaudy owl made from tiny crystals. Not something Emily would usually wear but the thought Chantelle had put into getting it made it extra special.

"I love it," Emily said, clutching it to her chest. "It will look beautiful on my jacket."

Chantelle grinned happily. Then Emily looked over at Daniel to see what the little girl had gotten him. It was a small porcelain figurine of a dark-haired man holding a fishing rod in one hand, his other hand slipped into the hand of a blond-haired girl in an oversized fishing hat.

"It's us," Chantelle exclaimed. "We're going fishing."

"I can see that," Daniel said, emotional. "It's just... uncanny. Isn't it, Emily?" He held it up to her so she could get a better look.

"What does uncanny mean?" Chantelle asked. "Is it bad?"

Emily peered at the statue. It really was a remarkable likeness. She wondered where Chantelle could have found something so utterly perfect. Daniel was so clearly touched.

"Do you like it?" Chantelle asked, frowning.

Daniel reached for her and hugged her tightly. "I love it."

Emily looked on at the happy scene, of the fire glowing and her beautiful family embracing one another. It was the best sight her eyes could have been graced with.

"My turn," Emily said to Chantelle and Daniel.

She went over to the tree and grabbed a box for Daniel. Then she took out not one, not two, not three, but four different gifts for Chantelle. The little girl looked shocked.

"All for me?" she asked, surprised.

Clearly she'd never had so many gifts in her life. It made Emily sad to think of the child's neglectful past.

Chantelle opened the first gift, taking care as she removed the wrapping, which she then folded beside her neatly. It was a set of pastel pencils and a sketchbook.

"I love it!" she cried.

Emily smiled, relieved. "Keep going," she encouraged.

Chantelle opened the next present with the same level of care. She gasped with delight as she saw the ten-piece set of Beatrix Potter books. Emily remembered her commenting once on the illustrations and how much she loved them, and Emily herself had adored the books when she was younger. She couldn't wait to read them to Chantelle.

Chantelle carefully placed the books beside her and moved onto the next gift. This was larger than the last two, and Emily realized that Chantelle was opening them in size order, which was so typical of the highly organized child.

"Boots!" Chantelle cried, as she pulled out the cute leather animal-designed boots. They were from the same collection as Bailey's, although her friend had a frog design and Chantelle's was a fox. But she'd always remarked on how much she loved Bailey's boots, and now they could be like twins.

"They're sooooo soooo nice!" Chantelle added. She slid the boots right on there and then, even though she was in her pajamas. It was a funny sight to behold.

"And your final gift," Emily said, nodding to the largest one of them all.

Chantelle's fingers moved slowly as she unwrapped the gift, almost as though she were savoring the moment and didn't want it to end.

"Oh wow!" Chantelle cried as she removed from the paper a Polaroid camera complete with film refills. "A camera?"

Emily nodded. "You enjoyed taking pictures so much when we went sledding I thought you might like to have your own camera. And since your dad loved photography when he was young I figured there might be some kind of genetic talent, an inherited flair."

"You liked taking photos?" Chantelle asked Daniel.

"When I was younger," he said, looking a little embarrassed.

"Here, look," Emily said, reaching out for the camera. "Say cheese!"

Chantelle grinned and Emily snapped a picture. Then it popped out of the top and Chantelle exclaimed. She grabbed the Polaroid.

"What's this?" she said, staring at the gray shiny square in her hands.

"That's the photo," Emily explained.

"But I can't see anything."

"Just wait," Emily said. "It's like magic."

Chantelle sat on her knees, her elbows propped onto the rug, staring at the picture as it developed. She looked utterly delighted as her image emerged before her.

Chantelle threw her arms around Emily's neck. "That's amazing!" she exclaimed. "I can take pictures of you and Daddy and Bailey and Toby and the dogs and chickens and decorate my walls."

Her neck thoroughly squeezed by Chantelle's vise-like hug, Emily was delighted that she'd managed to find Chantelle gifts that she could enjoy.

"My gift is nowhere as good as Emily's," Daniel said, looking coy as he produced a gift from behind his back.

It was poorly wrapped, but Chantelle didn't notice. She took the gift eagerly and unwrapped it gently.

"What is it?" Chantelle asked, holding up a telescope.

"It's for looking at the stars," Daniel explained. "You can set it up in your window and then when the sky gets dark you can look at the stars. If you're lucky you might even see a shooting star."

Chantelle's mouth dropped open. "Really?"

Daniel nodded, looking a little relieved that Chantelle seemed so interested in the gift he'd gotten her. "You can even see the craters of the moon."

Chantelle looked at the telescope in her hands like it was a magic wand. "Wow," she gasped.

Daniel looked over at Emily and gave a sheepish grin. She smiled at him reassuringly. They'd done an excellent job of gifting on their first ever Christmas, and they had one happy kid on their hands.

"It's still dark now," Chantelle said, looking up, eyes wide and eager. "Can we go and look for shooting stars?"

Daniel nodded and stood, just as enthusiastic by Chantelle's excitement. Emily smiled as she watched them run off, hand in hand, Chantelle in her cute little nightdress and boot combo, the telescope tucked under her arm, and thought about how much she loved them, how she really had struck gold.

*

Emily was exhausted by the time day turned into evening and the dinner guests were due. Chantelle had kept her and Daniel on their toes all day, running round with excitement, snapping photos.

But it was with renewed energy that she opened the door to Suzanna and Wesley that evening. Toby was with them and he rushed off to find Chantelle.

"This way," Emily said, leading them into the dining room.

"Oh, it looks fab in here," Suzanna said, glancing at the beautiful fairy lights and snowflake decorations.

More and more guests arrived, until the table was heaving with guests, neighbors, and friends alike, from Owen to the Canadian family staying at the inn. Listening to their loud, happy chatter, Emily felt overwhelmed with gratitude and love.

Dinner was a loud, warm, and happy affair, and the food Matthew had prepared was utterly delicious.

Allison, who sat beside Emily, leaned in to her. "I noticed the menorah," she said. "Are you Jewish?"

"Daniel is," Emily explained. "He was lapsed but having Chantelle now has made him remember all the traditions and how much he loved them. They lit the menorah together last night, and again today. It's been really lovely to watch."

"We're Jewish too," Allison explained, gesturing to her husband, Saul, who sat across from her. "That's why I was so pleased to see a menorah. And sufganoit." She winked, holding up a little ball of fried donut.

Emily laughed. "I had no idea."

Allison nodded. "That's one of the lovely things about Sunset Harbor. The whole spectrum is represented."

"What do you mean?" Emily asked. She knew Raj and Sunita Patel were Hindu, and her close friend Serena was Sikh, but other than that she'd just assumed everyone was Christian.

"Well, Suzanna and Wesley are Buddhist, aren't they?" Allison said, nodding at the couple.

"They are?" Emily exclaimed. She'd had no idea. How could something like that have not come up in conversation?

"Oh yes. Suzanna's parents are from Thailand originally. I think Wesley is Sri Lankan. But you should check with them, I might be wrong."

Emily shook her head, surprised. Despite knowing Suzanna and Wesley for several months, somehow this information had passed her by. She felt like a terrible friend for not knowing. At the same time she was even more touched than before that they'd come to her Christmas dinner, since neither of them celebrated the festival themselves!

And at the same time she thought about how welcome everyone was at the inn, and how much she loved the way the space had become so inclusive for everyone.

But as Emily glanced around the table, a moment of sadness overcame her. She hadn't heard anything from her dad. Perhaps it had been wishful thinking on her part, but she'd really thought that if he'd read her email, if he knew he was forgiven, then today of all days he'd be in touch. Emily found herself discreetly checking her phone throughout the meal to see if there were any new messages but there never were.

Likewise, Sheila hadn't been in touch either. And though Chantelle hadn't asked after her mother aloud Emily knew she'd be wishing for contact deep down, that when the thrill of Christmas faded she'd be wondering why she hadn't heard anything for her own mother.

Emily felt suddenly overwhelmed with emotion. She excused herself from the table and ventured outside onto the porch, wrapping herself in her jacket where she'd pinned the diamond owl. The sight of it was enough to reduce her to tears.

Emily sat on the swinging chair and tucked her legs up under her, gazing up at the moon. As she did so, she felt the now familiar sensation of being sucked into the past.

In this memory she was with Charlotte again. They were on a swing that her father had made out of a piece of wood and rope, which he'd strung up between two trees. They were sat together because the swing was just big enough to accommodate them both, and their arms were linked.

"I love my dolly," Charlotte said.

They'd both been gifted rag dolls, which were sitting upon each of their knees. Charlotte's wore a gorgeous patchwork dress and had hair made of ginger wool. She'd immediately decided to call hers Michelle. Emily hadn't named her own doll yet. She was taking her time with the decision because she wanted it to be perfect. Her own rag doll was more delicate, with blond hair and a pale blue dress. She had pink cheeks which were made of felt circles sewn onto her face with big woolen stitches. She needed an elegant name, like one of the girls in those books about Victorian British orphans that Emily loved to read.

"It's midnight," Emily told Charlotte, as she looked down at the face of her new pink watch. "That means Christmas is over."

"It was the best Christmas ever," Charlotte replied.

Emily nodded. "Yes. It was."

The two girls hugged their dollies tightly, swinging back and forth between the branches of the tall, strong oak tree.

Then suddenly Emily was back on the seat on the porch. No dollies. No Charlotte beside her. Just herself, swinging alone twenty-five years later. She didn't even try to stop her tears from falling.

The sound of footsteps from behind startled her out of her upset. Daniel came and sat beside her.

"You're sad," he stated.

Without explanation, Emily just nodded and rested her head against his shoulder. No words were forthcoming and so she said nothing at all. But Daniel held her tightly, reminding Emily that she wasn't alone, that although things changed, time passed, and the people around her were not the same as they had been all those years ago, she was certainly not alone.

"I have an idea," Daniel said.

Emily moved out of his one-armed hug and looked up at him. "What's that?"

"The New Year's party," he said. "How about we throw a Prohibition theme? I'll get the bar fixed up as a speakeasy."

He smiled encouragingly. Emily knew he was trying to cheer her up and greatly appreciated the effort. Maybe he was right. Having something to plan over the next week would certainly keep her preoccupied, and the Christmas party had been a resounding success after all, as had the Thanksgiving party just a month earlier.

"We'll start getting a reputation," Emily laughed.

"Isn't that a good thing?" Daniel replied.

"I guess. But won't it be too much work for you? You're supposed to be having a vacation from Jack Cooper's! Where will you find the energy?"

She didn't want to mention her other concern, that there would be no time left to plan their wedding.

Daniel cupped her face and kissed her gently. "For you, Emily, I can do it."

Despite her upset, Emily felt humbled with gratitude and love. It had been a wonderful Christmas.

CHAPTER SIXTEEN

Emily woke the next morning to find the other side of the bed empty. Her initial panic that Daniel had left her during the night was quelled when she heard the sound of hammering coming from downstairs. He must have woken early to keep his promise of working on the bar.

Emily dressed and went to fetch Chantelle for breakfast. When she found the child in her room, she could instantly tell that Chantelle was upset.

"What's wrong?" she asked as she held her hand and led her downstairs to the kitchen.

"Nothing." Chantelle shrugged. She hopped up onto one of the stools. Then she wrinkled her nose in distaste. "Is Daddy going to be making that noise all day?"

Emily laughed. "All week, actually."

She brought a glass of juice and a bowl of cereal over to Chantelle and set them down in front of her, then took the stool opposite.

"Are you sure you're okay?" she asked, again.

Chantelle began pushing cereal around her bowl with her spoon. "I just thought I might get a call from Mom," she said.

Emily felt a sinking sensation in her chest. Not just because Chantelle was sad, and that Sheila had disappointed the child again, but because it was the first time in a while she'd heard her express any kind of desire to have contact with her mom. For the first time, Emily felt filled with doubt over whether pursuing adoption was the right course of action after all.

"Why are *you* sad?" Chantelle asked.

Emily looked at the sweet, caring child. "I just have lots of things on my mind," she said.

"Is it because your mom didn't call on Christmas?" Chantelle asked. "Or because your daddy didn't write back to you?"

Emily frowned. "How did you know I'd written to him?" she asked.

"Because you're always checking your emails," Chantelle replied. "I figured if it was anyone else you'd just call them."

Emily raised her eyebrows, impressed with how astute the child could be.

"Come on, clever clogs," she said, "Let's go draw some invitations for the party."

Chantelle jumped down from the breakfast bar and they headed down the hallway. The sound of Daniel's hammering grew louder.

"Do you really think Daddy will be finished in time for the party?" Chantelle asked as they passed the living room, where a sheet had been hung across to stop anyone from snooping.

"I do," Emily said, smiling. "When your dad puts his mind to something, he doesn't give up."

But her smile faded as she realized there was one thing Daniel seemed to have given up on, and that was planning their wedding. She took a breath to calm her mind. There was a week until New Year's. Then after that, their calendar would be blank once more. No more distractions. Emily made a decision then that she wouldn't mention a single thing to do with the wedding until New Year's. That was Daniel's deadline. After that, it was full steam ahead whether he liked it or not.

*

Once the chaos of Christmas began to die down, Emily took the first opportunity she could to visit Trevor. When she reached his front door she found it partly ajar. A bolt of anguish struck her.

Emily pushed the door fully open and rushed inside, calling, "Trevor! Trevor?"

A small voice called back. "I'm over here!"

Emily gave herself a moment to slow her racing heartbeat, then followed the direction Trevor's voice had come from. She walked through the kitchen, the utility room, then out through the conservatory. No wonder Trevor's voice had sounded so quiet; he was all the way outside!

"Trevor, what are you doing out here?" Emily asked as she entered the conservatory and found him sitting in a garden chair wrapped up in blankets.

"Just admiring at the view," Trevor replied with a knowing smile.

Emily looked out the conservatory windows and saw then that Trevor had a clear view into the greenhouse where the four spindly fruit trees stood.

"You knew it was us?" Emily said.

Trevor nodded. "And I love it. The most thoughtful gift I could imagine."

Emily wasn't sure, but she thought she might have seen a sparkle of tears in the corner of his eye.

108

"Now, if you have the time, come and tell me about your Christmas," Trevor said. He patted the seat beside him. "How was the choir service? How is the wedding planning going? I want to know everything."

Emily sat and took a deep breath. "Chantelle sang beautifully. It was truly wonderful. The Christmas dinner was a success, although we missed you being there, of course. And wedding planning has taken a back seat. I'd rather not talk about it."

Trevor seemed to understand. "May I ask, did you hear anything back from your father?"

Emily shook her head. "I was hoping that Christmas would be the prompt but no. Nothing."

"You're disappointed," Trevor said.

Emily nodded, and for the first time she realized just how much Trevor had taken on the role of a counselor, offering her sympathy and care, listening with patience to her troubles. All this time she thought she'd been the one caring for him but he had been caring for her just as greatly. She would miss his camaraderie so much when he was gone.

"But you still have hope?" Trevor asked. "Hope that he will get in touch one day?"

"I don't know if I do."

"But you must," Trevor replied. "You've gotten closer to him than ever before. You are almost there. Just hold onto that hope. Because there is always a chance things will change. Even when things look hopeless, you must have hope."

Emily sat and absorbed his words. Trevor was right. She shouldn't give up on her father, especially not now, when she was so close. Perhaps her dad would surprise her yet.

CHAPTER SEVENTEEN

Daniel's hands covered Emily's eyes as they stood beside the white curtain concealing the living room. Daniel had worked flat out all week on the renovation work and, despite the tight deadline, had gotten everything ready in time for the party. He was ready now for the grand reveal.

Chantelle was beside them, covering her eyes with her hands, jiggling up onto the balls of her feet and back down again with barely contained excitement.

"Ta-da!" Daniel exclaimed, and he tore the curtain down.

Emily and Chantelle rushed into the living room.

Daniel's renovation work was spectacular. Emily could hardly believe how talented he was. The whole fake wall had been removed and replaced with a dark red velvet curtain which Daniel had tied to the side with a golden cord so that it looked like the curtain of a theatre stage.

He'd varnished and polished the wooden bar, as well as all the stools, tables, and chairs that they'd found originally in the secret room. He'd reupholstered the red velvet fabric of the booths and stools, had dusted all the old bottles, filled the optics, buffed the mirror so it was gleaming, restocked the shelves with glasses, scrubbed the dark red carpet so it was bright and welcoming.

"Wow!" Chantelle exclaimed. "It's awesome!"

Daniel looked very pleased with himself, and quite rightly, Emily thought. He was so talented and she could not have been more proud of him.

"This is going to be the best party ever," Chantelle said. Then her eyes widened with a sudden spark of inspiration. "Are there going to be fireworks?"

Emily nodded enthusiastically. "They're already set up in the garden."

"All ready for the stroke of midnight," Daniel replied. "I'll light them just as soon as I've finished smooching Emily."

Chantelle pulled a disgusted face. "Gross."

Emily laughed.

"Well, we'd better start getting everything ready," she said.

They ran upstairs and changed into their 1920s attire. Emily helped Chantelle change into a dark purple vintage purple dress and styled her hair with a side parting and gelled kiss curl. Then as the little girl played in her room, Emily got herself ready. She wore dramatic makeup, with ruby red lips and fake lashes. She gelled her hair in the same style as Chantelle's and then slid on some lace elbow-length gloves.

Her look complete, she twirled in the mirror, the fringes on her flapper dress shimmying as she did.

"You look gorgeous," Daniel said, appearing in the bedroom behind her.

Emily took in the sight of his tux and flashed him a grin. "You don't look so bad yourself."

She glanced at her watch. The guests would be arriving any minute for the evening meal. Hopefully none of them would have guessed why the theme for tonight's party was Prohibition era, though Emily had received several queries as to whether that meant it was a liquor-free party. Little did they know what they were in store for.

Right on time, the doorbell rang. Emily answered it. It was Wesley and Suzanna.

"Happy New Year," Wesley said. He handed Emily a bottle of champagne.

"This looks expensive," Emily said.

"Oh, it is," Wesley informed her. Then he added in a conspiratorial whisper, "I won it in a wine merchants auction."

He winked and Emily laughed.

Wesley removed his coat to reveal his pinstripe suit. Emily clapped with delight.

"He does scrub up rather well," Suzanna said in her usual timid voice. She herself looked divine in a peach fringe dress and kitten heels. She had slicked her hair over into a side parting. It suited her.

"You look gorgeous," Emily said. "Positively glowing."

Suzanna blushed.

Daniel greeted them both and led them into the dining room to take their seats. As he went, the doorbell rang and Emily answered the door to Serena.

"I'm so happy to see you!" Emily cried, pulling her friend into a tight embrace.

"I've only been gone a week," Serena laughed, her voice strangled by the force of Emily's hug.

"Some weeks are longer than others," Emily replied.

Serena looked incredible as always, and had put a lot of effort into her 1920s outfit. She'd even handmade her own sequined headband.

"So, are we having this party in the speakeasy?" Serena asked.

Emily put a finger to her lip to shush her. "No one else knows. It's a surprise."

"Oh!" Serena said, lowering her voice. She winked. "Got it."

As Serena headed toward the dining room, Yvonne and Kieran arrived at the door. Emily was overjoyed to see them. She hugged them both tightly.

"How was Paris?" she asked Kieran, who looked very dapper in a gray suit.

Kieran rolled his eyes. "Well, my girls are teenagers now so their conversational skills have diminished to unhappy grunting." Everyone laughed. "But it was lovely, really. Although I missed this one." He slung his arm around Yvonne and kissed her. "And our little monster, of course."

"Speaking of, where is Bailey tonight?" Emily asked.

"We left her with the sitter," Yvonne explained. "It's been just the two of us for weeks. Mommy needs a break. And a stiff shot of liquor."

Emily laughed. "Well, there's plenty of that."

The couple went off to join the others in the dining room, leaving Emily in the hall to greet the remaining guests. Then once everyone had arrived, they all congregated in the dining room for a glass of champagne before settling down for a meal.

Chantelle fidgeted all through the meal. She was too excited about seeing the renovated bar and was struggling to continue to keep it a secret. Emily kept glancing over at her as she bounced on her seat and pressed her lips together as though keeping them sealed was a physical impossibility. As soon as everyone had finished their dessert and had their glasses topped up with champagne, Emily went over to Chantelle's seat.

"I think it's time to make the announcement," she whispered in Chantelle's ear.

The little girl's eyes pinged open, a mixture of excitement and fear. "Now?"

Emily nodded with encouragement. "Just say your lines, exactly as we practiced them." Then she stood and tapped her glass with a spoon to get everyone's attention.

Chantelle gulped, all eyes on her.

"Ladies and gentlemen," she began, "we would like to invite you to a very special, secret event. The most exclusive club in Sunset Harbor. You are hereby welcome to the grand opening of the Sunset Speakeasy." Everyone looked around at each other in bemusement. "Please, follow me," Chantelle finished.

She led the way out of the dining hall, a line of intrigued guests following her. Then she opened the living room door and everyone streamed in, gasping with surprise and wonder.

Emily swelled with pride as her friends glanced around the speakeasy with shock and awe. They looked so fitting in their outfits. The sight delighted Emily.

"This is just fabulous," Yvonne exclaimed. "I can't believe what I'm seeing."

Kieran put on an exaggerated Boston accent as he leaned against the bar and said, "Can I buy you a Manhattan, little missy?"

Behind the bar, dressed up for the occasion, was Serena's friend Alec, who had been more than happy to work for triple time on New Year's Eve. He made up a batch of Manhattans for everyone and they began milling around, gushing over the amazing restoration work.

"Aren't you drinking?" Emily asked Suzanna when she realized her friend wasn't holding a cocktail glass.

Suzanna shook her head. "I'm too much of a lightweight for liquor!"

"I can get you something else," Emily said. "There's rosé if you'd prefer."

Suzanna shook her head again and dipped her eyes. Emily suddenly realized why her friend was refusing alcohol.

"Are you...?" she began to ask.

But she didn't need to finish her question because Suzanna's eyes lit up and she nodded her head vigorously.

"Eleven weeks," Suzanna said, touching her belly with a protective hand. "We wanted to wait one more until announcing it."

Emily could hardly contain her excitement. "This is amazing!" she squealed. "I'm so happy for you!"

It wasn't that long ago that Suzanna and Wesley had been stagnated with their lives, he in a job he didn't like, she with only one child because their finances were too tight for a second. Now Wesley had started his wine business and Suzanna was pregnant! Emily couldn't be happier for them.

As the evening drew on, the liquor flowed freely. Kieran instigated a dance-off, which involved lots of hand jives and attempts to Charleston.

"Want to try a Lindy-hop?" Daniel asked Emily as he twirled her on the spot.

"Absolutely not!" she laughed.

Then a sleepy-looking Chantelle was tugging at the hem of Emily's dress.

"What's up, sweetie?" Emily asked. "Do you want to go to bed?"

Chantelle shook her head. "I want to stay up for the fireworks," she said.

"Of course," Emily said. She picked Chantelle up in her arms so the sleepy girl could be part of the dancing with Daniel.

They danced, giggling, until they were exhausted and out of breath.

"We'd better get everyone outside," Daniel said, noticing that the time was nearing midnight.

"Good idea," Emily agreed.

Emily shooed her giddy, tipsy guests out onto the porch, where they all huddled together for warmth.

"Let the countdown commence!" she cried.

Everyone joined in counting down from ten.

"Three...two...one! Happy New Year!!!"

Daniel planted a sumptuous kiss on Emily's lips, holding her tightly against his body.

"The fireworks," she prompted when they finally pulled apart.

Daniel quickly lit them and the rockets flew into the air, bursting with color. Everyone clapped and cheered.

"What's your New Year's resolution?" Emily asked Daniel.

"Making even more memories to cherish," he said, kissing her. "What's yours?"

"Marrying you," Emily replied.

She hadn't forgotten her resolution to herself, to pin Daniel down to some wedding details. Now she just had to make sure she followed through.

Just then, Suzanna maneuvered herself to the front of the crowd.

"My resolution is to be more fearless," Suzanna said. "So I may as well start now. We're pregnant!"

An even louder cheer went up, so loud it could probably be heard from any spot in Sunset Harbor. To a backdrop of sparkling color, everyone hugged and cheered, filled with love and gratitude to have each other.

CHAPTER EIGHTEEN

The next morning Emily awoke to a pounding head and a mess of a B&B. She went down to the porch to get a bit of fresh air, where empty champagne glasses were still strewn, with popped balloons and streamers blowing gently in the breeze.

As she stood there surveying the carnage, Emily felt her phone vibrate in her pocket. Amy's name flashed up on the screen. Emily answered the call.

"Happy New Year!" Amy screamed into the phone, so loud Emily almost dropped it.

"Happy New Year to you too," Emily replied, wincing.

"Are you hung over?" Amy probed.

"Of course I am!" Emily exclaimed. "We had the grand unveiling of the speakeasy bar last night. There was lots of jazz and Manhattans and attempts at doing the Charleston."

"Sounds fab," Amy replied. There was a lilt to her voice.

"What did you get up to?" Emily asked with curious suspicion.

"Well, I met a very handsome man at midnight," Amy replied, giggling.

"You did?" Emily exclaimed. "Tell me everything!"

"Later," Amy replied. "First I want to know how everything is going with the wedding planning. Have you decided on a venue yet?"

"We still haven't seen anywhere else," Emily confessed. "Daniel's been diverting my attention with parties." She couldn't help her fear that Daniel had been trying to keep her mind away from wedding topics. "But it's a new year and a new me. I won't stand for any more shirking!"

"Good," Amy said. "So when do you start?"

"Today. He won't be up for it, though. He's even more hung over than I am."

"Never mind about that," Amy replied. "You're booking a venue appointment, not running a marathon. I'm sure he can cope."

Encouraged by Amy, Emily took a coffee up to Daniel in bed. He groaned as he accepted it. Then she pulled back the curtains and light streamed into the bedroom.

"Why are you torturing me?" Daniel said, covering his head with the duvet.

Emily pulled the cover away. "You're not a vampire. You can handle a bit of light."

"Why are you trying to wake me up?" Daniel asked, somewhat suspicious.

"Wedding," Emily stated, trying to remain confident. "I would like to make an appointment to look at another venue."

Daniel tried to keep his weary eyelids open. "Now?"

Emily immediately felt her resolve begin to weaken. "Yes. Now. We haven't made any plans for weeks."

"Well, we've been a bit busy," Daniel replied a little tersely. "Christmas. New Year. Renovating the bar. It's not exactly like we've been short on things to organize."

"I know," Emily replied, feeling herself grow irritated. "But this is important."

Daniel rubbed the place between his eyebrows. "Okay. Fine. Where do you want to look?"

"That place I saw while shopping in Kittery," Emily began.

Daniel looked nonplussed. "Kittery is quite a long drive away. And it's not like it has anything particularly different to offer. Harbor town. Coastal views. We have that here."

"But it looked nice," Emily replied. "Look." She grabbed the wedding brochure of venues in Maine from the bedside cabinet and flicked through until she found the pictures of the beautifully converted orangery. The glass canopy looked amazing in the sunlight.

"We'll have to have a summer wedding if we go here," Daniel said. "Can you imagine how awful it would be if it was raining?"

Emily could tell he was trying to make a joke but she wasn't in the mood.

"Is that all you have to say?" she replied, snapping the magazine shut.

Daniel gave her a confused expression. "We can look there if you want. I was only joking."

"Well, I do want," she replied with a pout. "I'm going to call them right now and make an appointment."

Emily shuffled off the bed and took her phone to the porch in order to give herself a bit of distance from Daniel. Before she called the venue she quickly texted Amy to tell her of her success. Her friend wrote back immediately, congratulating her for finding the confidence to address the issue.

Emily typed in the venue's number and listened to the dial tone. A woman answered in a cordial manner, introducing herself as Simone.

"I'd like to book an appointment," Emily told her. "As soon as possible, really."

"I actually have a free booking today," Simone explained. "Not many people want to look at venues on News Year's Day, as you can imagine."

Of course no one would want to book a meeting on New Year's. Everyone knew they'd be too hung over to attend. It was only she and her sheer persistence that meant she and Daniel could make themselves available.

"That's perfect," Emily said. "We'll head straight there. See you in an hour?"

"I look forward to it."

Emily ended the call and rushed back up to the bedroom to discover that Daniel had pulled the covers back over his head. She plopped down on the bed beside him.

"Great news," she said. "We have an appointment in an hour."

Daniel looked surprised. "An hour? But what about Chantelle? We won't be able to book a playdate for her on such short notice."

"She can come with us," Emily replied. "You know how much she enjoys it."

Daniel seemed flustered by the sudden booking and sighed heavily as he went to wake up Chantelle and get her ready for the day. Emily felt frustrated by his attitude. Why was he such a nightmare every time they did anything wedding related? His attitude filled her with self-doubt.

As she got herself ready for the journey, she received several texts from Amy about the venue they were about to see. Amy had clearly immediately gone online to research it. Emily wanted to feel excited too but in actuality she was quite stressed about the whole thing. Amy's enthusiasm was in such contrast to Daniel's flatness. She would prefer it if their attitudes were switched, if Daniel was the one excitedly researching the venue.

Once the family was ready they piled into the pickup truck. Chantelle was sleepy in the back car seat, and looked less than thrilled by the trip. Emily couldn't help but feel irritated. No one was even remotely enthusiastic, not even Chantelle who was excited by everything!

As Daniel drove, they all remained silent, just listening to pop hits on the radio. Emily knew he was hung over but she wished he would at least make conversation with her. It would go some way in reassuring her frantic mind.

They reached the venue, which was even prettier than in the pictures, and then Emily remembered. Something about the sparse winter branches of the trees surrounding the small stone structure delighted Emily. It looked like something from a postcard. She could imagine it covered in snow. Maybe she wanted a winter wedding after all.

There was a woman waiting for them on the steps, holding a clipboard.

"Hello, I'm Simone," she said, shaking each of their hands, including Chantelle's. "Please come in."

She opened up the large oak door and led them inside.

Emily gasped as she looked around the venue. It was small and would only accommodate their closest friends, but it was gorgeous. Glass windows stretched from floor to ceiling, which was also made of glass. There was vegetation everywhere, making it feel as though they were as much outside as inside, giving the place a fresh smell and cool feel.

Daniel chuckled. "It's like being in a greenhouse."

Emily shot him a warning glare. Now was not the time for his "funny" quips.

"We can change the foliage to meet your needs," Simone explained. "Of course it's seasonal so at the moment it's our winter selection. We can remove it altogether also if that's preferred."

"No, I love it," Emily said, touching her fingers delicately against the sprigs of holly and the twisted wreath-like bark.

Daniel didn't seem as awestruck by the vegetation as Emily was, which she thought strange since he was such an outdoorsy type, what with his rose garden and the patches of vegetables he tended to at the inn.

"What season were you hoping to arrange the wedding for?" Simone asked.

"We're not sure yet," Emily said. "Of course I'd always imagined a summer wedding when I was a kid, but Maine is so lovely in the winter. Then I love the colors of fall. The weather of spring." She laughed. "I guess every season has its advantages."

"A fuss-free bride-to-be," Simone joked. "You're just my type."

Emily laughed along with Simone's humor. But Daniel was standing a little ways apart, staring up at the domed glass roof, his arms folded.

"Is it noisy when it rains?" he asked.

Emily tensed. Daniel was in practical mode, thinking of things logically rather than with his heart.

"The glass is double glazed," Simone explained. "Even though you'd never know to look at it. So, no, it's never that loud. You'll always be able to hear the vicar." She smiled.

"I love it here," Emily gushed.

118

"Please, do take your time. Have a look around," Simone said, and Emily wondered whether she sensed the disparity between her own and Daniel's desires. "I'll be here if you have any questions."

Chantelle was already exploring the spherical space. She seemed to like it, despite her sleepiness dampening her usual enthusiasm. It was only Daniel who appeared nonplussed. Emily was disappointed that he wasn't more enthused by the location.

They stepped away together to talk privately.

"What are you thinking?" Emily asked in a hushed voice.

"I'm thinking I need a Bloody Mary," Daniel replied.

"I mean about the venue," Emily hissed.

Daniel shrugged. "It's hard to make a decision when my head is pounding so hard."

Emily felt herself pull her hands into fists. Daniel was being infuriating.

She walked up to Simone. "Thanks so much for showing us around. We'll take all your pamphlets and brochures and be in touch."

"Of course," Simone replied, handing her their marketing materials. "I look forward to hearing from you."

"Come on, Chantelle," Emily called to the girl, whose head seemed to be as in the clouds today as her father's was.

They piled back into the pickup truck. Emily couldn't help but slam her door shut and sulk.

Daniel started the engine and watched her from the corner of his eye. "Is everything okay?" he asked as he began to back out of the parking space.

"Why don't you like it?" Emily asked, launching straight into the confrontation.

"It was nice," Daniel admitted. "But it's quite a long way to drive for basically some indoor trees."

Emily looked at him coolly.

"I just mean I'm sure there's somewhere closer to home that has the same thing going on," he added, attempting to clarify his words.

Emily sunk down into her seat and turned her gaze out the passenger side window. "Sure," she mumbled. "I'll look closer to home."

As Daniel drove them along the streets of Kittery, Emily composed a text to Amy, who she knew would be waiting on tenterhooks for some news about the venue.

Well, that was a complete bust.

Emily twiddled her ring tensely as Daniel parked the truck back at the inn. Chantelle had napped the entire way and now finally had some energy. She rushed out into the backyard to play and stretch her legs.

Quietly, Emily and Daniel walked up the porch steps. They'd barely spoken a word to each other the whole drive home.

To Emily's relief, Vanessa and Marnie had already cleared the downstairs area of the New Year's party detritus. It was like someone had waved a magic wand and restored the inn to its former glory.

Lois was on shift, sitting at the reception desk.

"You have mail," she told Emily, hopping up to attention. "Well, Chantelle does anyway."

She handed Emily a bundle of letters. Emily took them with a frown. Immediately, she noticed the watermark on the envelopes. They'd been posted from Tennessee. Sheila? That was the last thing she needed right now!

"What are those?" Daniel asked Emily.

She held the letters to her chest. "I think they're from Sheila," she replied, her clutch on them tightening.

Daniel's expression immediately became drawn. They headed into the living room where they could speak more privately, away from Lois and the guests who roamed the halls.

There were four letters in total. Emily wondered when Sheila had written them and why she hadn't sent them immediately, why she'd waited to send them together. It seemed peculiar. She felt them and realized that three of them must be cards. Perhaps a birthday card for Chantelle's birthday in October, a Thanksgiving day card and a Christmas card? But what was in the fourth envelope, which was more pliable than the others?

"Should we show them to Chantelle?" Emily asked Daniel.

But no sooner had the words left her lips than Chantelle walked into the living room, red-cheeked from her dash around the yard.

"Show me what?" she asked.

Emily and Daniel froze. There was no option now. They had to show her what they'd considered concealing and risk the emotional fallout.

"Cards, sweetie," Emily said softly. "From your mom. And maybe a letter."

Chantelle visibly paled. "Give them to me," she demanded.

"Okay," Emily said with trepidation. "But remember your mom isn't well. What she's written might be disappointing."

Chantelle remained emotionless. Emily handed her the four envelopes.

The little girl slowly walked over to the couch, sat down, and opened the first. Emily craned her head, trying to see what it was, and assumed from the bright pink color that it was indeed a birthday card. Chantelle moved on, opening the second envelope, then the third. From here, Emily couldn't make out any of the writing contained within them, and Chantelle kept them very private, returning the cards neatly to their envelopes once she'd quietly read them.

Then she opened the fourth envelope. As Emily had predicted, this was indeed a letter. Emily and Daniel watched as Chantelle unfolded it, rested it on her knees, and took a considerable amount of time reading it. Like the others, she returned it neatly to its envelope. Then all at once, she began to cry.

Emily rushed to her side. "Sweetie, is everything okay?"

Chantelle nodded, but her tears kept on falling.

"What did your mom say?" Daniel asked.

Chantelle refused to speak.

"I'm going to my room now," was all she said.

Silently she stood up and left the room, leaving Daniel and Emily floundering. They looked at one another.

"What should we do?" Emily said.

Daniel shrugged. "I don't know. Maybe I should call Sheila? Find out what she said in the letters?"

Emily didn't like the idea of Daniel speaking to his ex. Sheila liked to flirt with Daniel and it made Emily uncomfortable to think of them talking on the phone.

"I don't think that's a good idea," she said.

"We can't exactly sneak into Chantelle's room and read them when she's not looking," Daniel countered. "It would be an invasion of privacy."

"And calling Sheila to ask what she wrote wouldn't be?" Emily replied.

Daniel frowned. "You just don't want me to speak to her, do you?"

Emily folded her arms and exhaled. "No. Okay. I don't," she admitted.

"You don't have to be so insecure all the time," Daniel replied. "I'm not about to rekindle my relationship with my drug-addicted ex-girlfriend who hid my child from me for six goddamn years."

His words weren't exactly a comfort to Emily, nor was the tone in which he spoke them. Daniel seemed to grow more exasperated at her lack of response.

"We're engaged, Emily," he said. "Doesn't that mean anything to you? I'm about to commit to spending my entire life with you and you're worrying about *Sheila*?"

All at once, Emily began to weep passionately. It was as if all of her fears and anxieties over the last couple of months were bursting out of her in one go.

"Do you really want to get married, Daniel, or was this whole thing just for show?"

Daniel stared at her, astounded by her sudden outburst. "I can't believe you'd even ask that," he said, astonished.

Then, without uttering another word, he turned on his heel and stormed out of the room.

CHAPTER NINETEEN

The next day Emily was trying to keep her mind busy with the inn rather than letting it drift back to the argument with Daniel. But she found it difficult to focus on anything.

She was so preoccupied with her own thoughts she didn't even hear the telephone ringing until Lois rushed up to the reception desk to grab it.

"It's for you," Lois said, handing the receiver to her. "Chantelle's teacher."

Emily felt an immediate jolt of concern.

"Ms. Glass?" she said into the receiver, sounding more than a little surprised. "Is everything okay?"

"Well, that's why I'm calling," Ms. Glass said. "I wanted to speak to you about an incident with Chantelle."

"What?" Emily gasped. "What's happened? Is she okay?"

A thousand thoughts raced through her mind. Was the child injured? Bullied? Lost?

"She's fine," Ms. Glass continued. "It's just that she got into an altercation with one of her friends. Toby."

Emily frowned at the news. Suzanna and Wesley's son? But he and Chantelle were the best of friends.

"What kind of altercation?" Emily asked.

"There was a spat in the playground," Ms. Glass explained. "Chantelle became somewhat aggressive. She hit Toby."

Emily gasped. She'd seen firsthand Chantelle's explosive rage, but it had never been directed at a person, just inanimate objects. She couldn't imagine the sweet, gentle child hitting anyone.

"She's going through a lot," Emily explained, stammering. "With her mom."

"What kind of things?" Ms. Glass asked gently.

Emily had no answer to give. She had no idea what was in Sheila's letter but she was certain it was the reason Chantelle had flown off the handle at Toby.

"Well, I don't know all the ins and outs, to be honest," Emily explained. "Her mom got in touch for the first time in a long while. The last time that happened Chantelle acted out so I'm sure it's related. Is Toby okay?"

"He's a little shaken. His mom's taken him home for the rest of the day."

Emily wondered whether Suzanna would be outraged by the incident. She wanted to call her ASAP and apologize but Ms. Glass hadn't finished.

"I think it would be really helpful if you and Daniel came into school today to talk about it," she said.

"Is that necessary?" Emily began. "I'm sure it won't happen again."

"Actually, I really think it would be a good idea for everyone to sit down with a counselor. Chantelle's background is clearly having a significant impact on her."

Emily snapped her lips shut. She was trembling, unable to speak. Chantelle had been coping so well. She'd been flourishing. And now Sheila had crawled out of the woodwork and ruined everything.

"It will calm down," Emily replied. But even as she said it she could tell she'd lost her resolve. What if she didn't?

"I know this is difficult," Ms. Glass continued, "but it may be a delayed reaction on Chantelle's part. We needn't approach this like a stand-off. There's nothing shameful about your situation, no one is criticizing you. You're doing a great job in pretty difficult circumstances. We're all on the same team. We all want what's best for Chantelle."

"Yes, of course," Emily whispered, her mind a blur of worries. Could this incident affect the adoption claim? What if Chantelle's behavior at school was taken as an indication that she wasn't best placed in her and Daniel's care? What if seeing a counselor acted against them, like a blemish on their permanent record? Or, conversely, what if refusing to see one did?

Emily's head spun. She had no idea what to do. Calling Richard Goldsmith for advice would be lunacy. She had to make her own call on this one, trust her own judgment as a parent.

"Fine," she said, finally. "If you think it's necessary. When did you want to do it?"

"As soon as possible," Miss Glass replied. "This afternoon. Can Chantelle's father join us as well?"

Emily hadn't expected it to be so immediate. "Daniel's at work. He won't be able to leave at such short notice."

There was a moment's pause from the other end of the line. Then, "Perhaps you could give him a call?" Ms. Glass suggested. "See whether he might be able to make an exception on this one occasion?"

Emily floundered. Ms. Glass was treating this so seriously. Were things with Chantelle really so terrible that she needed to drag Daniel out of work just for a meeting?

But she decided it best to. This was about Chantelle and doing what was right for her.

"Okay. We'll be there."

After arranging the meeting with Ms. Glass, Emily hung up and immediately drove speedily to Jack Cooper's workshop. She parked haphazardly beside it, then jumped out of the car and ran up to it.

She knocked on the garage-style door, making the metal rattle. From inside she could hear the sound of a radio. A moment later the door was heaved up from the other side with a rattle. There stood Daniel.

"Emily?" he said, sounding shocked. "What's wrong?" He reached out and touched her arm.

"It's Chantelle," Emily said, rubbing her forehead. "She hit Toby. We have to go and see a school counselor."

Daniel looked concerned. "Now?" he asked, glancing over his shoulder at the other people working in the woodshop, bent over sanding machines and jigsaws, all absorbed in their work.

"I'm afraid so," Emily said. "Will you be able to leave?"

"Sure," Daniel replied, though he didn't sound particularly happy about it.

Emily watched from the doorway as Daniel went and explained the situation to Jack. Then he came back and led Emily out with a protective hand on the small of her back. He shut the garage door behind him.

Clambering into the passenger seat of Emily's car, Daniel's expression turned into one of concern. Emily wondered whether the same worries were flitting through his mind as they were hers: that this could impact negatively on the legal proceedings.

Emily drove them to the school parking lot. They got out and walked the path quietly, wearing twin expressions of self-doubt. Then they climbed the steps up to the main doors and Emily pressed the intercom button.

"We have a meeting with Ms. Glass and the school counselor," she explained to the secretary. "We're Chantelle's parents."

There was a buzzing sound and Emily tugged on the door, opening it. It felt so strange for her entering the school with such negative emotions. Usually Emily found coming here a pleasant experience.

Daniel and Emily stopped by the reception desk to collect their visitors' badges.

"The counselor's office is just down the hall, third on the left," the receptionist explained.

Attaching their stickers to their shirts as they walked, Emily and Daniel followed the directions and drew up outside the counselor's office. They peered in through the small glass window in the door. Inside, the room looked cozy. It was filled with toys and craft stations. Chantelle was sitting cross-legged on a rug, painting a picture on a low, round table. There was a portly woman sitting in a chair beside her, looking down and speaking with her as she painted. She had a long gray braid hanging down over one shoulder. Ms. Glass was there as well, and she looked up at the window.

"Come in," she called, beckoning.

Daniel opened the door, taking the lead, for which Emily was grateful. She was feeling intimidated by this whole situation and needed him to take the reins.

Chantelle looked up as they came in. When she realized it was them she seemed to shrink, as though she could tell she was in trouble.

Ms. Glass was all smiles as she shook Daniel's and Emily's hands in turn.

"This is Gail, the school counselor," she said, gesturing to the portly woman.

Everyone sat. Emily found the setting very strange and stilted and felt immediately uncomfortable.

"Chantelle has been doing some lovely paintings for us," Gail explained in a soft, lilting voice. "Would you like to see?"

She handed one of the pictures to Emily. Chantelle had painted a woman with white blond hair and blue jeans. In her arms was a baby.

Frowning, Emily handed it to Daniel. When he saw the picture his gaze snapped up to meet hers and she wondered what he was thinking. Chantelle seemed tense as she watched the two of them studying her painting.

Gail continued. "And we've been talking a bit, haven't we, Chantelle? You were telling me about how you were feeling upset before you hit Toby."

Chantelle nodded but kept her gaze in her lap.

"Can you tell Emily and your daddy a little more about that?"

Chantelle just shrugged. "I was upset, that's all," she mumbled.

"There was something else you told me, wasn't there, Chantelle?" the counselor pressed. "About Toby and his family?"

"Toby said his mommy was having a baby," Chantelle said, her bottom lip trembling. "He was excited to have a brother or sister."

Gail looked at Daniel and Emily with a sympathetic look. Emily felt her heart clenching as all the pieces clicked into place. The woman in Chantelle's painting was Sheila. Was she holding a baby because she was pregnant? Was that what she'd revealed to Chantelle in her letter? It would certainly explain why Chantelle had become aggressive toward Toby, because somewhere far away a sibling she may never get to meet was growing inside Sheila's belly. The thought broke Emily's heart.

She looked over at Daniel. The pieces must have fallen into place in his mind too because he'd become pale.

"Is that what your mom said in her letter?" Daniel asked Chantelle. Emily could tell he was trying to speak softly but there was an edge to his voice.

Chantelle remained mute.

"We're not angry with you," Emily added, gently. "You haven't done anything wrong."

Ms. Glass interjected at that moment. "Although Chantelle does need to understand that hitting isn't the right way to handle her feelings."

Daniel glared at her. "I'm sure she understands that," he retaliated.

Gail became the mediator. "Let us give Chantelle a chance to speak," she said. "If she's ready."

But Chantelle just shook her head. Emily didn't want to feel frustrated with the girl but she couldn't help it. They hadn't read Sheila's letter and Chantelle hadn't told them what was in it. Did Gail know? Had some stranger been able to crack through Chantelle's exterior while they themselves had failed to?

Gail swished her long braid over her shoulder and sat back in her chair, looking calmly at Daniel and Emily. "Perhaps now would be a good point to end this session? We can pick it up again next week."

"Next week?" Daniel said, sounding irritated. "I thought this was a one-off."

Ms. Glass became awkward at that moment. "We actually thought Chantelle might benefit from seeing Gail for weekly thirty-minute sessions."

"Who's we?" Daniel said, folding his arms. "Because I certainly wasn't consulted."

Emily could tell he was becoming more fraught. She felt anguished at the thought that his behavior may be noted and put forth during their court custody battles.

"Could you give us a little bit of time to think about it?" Emily said. "Just to get our heads around the idea?"

Gail nodded. "It can be very helpful for children like Chantelle to have the chance to take a bit of time out of the day to draw and play and really think about how they feel."

"Children like Chantelle?" Daniel repeated, his voice becoming slightly acidic. "What do you mean by that?"

Chantelle was clearly picking up on all the negative emotions flying around the room. She curled her arms around her knees, almost as though attempting to occupy less and less space, to make herself invisible.

Emily touched Daniel's arm. She was worried about what effect his attitude might have on Chantelle, and on Gail's and Miss Glass's opinions of them as a family. She quietly but firmly said, "Let's talk about it this evening."

Daniel nodded.

Everyone stood. Gail held the door open for them to stream out. They left the room as a united family, shaken by uncertainty but still standing strong.

Emily paused at the door.

"Thank you for everything," she said to Gail.

Gail nodded. "It's all going to be okay. But if we can encourage Chantelle to express herself through her pictures instead of with her fists that would be a good start."

Emily nodded, certain in her own mind that counseling sessions would be the right thing for Chantelle. It was convincing Daniel that would be harder.

CHAPTER TWENTY

That evening, Emily decided they should all eat dinner together. Daniel had been so busy recently it wasn't unusual for him to just grab something on the go, and Emily had fallen into a lazy habit of giving Chantelle a small meal immediately after school. But today was different. Today they needed to be together as a family and talk.

She set up the table in the living room with flowers and candles, making sure that the environment was as relaxing as possible, and then, while Chantelle played up in her room, she cooked a big batch of spaghetti Bolognese. As she placed it in the oven to stay heated, Parker arrived for his shift.

"That looks nice," he said, peering in the oven. "Special occasion?"

"Kind of the opposite," Emily replied. "Chantelle had a bit of trouble at school today."

"So you're bribing her to behave with Bolognese?" he said with his usual mischievous smile.

Emily rolled her eyes. "I'm just trying to make sure we have a proper meal together as a family. Spend some quality time together."

"You know, nothing says quality time like Jell-O for dessert," Parker said. "I made some yesterday; there's plenty left over for you all." He was already putting on his chef's jacket, turning up the sleeves so he could wash his hands thoroughly before starting work.

"That would be great," Emily said.

Parker flashed her his cocky smile. "Good," he said. "Strawberry okay?"

"That would be great, thanks," Emily said, turning to leave the kitchen.

"Oh, and I'll put the private sign up on the living room door," Parker added. "Make sure none of the guests wander in and interrupt."

Emily was grateful to have support from Parker. Thanks to his help she now had a few spare minutes to spruce herself up before Daniel got back from work, so she went up to the bedroom to change and fix her hair. Finally, she slicked on some mascara, then went to Chantelle's room.

"Dinner will be ready in five minutes," she said, poking her head around the door.

But instead of finding Chantelle playing, she discovered that the little girl was curled up in a ball in her bed, weeping.

"Oh, sweetie," Emily said, rushing in.

She sat on the bed and tried to hug Chantelle. But the girl moved away from her embrace.

This had happened before, Emily recalled, and it had hurt just as much then. When Chantelle recoiled from her affection it felt to Emily as painful as being slapped. All she wanted was to comfort her, but Chantelle blocked her out. Emily sat there, uncertain of what to do.

Just then, Emily heard the sound of the front door slamming. Daniel was home. But it didn't look like she was going to be able to coax Chantelle out of her misery for the sit-down meal she'd planned for them.

"You don't have to talk about it if you don't want to," Emily said softly. "I'm not going to interrogate you. Daddy and I just want to eat together, is all. You can do that, can't you?"

But Chantelle remained mute, locked in her ball.

The bedroom door opened then and Daniel looked in. "Parker told me that we're having a treat tonight. Bolognese and Jell-O! Sounds amazing." He stopped then, clearly noticing Chantelle's state. "What's going on?" he asked.

Emily shook her head. "I think Chantelle's just feeling a bit emotional, aren't you, honey? She just needs to have a cry and then we'll all head down for dinner." She could hear her false reassurance, the pretend breeziness in her voice that her mind was sadly lacking.

Daniel frowned, not buying it for a minute. He sat on the bed beside Emily and the crying ball of Chantelle.

"Now, listen," he said in a caring but authoritative manner, "you need to sit up."

Miraculously, Chantelle responded to her father. She sat up, her face red with anger and tears, her cheeks puffed. The scowl she wore was piercing.

"Good," Daniel said. "Now I want you to tell us what's making you so angry. Is it your mom?"

"Yes," Chantelle mumbled.

"What about her, sweetie?" Emily asked softly. But her gentle approach didn't work. Chantelle was in no way responsive to her. It was Daniel's more demanding tone she seemed to respond to.

"Answer the question, Chantelle," Daniel commanded. "Was there something in her letter that upset you?"

Chantelle nodded.

"Tell me," Daniel said.

Chantelle's bottom lip trembled. "She told me that she was going to have a baby and that once the baby was born she would be able to get a house and then she'd come and get me and we would be a family again."

Emily felt her throat constrict. So Sheila *was* pregnant. Chantelle was going to be a big sister, but not because Daniel and Emily had conceived, but because Sheila had. Emily couldn't help but feel bitter about it.

If the news of Sheila's pregnancy had affected Daniel in any way he didn't show it on his face.

"She can't do that," he told Chantelle using his matter-of-fact voice. "She can't just come and get you whenever she feels like it."

Emily could tell by Chantelle's expression that she just didn't believe him. Her fear was so great that even the reassurance of her father wasn't enough to placate it.

"Even if she has a real house?" Chantelle asked. "Because she always said that was the problem. That if we just had a real house and didn't have to move all the time then everything would be okay and she would be happy and a better mom."

Emily felt emotion rise in her throat. Chantelle talked rarely about her childhood, but when she did, it always upset Emily. There was always some new way in which the child had suffered that Emily had never even considered.

"Did you move a lot?" she asked.

Finally, Chantelle seemed to respond to her. She nodded. "All the time. We'd stay with mom's friends. Then they'd kick us out and we'd go and stay with some other ones." She started to cry again. "I always wanted her to get a house and now she's going to because of the baby!"

Emily sighed, her heart aching as she listened to the complex emotions Chantelle was experiencing. Jealousy that her mom was getting her life in order for her new sibling-to-be when she'd failed to do so for her. Fear that in getting her life in order she'd be taken away from the new home she had found here. No wonder she'd lashed out at Toby and his thoroughly uncomplicated version of a parallel situation.

Just then, there was a knock on the door. Emily looked up, confused, to see Parker peering round the side.

"I had a feeling you guys might be in the mood for dinner in bed with a movie. So I took the liberty of…"

He walked into the room with a tray in his hands, upon which were three bowls of steaming Bolognese, three glasses of juice, and three bowls of Jell-O topped with whipped cream.

Chantelle seemed to brighten at the sight of the food. Parker set the tray down on the bedspread.

"And let's not forget this," he added, pulling a DVD out of his large chef's pocket. It was a Disney cartoon, one of Chantelle's favorites. He popped it in the player for them and pressed play.

As he left the room, Emily gave him a meaningful look and mouthed, *thank you*, touched that he'd gone to such effort for Chantelle, for them all.

She picked up her bowl of food and settled down to share a meal with her two favorite people. Whatever troubles they faced in their future, they could handle them, just as long as they stuck together.

*

"You seem quiet," Emily said to Daniel later that night.

He was sitting in bed, his contemplative face lit by yellow lamplight. Emily came and sat beside him, crossing her legs in front of her on the bedspread.

"I was thinking about Chantelle," Daniel said. "About what we should do about her."

Emily reached out and rubbed his shoulders, feeling the tension pent up within them. "I don't think we need to do anything in particular. We just need to relax for a day or two. Spend some time together in the house, play games, walk the dogs. Do things as a family."

Daniel remained quiet. Emily hoped she hadn't hurt his feelings, that he wasn't thinking her comments were in any way blaming him for always being busy at Jack Cooper's.

"I was actually thinking it might be better to take a bit of time away somewhere quiet," he said, finally.

"A vacation?" Emily asked. "I don't think the school would agree to Chantelle taking time off. They'd think we were rewarding her for hitting Toby." She chuckled at her conjured mental image of Gail and Ms. Glass shaking their heads in disapproval.

"No, I mean…" Daniel's voice faltered. "I mean that the inn might not be the best environment for Chantelle right now."

Confused by the comment, Emily stopped rubbing Daniel's shoulders. He turned to face her and took both her hands in his.

"I've been reflecting on what Ms. Glass and Gail were saying in the meeting. Maybe Chantelle's behavior would be more settled if she herself was more settled. With all the people coming and going and all the parties, it's a lot for a child to take in." He sighed, as if merely uttering these words was painful for him. "After what Chantelle told us about her start in life, living with all those different people all the time, I just don't want her to think it's normal to always be sharing her space with strangers. How will she ever feel secure? How will she ever get any privacy? I don't want her always feeling like she has to adapt herself to whatever random events may be happening around her." He exhaled loudly. "Does that make any sort of sense?"

Was Daniel blaming the inn—and by extension, Emily herself—for Chantelle's problems? She didn't want to wade in with her insecurities, but Daniel was making it pretty clear that he was, even if he was attempting to veil it.

"You didn't say anything about this after the meeting," Emily said, trying to remain calm despite the anger building within her. She rested her back against the headboard, no longer wanting to be quite so close to him. "I thought you disagreed with just about everything Ms. Glass and Gail were saying."

"As a knee-jerk reaction," Daniel admitted. "I felt like I was being criticized. But I've had time to think it through and, well, I agree with them."

"But agree with them over what exactly?" she asked, her throat tightening.

"Over how the disruptions in Chantelle's life are affecting her behavior and about minimizing those disruptions as much as possible."

"And how do we minimize them?" Emily asked. She could tell just by reading between the lines that Daniel had come up with a plan, some way of helping Chantelle that he was now anxious to share with her. She braced for the impact.

Daniel took a deep breath. "I was thinking about moving into the carriage house. It's empty now that Colin's checked out. It would be quieter and far less hectic."

"There's nothing hectic about the inn," Emily said defensively, cutting in. The thought of moving out of the happy home they'd constructed filled her with dread, not to mention the fact that she *needed* to be at the inn in order to run it effectively. "And Chantelle loves it here. Her behavior has just taken a momentary blip because of Sheila's letters. The inn is the most stability she's ever known.

Taking her away from home would be harmful. She'll bounce back in a few days, I'm sure of it."

Daniel seemed to grow exasperated. "You're not listening to me. I'm saying that I don't think she will 'bounce back' if we keep living here. I'm saying she'll keep having these blips because she'll always been dealing with change and fluctuation and all these people traipsing in and out of her life, appearing and disappearing again. I'm not talking about cutting the inn or you out of her life or anything."

Suddenly, it started dawning on Emily what Daniel really meant, what he was implying without saying it directly. He wasn't talking about the whole family moving, he was talking about him and Chantelle moving without her!

Emily started to feel cold all over as she broke out into a clammy sweat.

"I just want to do what's best for Chantelle," Daniel continued. "You understand that, don't you, Emily? And, well, this isn't my house. It never has been. For you it is, sure, but sometimes for me I feel a bit like I'm camping out in your business, and that I've brought my daughter along for the ride."

If she'd felt bad before, Emily now felt as stunned as if she'd been slapped in the face. Had Daniel really just said *my* daughter? After everything she'd put into raising Chantelle, did he really view himself as her sole parent?

"I didn't mean that she wasn't your daughter, too," Daniel backtracked suddenly, clearly realizing his mistake.

"Yes, you did," Emily accused, and she could hear the utter pain in her tone as she spoke. "You meant exactly what you said. You think of Chantelle as yours and yours only, don't you? Admit it."

Daniel's expression turned suddenly very dark. When he spoke his tone was sharp. "Okay, I do. Because she is. She's my flesh and blood. My biological child. Doesn't that give me the right to raise her my way? In my own home?"

Emily couldn't believe what she was hearing.

"How long have you been harboring these resentments?" she demanded, wincing at the spite she heard in her voice. "You know things could be much simpler if you spoke to me openly and honestly about your feelings rather than keeping everything bottled up."

"This doesn't need to turn into a character assassination," Daniel snapped back. "Let's stick to talking about Chantelle and about what's right for her."

But Emily couldn't help herself. Her pride had been wounded by Daniel's words. Her reflexive response to that was to lash out.

"Okay then," she blurted out. "Tell me what *you,* her father, think is best for her, since my opinions no longer count."

"You're being childish," Daniel retorted. "I'm just talking about moving to the carriage house, having somewhere distinct from the inn."

"More like distinct from me!"

"Only because you need to be on site in the inn!" Daniel replied, clearly exasperated by the way the conversation had so quickly soured. "Only because I know how attached you are to this place, and how much you need to be here at the moment. You wouldn't be happy in the carriage house! If you really think about it, you'd be miserable in that place rather than here. I'm not saying we should split up or anything like that, Emily. I'm just saying that we rushed into creating this family unit for Chantelle and it might have been more sensible to take things a little more slowly, to have her settle in the carriage house rather than suddenly having this huge mansion at her disposal. The culture shock itself would be enough to disrupt her behavior."

But Emily couldn't help but feel as though Daniel's words were just attempts to patch up the damage he'd already done. He was backtracking, thinking of excuses as to why he didn't really want her around, and why he wanted Chantelle to himself.

"Daniel, why don't you admit that what you are really saying is that you want to get away from me, too? Otherwise you'd invite me to live with you both in the carriage house." She folded her arms.

"I've already explained why I didn't invite you. You have to be here."

"And if I say I don't need to be here? That I feel as if the inn would run smoothly without me being on site one hundred percent of the time?"

Daniel seemed stumped and Emily felt the bittersweet sting of vindication. She was right.

"Look." She rubbed the tension frown on her forehead. "If you feel so strongly about raising *your* daughter *your* way in *your* house then I'm not going to stop you. Because I do want what's best for Chantelle. But the carriage house isn't your property, Daniel. I need the income from its rental, so you can't just move in there."

Her heart ached as she spoke the words. But it was true. She couldn't just cut off that source of income. Colin Magnum's month in the carriage house had single-handedly kept the inn afloat over winter. Its page garnered the most views on their website, it got the most requests for more information over the telephone. If someone requested to book it out she couldn't exactly downgrade them. It would be bad for business. No, not just bad, it would be the death knell.

But she knew what she was saying, what the consequence could possibly be. If Daniel really was serious about this then she was essentially evicting him. She looked away, not wanting to see his face. Not wanting to hear his answer. Hot tears welled in her eyes.

When he spoke, Daniel's voice was as cold as ice. "You're being ridiculous. All I was suggesting was that we get a bit of space from this place. And now you're kicking us off the grounds?"

Emily turned to him. "I'm not *doing* anything! This is all coming from you, Daniel. This is what you're telling me you want."

"You're giving me an ultimatum."

"You're forcing my hand."

Daniel was growing increasingly angry. "Where are we supposed to go?"

"I don't know," Emily said, feeling her whole body deflate with defeat at the realization that Daniel was serious, he meant this, he was really going to go.

Daniel yanked the covers back and grabbed his sweatpants from where they were slung across the chair. In the darkness, Emily could make out his silhouette as he yanked a shirt over his head, his movements exaggerated and aggressive. Then he snatched up a travel bag.

Emily couldn't take it anymore, couldn't sit there watching him pack up his things. She wanted to reach for him, to pull him back to her and beg him not to take their child away. But he'd made up his mind, and so she did none of those things. Instead, she stood up and rushed away from a sight she never wished to see.

CHAPTER TWENTY ONE

Her eyes blurred with tears, Emily hurried down to the porch with her cell phone. She just managed to type out a text message to Amy. A second later her cell lit up with an incoming call from her friend. Emily answered it with trembling hands.

"What's going on?" Amy asked, panicked.

"It's Daniel," Emily replied, her voice warbling. "He's leaving."

Out on the porch in the darkness of night, under a winter moon, Emily shivered. But it was as if the cold was internal, not coming from the icy breeze but from some deep, dark place that was opening up inside of her.

"I don't understand," Amy said. "Where is he going?"

Emily looked up at the light glowing from her bedroom window, knowing Daniel was inside packing his things.

"It's a long story," Emily stammered, trying to unpick the series of events that had led to this place. "Sheila got in touch with Chantelle and it made her behavior go off the deep end. Then Chantelle told us about being moved around a lot as a kid, and now Daniel's got this idea in his head that the hectic pace at the inn is bad for her. He thinks she needs to be raised somewhere more calming. I mean where the hell could be more calming than Sunset Harbor!"

She could hear her voice becoming shriller and more panicked.

"Okay…." Amy said, drawing the word out as though trying to calm Emily. "So if he thinks the inn is too hectic why don't you rent a cottage together down by the harbor? I could wire you some money if you're worried about rent."

Emily wished she could have Amy's pragmatic mind rather than her own emotional, hot-headed one. How different things would be right now if she'd suggested she and Daniel move to a harbor-side house together and leave the inn to run itself, instead of throwing insults and barbed comments at him?

Emily shook her head. "It's too late for that. He wants to leave. He wants it to just be the two of them." She held her anguished breath in her lungs, unwilling to say the next words. When she finally spoke them, they flooded from her with her exhalation. "He referred to Chantelle as *his* daughter."

"Ouch," Amy replied sadly. Then, in her calming voice, she added, "I'm sure he just needs a bit of time to cool down and think things through. He'll realize it's not a good idea soon enough."

"He's packing right now," Emily replied, and now her anger ebbed away to be replaced by grief.

"He's not going to leave in the middle of the night," Amy replied. "He wouldn't be so stupid."

"Him stupid?" Emily scoffed. "This all happened because of my stupid mouth!"

She deeply regretted the words she'd spoken, words that could not be unsaid.

Amy kept using her calm tone, though it didn't calm Emily one iota.

"Where do you think they're going to go?" she asked.

"I don't know," Emily confessed.

Surely Daniel wouldn't be so prideful as to whisk Chantelle out of her life to some unknown location? But the carriage house had been his home for the last decade and there was nowhere else for him to go.

Then the thought struck her. There was another place Daniel had called home, many years ago. Tennessee. Had she inadvertently forced him back to Sheila, back to the life he'd left behind?

"Babe," Amy said, "I think you need a break. I mean, clearly you do. Come to New York. You, Jayne, and I can go to a spa, get massages. You're running yourself into the ground trying to juggle a business and a family."

Emily pressed her face into her hands, feeling tears roll across her fingers. "I can't."

"Why?" Amy challenged.

Emily stopped herself from saying Chantelle, because that clearly wasn't the case anymore. And the inn was more or less self-sufficient these days. There was Trevor to worry about, but was that really a reason to remain in Sunset Harbor, miserable and riddled with anguish?

"You have a cell phone, don't you?" Amy prompted gently. "You can call them whenever. It's not like you'd be unreachable."

Emily realized then that Amy was right. New York was only an eight-hour drive away. If some unforeseen emergency befell the inn she could just drive back. Not that she was particularly needed in Sunset Harbor right now…

"Okay," Emily said meekly. It wasn't easy for her to admit defeat. "I do need a break from this."

"Good," Amy said, breathing a sigh of relief. "When can I expect you?"

Emily took a deep inhalation. "There aren't any guests due to check in tomorrow and all the shifts are covered, so I guess there's nothing stopping me from heading off right now." She hated that it was true, that she didn't need to factor in who would be taking Chantelle to school tomorrow. "If I drove through the night, I could be with you in the morning."

"You don't need to sleep?"

"I'll drink coffee."

"That's my girl," Amy said.

Emily could hear the smile in her friend's voice. But she herself was unable to match it. There was nothing to smile about.

She stowed her phone in her pocket and climbed the porch steps before stepping back inside the dark inn. She ascended the stairs quietly and entered her bedroom. Daniel was there, still packing. He didn't even look up at her as she walked in.

Emily searched for her courage and took a deep breath before proclaiming, "Daniel. I'm leaving. I'm going to New York City to stay with Amy for a bit."

That got his attention. He looked up from the case, a stunned expression on his face.

"For how long?" he asked.

Emily shrugged and flopped down onto the bed. "I don't know. I don't know anything anymore. I just need some headspace."

"Then take Tracey's yoga class," Daniel said sarcastically. "Don't run off!"

Emily sat up, furious. So when Daniel said he was leaving for some unspecified length of time taking his daughter away from her she was supposed to just accept it, but god forbid she take so much as a vacation!

"I want to be with my friends, that's all," Emily replied. "I want to remember what it felt like to be free of responsibility, to have fun."

"And what should I tell Chantelle?" he said, folding his arms.

At the mention of the child, Emily felt tears welling in her eyes. She didn't want to look weak in this moment in front of Daniel but there was no use. The tears rolled down her cheeks, one after the other, in an ever quickening pace.

"How about whatever it was you were going to tell her when you decided to take her away from me?" she sniped back.

But despite her angry words, Emily felt terrible at the thought of abandoning Chantelle. Even if it was just for a week or two, she didn't want Chantelle to think it had been her bad behavior that had driven Emily away.

Emily wiped the tears away and rubbed her eyes. "I don't know what you should say," she added, her voice meeker now, the fight having left it. "I just know I can't be around you right now."

Then she stood and rushed out of the room, heading next door to Chantelle's. The child was in a deep slumber. She sat beside her on the bed, looking at the beam of moonlight that lit her sweet, peaceful face.

Was she being foolish? Would it be callous to leave Chantelle while she was still asleep, to not be there in the morning to share breakfast with the girl? The argument with Daniel had so quickly escalated, but how could it not have? In what world could Daniel have told her he wanted to take Chantelle away without it turning into such a huge fallout?

The last thing she wanted was for Chantelle to be caught in the middle of all this.

Just then, the girl stirred. She looked up at Emily with her huge blue eyes and smiled a sleepy smile.

"Is it morning?" she asked.

Emily could feel tears well in her eyes, but she would not let them fall in front of the child. She shook her head. "Not yet, sweetie."

"Why are you here then?" Chantelle asked. She yawned. "Are we watching movies in bed again?"

In spite of her sadness, Emily managed to laugh. "No, I just remembered that I'd forgotten to tell you about my trip to see Amy and Jayne."

"You're going to New York City?" Chantelle asked, somehow looking excited and sleepy at the same time.

"Uh-huh," Emily replied, her voice cracking. "So I won't be here when you wake up tomorrow morning. Is that okay?"

Chantelle nodded. "Will Daddy make me pancakes for breakfast like you do?"

Emily snuggled the child, never wanting to let go. She buried her face into Chantelle's hair, smelling her scent, and allowing just a few of her tears to fall into the crown of her head. "Better," she managed to say. "He'll let you put syrup on them."

She heard Chantelle make a noise of delight and, confident the child would suffer no ill effects from her sudden unplanned vacation, let her go from the tight embrace. She tugged the covers up and stroked Chantelle's hair until she was asleep.

Emily stood and left Chantelle's room, her mind now set.

CHAPTER TWENTY TWO

Emily pulled up outside Amy's East Village apartment and killed the engine of her car. It had been a long drive through the night and she was exhausted.

She took her cell from her purse and dialed the inn, not wanting to speak to Daniel. It was Lois who answered.

"Can you put Chantelle on the line?" she asked.

"Sure," Lois replied. Then, through the muffled sound of her hand on the receiver, heard Lois shout out, "Chantelle! It's Emily!"

Emily cursed inwardly. She hadn't really wanted Daniel to know she was calling.

Chantelle's voice appeared on the other end of the line, as bright as ever. "Are you in New York now?"

"Yup," Emily replied. "Did Daddy let you have syrup on your pancakes?"

"No," Chantelle said glumly. "But he let me have strawberries."

"That's nice." Emily tried to keep composed through the conversation, to make sure Chantelle continued to have no idea what was going on behind the scenes, but her mind was reeling at the thought of how long it would be before she saw the child again.

"I have to get my shoes on for school," Chantelle said. "Do you want to speak to Daddy?"

Emily felt she had no choice but to say yes, to maintain the charade. "Yes, please. Have a good day at school, sweetie."

"I will."

She listened to the sound of the phone exchanging hands. But Daniel didn't say a word. Clearly, the lack of desire to speak was mutual.

She hung up and threw her phone back in her purse with frustration, still fuming that Daniel was doing this to her, to Chantelle, and wondering how long they'd be able to keep the pretense up before she realized something was wrong.

Amy had promised to be home when she got there, so Emily went ahead and buzzed the bell to her apartment.

"Em?" she heard the voice of Jayne crackle through the intercom.

Emily hadn't expected to see Jayne. Suddenly, the thought excited her.

"Yes!" she cried. "Buzz me in."

She heard the door unlock and hauled it open. Rushing inside, she practically slammed her palm on the elevator call button. Suddenly everything felt so familiar, so nostalgically exciting. With adrenaline coursing through her, it felt to Emily like the elevator was taking a very long time to arrive, then when it finally did, it felt like it took an absurdly long time to take her to the top floor where her friend lived.

When the doors of the elevator finally opened, Emily was surprised to discover Amy and Jayne there waiting for her. They burst into the elevator, yanking her into a fierce embrace.

"I can't believe we finally managed to pry you away from that B&B!" Jayne exclaimed into Emily's ear. "It only took a year!"

They drew apart and Emily couldn't stop herself from grinning. Even Jayne's blunt and inappropriate joke wouldn't dampen the surge of joy she currently felt.

"Come in," Amy said, leading her by the hand through the corridor. "You must be exhausted."

"I am," Emily confessed. "But I'm also so, so happy to be here. Everything looks exactly as it did when I left."

Jayne gave her a look. "Wait 'til you see what Amy's done to her apartment."

Curiously, Emily walked into Amy's apartment to discover it had been completely redesigned. The old kitchen had been ripped out and replaced with new, swanky, modern fixtures. The wall that had separated it from the living room had been removed, so that the space was now open-plan. Amy's old leather couch had been replaced with a huge new chaise lounge that took up the entirety of one of the walls. All the walls had been painted the same colorless crisp white, and huge light bulbs hung down from the ceiling.

"Wow," Emily gasped. "Talk about redecorating."

"Oh, I know," Amy said, a little embarrassed, brushing off the compliment. She went over to the fridge and pulled out a bottle of sauvignon blanc. "Too early?"

"Never," Jayne replied without missing a beat.

"Actually," Emily said, "I don't want to be a killjoy but I've been up for an absurdly long amount of time and if so much as a drop of that stuff passes my lips I'll become an emotional drunk."

Jayne gave her look. "Let's face it, you're going to be emotional. There's going to be crying. May as well do it drunk. Am I right?"

But Emily wasn't relenting on this one. It seemed far too reckless, even for someone who was supposedly on vacation.

"I don't think Emily wants to drink," Amy explained to Jayne, putting the bottle back in the fridge and closing the door. "And since she's the guest, she gets to call the shots. So, what do you want to do, Em?"

"I'd really like to stretch my legs," Emily replied. "I've been cooped up in my car for hours. How about a walk around Central Park?"

Jayne didn't seem impressed. "I literally just finished a run around Central Park this morning." Amy sent her a warning glance. "But I guess if Emily wants to…"

They gathered up their things and headed out to the streets of New York City. As they walked, Emily felt amazed by the city. She felt so nostalgic, with all the sounds and smells, the city bustle. It was hard for her to even comprehend how she'd once lived here.

At they reached the park, Emily checked her cell phone, wondering and hoping that Daniel had left her a text message professing his mistake, apologizing for his idiocy, and begging her to come home. There was no such text and Emily felt a sting of disappointment.

Clearly putting two and two together, Amy finally broached the subject of Emily's sudden appearance.

"We may as well get the crying and venting out of the way now," she began. "What's the deal with you and Daniel?"

Emily immediately tensed up. She'd spent an eight-hour car journey thinking about Daniel, mulling everything over, and while she wasn't exactly thrilled to go over it all again, it was always healthy to get things off one's chest.

"Yeah," Jayne added. "Like what the hell is going on? Amy told me a bit but it sounds like he's being a total jerk."

They began their walk around the park. Emily tried to keep breathing, to let the foliage of the towering trees keep her calm.

With her best friends, Emily knew she could say anything. She could rant about all of Daniel's flaws and know it would never get back to him, that her friends would listen patiently, would offer her advice and support and comfort.

"I just think he took on more than he wanted with me," she began, and immediately, as soon as the words were out of her mouth and she could actually hear her ruminations aloud, her tears fell once more. "I mean becoming a father was stressful enough. But then he moved in. And then we were talking adoption. Then he proposed. I mean, it's gone from zero to a hundred for him pretty quickly. I think he's just had this sudden realization that this is it, you know? That once he commits to me then he's settled down."

Amy held her hand tightly and Emily accepted her support. She needed it now more than ever.

"What about Chantelle?" Amy asked softly.

The sound of her name was like a knife piercing her heart. "He said that she was *his* daughter. After everything I've done for her. All the sacrifices I've made. It was like a kick in the teeth."

"I'm so sorry, hon," Amy said.

"So did you guys break up?" Jayne asked tactlessly. "How did you leave things?"

"I just walked out," Emily replied. "I just told him I didn't want to be around him anymore and got in my car and drove."

"That is badass," Jayne said, sounding impressed.

Emily smiled in spite of herself.

They continued their stroll, and Emily found her tears finally running dry. Despite her tiredness and emotion, being in the city again felt wonderful. For the first time in a long time, she felt the dark cloud in her mind start to lift. She remembered that life was full of possibilities, that it could change for the better in a heartbeat. When she'd lived in New York City, life had been simpler. Although things with Ben had been irrefutably crap, she hadn't had a home to worry about, or a business, or a kid. She looked back at those years with rose-tinted glasses, with a sense of nostalgia.

"Maybe I should just move back here," Emily said. "Leave all the heaviness behind."

Amy squeezed her hand. "You know I'd be the first to welcome you home, but I know that's not what you want."

Jayne echoed her sentiment. "Have you forgotten what it was like? You hated your job. Ben wasn't the nicest guy in the world. You worried constantly about whether you'd get married and have your own family one day."

Though Emily knew they were right deep down, she didn't recall it that way at all, or at least not now in comparison to life in Sunset Harbor.

"Well then maybe I'm supposed to be a wandering nomad," Emily said, with her tongue only half in her cheek. "I mean, it was *so* great at first, rushing off, leaving any sense of commitment behind. But what did I do? I immediately put down roots, tied myself to a new place. I rushed straight into another relationship. I'd only just gotten rid of my baggage and then I went and got myself a whole load more."

"But that's just life," Amy retorted. "Anywhere you go, anytime you get deep into a way of life or a place or a relationship, heaviness and responsibility and baggage will pile up."

Emily knew she was right, but she was feeling rebellious and didn't want to accept it. "Well, I don't want it. Just for like five minutes can I not be underneath a pile of baggage?"

Jayne laughed. "It's so much easier to just run from it, isn't it?"

She probably thought she was agreeing with Emily but in actual fact her words were enough to give Emily pause for thought. If Jayne thought something was a good idea, it probably wasn't!

Amy continued. "But anywhere you go, if you want to live life and invite it back in, then baggage will pile up again. That's what happens when you settle down, that is what it means to live life! If you run from that, you run from life."

Emily chewed her lip in contemplation. "When did you get so philosophical?"

Amy shrugged. "I don't know. I just know that it's easy to think that if you came back here it would all be less complicated. And yeah, it might for a little while but it will pile up again here, too."

"And let's not forget that you'd be closer to your mom," Jayne added.

"Oh God, you're right," Emily replied, smiling a little at Jayne's humor.

They walked in silence for a while, as Emily mulled things over in her mind. Coming back to New York City really wasn't an option for her. Or at least not if her goal was to minimize life's baggage. That she was stuck with.

"You look exhausted," Amy said finally. "Why don't we go back to my apartment so you can nap?"

Emily did feel very weary all of a sudden, like her feet were made of lead. She wondered if it was the adrenaline finally leaving her body, if the initial high at seeing her friends was ebbing away.

"I think that's a good idea," she said. "Sorry to be a nuisance."

She couldn't help but feel bad, dragging her friends out to the park only to turn around and head back home. Jayne especially, since she hadn't even wanted to come! But thankfully her friends were accommodating.

"Nothing to apologize for," Amy said. "Come on."

Arm in arm, they walked slowly back toward Amy's apartment. This time, Emily reassessed the New York City streets, seeing them not through the heady gaze of nostalgia, but with the harsh reality of her memories. She remembered places she'd been to on miserable dates with Ben, street corners upon which she and her mom had argued, sidewalks she'd paced back and forth while filled with work-related stress. Amy was right. New York City was filled with her baggage, just as much as Sunset Harbor was.

They made it back to the apartment and Emily was just about ready to drop. Her eyes were heavy and sore.

"Take the bed," Amy told her as she headed for the corner couch. "We'll wake you when it's time to party."

She smiled. Emily mumbled her sleepy gratitude, then shuffled off to the bedroom. As she undressed, she checked her phone again, praying for the groveling apology from Daniel that would end her pain right now. But there was nothing there.

Disappointed, she climbed into Amy's bed. The moment her head hit the pillow she felt herself slipping into slumber.

*

Emily fell into a disturbed sleep, her dream coming to her vividly and as sharp as reality. She dreamed she was back in her bed at the inn with Daniel sleeping beside her. She was watching him sleep, as she had done a thousand times before, with the moonlight streaking across his face, sharpening his features and making him look even more attractive. She reached a hand out to touch his chest but the second her fingers made contact with his skin she flinched away. He was cold.

"Daniel!" she cried, kicking the covers away as she heaved herself to a kneeling position beside him. "Daniel, can you hear me?"

Her voice was frantic, filled with desperation. She grabbed him by both his shoulders and shook. But his eyes remained closed. His skin beneath her fingers was cold. He was showing no sign of life.

She burst awake, almost hyperventilating. Sweat was pouring from her brow.

The door flew open and Amy rushed in.

"Em, what's wrong?" she said.

Disoriented, Emily looked around herself at the unfamiliar room. Amy's room. It was only she in the big double bed. No one else. No Daniel.

"Where's my cell phone?" Emily asked.

Amy looked concerned as she came into the room. "Is it in your jean pocket?"

Emily rummaged through the pile of clothes beside the bed until she found her jeans. Sure enough, her cell phone was inside the pocket. There were no missed calls from the inn, just one from a withheld number.

But as she held her phone in her hands, the screen suddenly lit up. A withheld number was calling again.

She immediately accepted the call.

"Could I speak to Emily Mitchell please?" an authoritative voice said on the other line.

"Speaking," Emily said, her chest fluttering with panic. Whether it was from the dream or some weird sense of premonition, Emily's voice had begun to shake. She had the feeling she was about to get some really bad news.

"Ma'am, I'm calling from the Maine State Police Department," the stern voice replied. "There's been a motorcycle accident involving a gentleman who had you listed as his next of kin. Daniel Morey. Do you know this gentleman, ma'am?"

Emily felt as if all the air had been sucked out of the room, like she'd been tackled by a quarterback. It took all her strength to keep hold of her phone.

"Yes," she managed, finding that her mouth had gone tacky. "Is he okay?"

She became suddenly aware of Amy beside her on the bed looking at her with concern.

"Mr. Morey is being taken to Maine Coast Memorial Hospital," the voice replied. "Will you be able to travel there?"

"I'm in New York," Emily said, speaking on autopilot, feeling hypnotized, numb with shock.

"Ma'am," the police officer said with a stern voice, "if you take my advice, I would recommend you travel back as soon as possible."

It was the worst thing Emily could have heard.

"Is he—" she began. But she stopped. She couldn't bear to utter the words.

"I'm not aware of the state of his condition at this point in time, ma'am. But I'd suggest you find a way to the hospital as soon as possible."

Feeling completely useless, completely dissociated, Emily ended the call. She looked at Amy standing beside her and the tears burst from her chest.

"It's Daniel," she wailed. "He's crashed his motorcycle."

Amy gasped, covering her hand with her mouth.

Then suddenly Emily was on her feet, grabbing her jeans and fumbling to get them on.

"I have to go," she said. "I have to go right now. Where are my car keys?"

147

Amy leapt to attention. "Hon, I don't think you should drive in this state. Take a flight."

"I can't leave my car," Emily snapped, turning around in circles in her vain search for her car keys.

"I can drive it back for you," Amy replied calmly. "Please, just fly. It will be quicker."

Emily paused as it sunk in that Amy was throwing her a lifeline. "You'd do that?" she asked. "Drive the car all the way back to Sunset Harbor?"

"Of course," Amy insisted. "Let me book you a cab to the airport, okay?"

Finally, Emily relented. In that moment she had no idea what she'd do without Amy in her life. But her brief respite of gratitude lasted only a moment before worry took over once more, and her mind filled with terrible images of Daniel bloodied and bruised in a hospital bed surrounded by tubes and ventilators.

Just hold on, Daniel, she thought. *I'm coming home.*

CHAPTER TWENTY THREE

Emily was a nervous wreck for the entire flight, her mind going through every possible scenario over and over. Terrified didn't come close to describing how she felt, it was closer to distraught. She'd never felt anything like it in her life.

"Are you a nervous flier?" the gentleman beside her asked, glancing at her white knuckles clutching the armrests.

Emily didn't even know how to respond, how to put into words that her fear was unrelated to flying, that it was potentially far more catastrophic. She decided it was easier to just nod and agree. At least that way she'd have an excuse not to utter any words.

The gentleman smiled. "It's the safest form of transport," he said, echoing a mantra she'd heard Kieran tell her time and time again.

"I know," she squeaked, and it was finally enough for him to leave her and her anguished thoughts in peace.

"Ladies and gentlemen, we're now preparing for our final descent," the air steward said over the intercom. "Please fasten your seatbelts."

Emily hadn't even removed hers since she'd spent the entire flight in a state of suspense anyway, with time moving around her painfully slowly and the whole world seeming to undulate.

"I hope we have a clean landing," the man beside her said with a smile. "If you've ever been in a bouncing Boeing it's not something that leaves you any time soon, let me tell you!"

Emily just nodded and returned to her blank, forward-facing stare. She felt the sensation of plummeting in her stomach that told her the plane was indeed landing. Then at last she felt a bump as the wheels met the runway, and the roar of them turning at high speed as they sped along. Then the plane slowed to a halt and Emily realized that her first hurdle had been overcome. She was back in Maine.

"We made it," the man beside her laughed. "Told ya we would."

Emily smiled politely and unclipped herself before the sign had been lit up because she wanted to make a dash for the door. She had no luggage on her, no carry-on in the overhead lockers, since she'd left all her stuff at Amy's, so she'd hopefully be able to make a beeline for the doors and beat everyone else off the aircraft.

As the steward thanked the guests over the intercom, Emily dashed for the exit. She reached it before they'd even finished their final announcement.

"Ma'am, it's not advisable to leave your seat before instructed," the flight attendant said with a warning note.

"My fiancé was in a motorcycle wreck," Emily said in something of a trance. "I don't know what state he's in. The cop didn't say. He could be critical for all I know. In the ICU. Maybe he died during my flight. I won't know until I reach the hospital. So… sorry, I suppose. I hope you can understand."

The words were tumbling from her mouth before her brain had even had time to think them through. For so many hours she'd been holed up in this aluminum capsule with no one to talk to, and everything had just come out.

The flight attendant's expression turned horrified. "I'm so sorry," she whispered. Then she reached forward, twisted the handle, and opened the airlock door. It hissed as it opened, letting daylight and fresh air stream in. "Good luck."

As Emily hurried out of the plane and along the corridor into the airport, she used her cell to call the inn. Thankfully, it was Serena that answered. Emily had called her with the news.

"Any word on Daniel?" she asked, the frantic edge in her voice clearly audible.

"Not yet," Serena replied. "Where are you?"

"I've just gotten back from New York. I'm heading to Maine hospital. Is Chantelle there?"

"She had a sleepover at Bailey's last night. Yvonne thought it would be better if she didn't know about Daniel's accident yet so she just thinks she was having an impromptu playdate. Yvonne took her to school."

Emily sighed with relief. At least Chantelle had not been suffering. For the millionth time, Emily felt so blessed to have friends like Yvonne, to know people who would rally around her through the hard times. She had no idea how she could express her thanks and gratitude for her.

Just then, Emily reached the frustratingly long line of people heading for the baggage claim area, where she needed to go despite having no luggage because that's where the exit was. She joined the back of the line and took deep breaths as she waited it out.

"Does Ms. Glass know what happened?" Emily asked, feeling terrified about the implications, the possible fallout.

"I don't know," Serena said. "I'm sorry, Emily, I have to go now. There are guests that need tending to."

"Sure," Emily replied, anguished at the thought of losing her only lifeline to Daniel and Chantelle. She briefly considered asking for Parker, just to keep some kind of connection with home, but knew there'd be next to nothing the young man could add to the conversation. "If you hear anything, will you let me know?"

"Of course," Serena replied. Then the line went dead.

Emily checked her cell for any messages from Daniel but there were still none. Whoever said "no news is good news"? What a load of junk. No news in this case was a painful stab through the heart.

Just then the rest of the passengers on Emily's flight reached the line and stood beside her. Emily became suddenly aware of the gentleman she'd been seated next to hovering over her left shoulder.

"Hello again," he said. "I couldn't help overhearing what you said to the flight attendant about your fiancé. I'm so terribly sorry. He'll be in my prayers."

"Thank you," Emily replied, touched to know even complete strangers were supporting her during this trying moment.

She finally passed through the baggage claim and ran full pelt out the main doors. Within a matter of seconds she'd thrown herself into the back of a cab and was whizzing away in the direction of the hospital.

The hypnotic state that had gotten her through the flight suddenly dissolved in the back of the cab, and she broke down in tears. Transporting weeping women to the hospital must not have been an irregular occurrence for the cabby because he didn't say a word about it.

Emily's cell phone buzzed. She looked down to see a text from Amy asking whether there was any news yet. She felt so grateful for her friend, especially since she'd stayed up until 5 a.m. just to stay in touch with her. Emily quickly replied that she was on her way to the hospital and would let her known ASAP.

The cab pulled up outside the hospital entrance. Emily quickly paid the driver and hurried out, in through the double doors, and up to the reception desk.

"Daniel Morey," she blurted at the woman behind the counter. "I'm his fiancée."

Luckily, the nurse was nice and accommodating of her brusqueness. "I'll just see what room he's in." She tapped into the computer then looked up at Emily from the screen. "Six-B. Over there on the left."

Emily thanked her and ran off down the corridor. When she reached Daniel's door, she threw it open wide, not knowing what she would see on the other side. Daniel was lying in a large bed, propped up by white pillows, his eyes shut and breathing shallowly. His hair was a mess, and there was a large gash on his chin. The skin beneath had turned a whole range of purples.

Emily felt her heart ache at the sight of him. She paced into the hospital room and sat heavily in the seat beside his bed. At least there were no heartbeat monitors, no tubes or ventilators. Whatever damaged he'd done to himself appeared to be superficial in nature.

She reached out and smoothed down the tufts of hair. Just then, Daniel stirred. He opened an eye.

"I didn't mean to wake you," Emily said, withdrawing her hand.

"You came back," Daniel slurred.

Emily could tell from his voice he was drugged up on painkillers.

"Of course I did," she whispered. Her throat became thick with emotion. "What did you do to yourself?"

Daniel used a slow-moving arm to pull back the cover, revealing that the other was in a cast. Across his torso there was a huge bruise, so dark it was nearly black.

Emily winced.

"I broke my arm," Daniel said in his sleepy, drugged voice. "And a couple of ribs." Other than that, he appeared completely fine and well.

"And there was me thinking the worst," Emily replied, only half joking. Of course she knew it could have been worse, but it was pretty bad, and the hours of silence hadn't helped matters. "Why didn't you reply to any of my messages?"

"My phone got crushed," Daniel said.

"You could have borrowed someone else's. The hospital's, for example."

"I don't know your number by heart."

"Then you could have told the inn and told them to get in touch!" She was letting the tears fall now. "Do you have any idea how terrifying it is to get a call from the cops saying your partner's been in an accident then have *no* more news? They didn't tell me anything! I spent the whole flight here thinking you might be dying."

"I'm sorry," Daniel said, sounding more lucid than a few moments ago. "I'd just wrecked my bike. I wasn't thinking straight." He maneuvered himself to a more upright position, grimacing in pain as he did so. "I didn't know the cops would call you. I guess when you cause an accident through reckless driving they drop you in hot water with your fiancée. They have to get their kicks somehow, I suppose."

Emily shook her head at Daniel's misplaced attempt at humor. She wanted to stay mad at him but in reality she was completely relieved to know he was okay enough to be making jokes, no matter how unwelcome they were.

Daniel's use of the term fiancée had not gone unnoticed by Emily. It gave her the courage to reach out for his good hand and wrap it in hers. It felt so good to be touching him again.

"I'm sorry for leaving the way I did," she said.

Daniel immediately grasped the olive branch she'd offered him. "Emily, no, I'm the one who should apologize. I don't know what I was thinking. Of course Chantelle is best off at the inn, with you and me. I just freaked out over her behavior and I didn't know what to do for the best and then suddenly I was saying all the wrong things."

Hearing those words was more than Emily could have hoped for. She found herself suddenly kissing his face, all over, again and again. Daniel pulled her into him, matching her kisses with ferocity.

Finally they broke apart.

"Daniel," Emily said, "I think I've been pushing you too much about the wedding. If you want to ease up on the preparations I completely understand."

Daniel looked shocked. Almost offended. "I was going to suggest the opposite. Being in that crash made me realize that more than anything in the world, I want to be your husband. I want to walk you down the aisle and make you my wife. If anything, I want us to plan the wedding quicker!"

Emily could hardly believe what she was hearing. Maybe Daniel had hit his head during his accident and gotten a concussion. Maybe once he'd recovered from it he'd return to the Daniel who dragged his heels. But then, maybe not. Maybe his brush with death had helped him see what really mattered in life.

"Well, I can get behind that," Emily replied, smiling for what felt like the first time in a long time.

Daniel sunk back against the pillow and nodded. He looked fragile, but Emily swelled with the love she felt for him. She was beyond relieved that they were reunited. And while she wished it hadn't taken a motorcycle crash for Daniel to realize what mattered in life, the important thing was that he'd finally come to his senses. They were together again, stronger than ever, and nothing would tear them apart again.

CHAPTER TWENTY FOUR

Luckily, Daniel was allowed to leave hospital that afternoon. Emily drove him back to the inn, then called Yvonne to tell her she didn't need to extend the playdate any longer.

"Oh, thank God he's all right," Yvonne said on the other end of the line. "When Serena told me what had happened I was so worried."

"He gave us all a shock," Emily replied. "Thanks for stepping in. I really appreciate it."

"Tell me to butt out if I'm being intrusive, but is everything okay with you two?"

"Intrusive?" Emily laughed. "More like intuitive. We had a fight. How did you guess?"

"Well, when I spoke to Serena she said you were in New York City with your friends but I thought a vacation would be the sort of thing you would have mentioned to me and figured you must have left in a hurry. What happened?"

Emily didn't much feel like recounting the events that had led up to her sudden trip away. "It doesn't matter now."

"As long as you're okay," Yvonne replied. "I'm just heading out the door to pick up Bailey. Want me to pick Chantelle up too?"

Emily hadn't realized the time. She looked over at Daniel slumped on the sofa looking sorry for himself. Leaving him didn't seem like a good idea. "Actually, that would be a great help."

"Do you want me to explain to her what happened?"

"That's okay. It should come from me."

Emily hung up the phone and went to tend to Daniel, feeling her trepidation at telling Chantelle grow as the minutes passed. Then she heard the sound of slamming car doors and glanced out the window to see Yvonne's car in the drive, her friend helping the children out.

Emily left the living room, heading Chantelle off in the corridor.

"Emily!" Chantelle cried, rushing forward and throwing her arms around her. "That was a quick trip!"

Emily hugged her back tightly. "I missed you too much so I came straight back." She looked at Yvonne. "Thank you so much for everything."

Yvonne nodded and led Bailey out, the little girls waving their goodbyes.

154

Once alone, Emily crouched down so she was eye level with Chantelle and took both her hands. "Now before we go and see Daddy, I want you to know that he got a little bit hurt."

"What did he do?"

"He just had a fall. It's nothing too bad. But he has a cut here." She pointed to her chin. "And a big bruise. He also hurt his arm."

"Poor Daddy," Chantelle said. "Can I see him?"

Emily nodded and led her into the living room. When Chantelle saw Daniel, bruised and bandaged, she gasped and ran to the couch, jumping up beside him. Daniel winced as Chantelle threw her arms tightly around his neck.

"Daddy, what happened?" she cried.

Daniel buried his face in her hair. "I fell off my bike."

"That was clumsy!" Chantelle said, making Daniel laugh.

Emily came and sat beside them. Chantelle turned to face her.

"I've decided that you two need to always be together," she said. "Because bad things happen when you're apart."

"You don't need to worry about that, kiddo," Daniel said. Then he reached out and took Emily's hand in his. "Emily and I are planning on being together forever."

*

Despite the bulky cast and sling constricting Daniel's left arm, he used his good arm to keep Emily close as they walked along the sidewalk together. He was holding her so tightly Emily felt as if he never wanted to let her go.

It was a cold, bright morning, with a thin sun attempting to struggle its way through the clouds. Chantelle skipped behind them along the sidewalk, becoming constantly distracted by bugs and leaves and all manner of things.

Emily felt like things were back to how they were supposed to be, to how they had been before all the bickering and fallouts.

They turned the corner and the wedding venue they'd made the appointment to see came into view.

"You know, you don't have to do this if you're not ready," Emily told Daniel for the hundredth time.

"Of course I want to," Daniel replied with a laugh. "I was the one who made the appointment!"

It was true. The transformation in Daniel since the accident was astounding to Emily. Now he was the one pushing it, wanting to get the wheels turning, acting like they couldn't get married soon enough.

Conversely for Emily, Daniel's accident had resulted in the opposite feelings for her. She almost wanted to slow things down, to enjoy the moments they had together without any kind of goal in mind. Still, she was resigned to go with him because it made him so excited and lifted his spirits, which had been noticeably lower since the accident.

They went inside the large town hall venue and were greeted by a woman called Adrianna, who would be showing them around. She was a beautiful Puerto Rican woman with dark, silky hair and nearly black eyes.

"Please, let's sit," Adrianna said, gesturing to a desk.

As they sat at the desk Adrianna handed them a brochure. They began flicking through the pages, looking at the items on offer, which included catering, table dressings, and flowers. All the prices were printed neatly beside them and Emily swallowed at quite how expensive it all was. This was by far the priciest venue they'd visited, as well as the largest. Daniel's desires had changed since the accident!

Bored by all the wedding talk, Chantelle got her coloring pens out of her backpack and started to decorate Daniel's cast with stars and flowers.

"What happened there?" Adrianna asked, looking at Daniel's arm. "If you don't mind me asking?"

Daniel blushed deeply. "I crashed my bike."

"He was expressing his anger through action rather than words," Chantelle said knowingly, clearly repeating something Gail the counselor had told her. She didn't even look up from her coloring.

"I'm so sorry to hear that," Adrianna said. "Does that mean you won't be working for a while?"

Emily didn't think Adrianna had meant to ask such a loaded question, but she suddenly went cold. It hadn't yet occurred to her that Daniel's injury would mean he'd have to stop working. Had he even called Jack to break the news? What would the setback mean for the adoption proceedings? For the wedding?

"Daniel, we can't afford this," Emily stated suddenly.

Daniel's blush intensified. He whispered out of the corner of his mouth. "It's fine."

"No," Emily said, shaking her head. "It's really not." She addressed Adrianna. "I'm so sorry, this is completely out of our budget."

"We can find the money," Daniel insisted. "We always come through in the end."

Emily shook her head. "I don't want us to. There's no point stretching things to the breaking point. We have to live within our means."

Daniel looked deflated. Emily hadn't wanted to hurt his feelings but he would have to adjust to his new reality and sometimes that involved a case of tough love.

Adrianna remained polite but Emily could tell she was beyond frustrated, that she was annoyed to have had her time wasted. Emily was as well. They should never have rushed back into all this wedding stuff. Daniel needed to recuperate. They needed to slow down.

"I'm sorry to have wasted your time," Daniel finally said, his voice meek and downtrodden.

He handed Adrianna back the brochure and they hurried out of the venue.

*

Once they'd returned home, Emily decided she needed a bit of space, so she went to check in with Trevor. He was looking a little perkier today, sitting in his greenhouse with his fruit trees as he'd recently taken to doing. Emily made them tea, as she always did, and they settled down for a chat. But of course, it was she who ended up divulging her woes, pouring her heart out about finances, about things not going right, about how it had taken Daniel a life-threatening experience to realize how much he wanted to get married, except, ironically, the very same accident had taken away his ability to pay for it!

"I'm sure there's more money to be made with the inn," Trevor said. "The evening meals are going splendidly, so why not introduce brunches?"

"I think Parker would burst a blood vessel if I put any more work on his plate, excuse the pun." Emily smiled.

"Then why not make more of that speakeasy? I hear it's quite popular with the locals but that you only have it open on Saturday evenings presently. Why not have it open all the time? The tourists would love it."

"I don't want the noise disturbing you," Emily said. "I like knowing who is coming and going. If it was open tourists all the cars and chattering could disturb you."

It wasn't that long ago, Emily recalled, that Trevor was shouting at Chantelle for playing too loudly in the yard!

"You ought not factor me in," Trevor said. "I won't be around much longer."

Emily shook her head. That was the last thing she wanted to be reminded of at this moment in time. She felt like there'd been so much upheaval recently, losing Trevor was one blow too many.

"I'm going to miss you when you're gone," she said. Then she suddenly realized how tactless it was to say aloud and held a hand up to her mouth.

But Trevor took it with good humor. "And I you, my dear," he said, patting her hand.

They finished their tea. Emily cleared everything away and then helped Trevor inside the house, settling him into his armchair so he could watch some TV.

"I'm sure everything with the wedding will sort itself out," Trevor told her as she left. "The universe has a way of putting things straight."

Emily noticed the way he looked into the distance, as though searching for something just out of his reach, something he was more than ready to touch. She didn't want to admit it but Trevor Mann was ready to let go of his mortal life. Soon, he would make the transition to the spirit world and once he was gone, Emily would lose the man who was the closest person she had to a father figure.

She wondered whether her own father would ever step up and take back his rightful position, whether the universe really would put things straight for her and send back the man who should be there to walk her down the aisle.

Which gave her a sudden thought. She paused in the doorway and looked back at Trevor. Before she gave her mind time to talk her out of it, she blurted out, "If I was getting married tomorrow, would you walk me down the aisle?"

Trevor turned his wizened eyes up to hers. "But you're not, are you?"

"Hypothetically?" Emily asked cheekily.

Trevor sighed, knowing she'd caught him out. "Hypothetically, of course. I'd be most honored to. But you and I both know you're not."

Emily shrugged and gave him a cheeky wink. "You never know," she said.

Then she skipped out of the house, hoping she'd given Trevor enough reason to keep fighting.

CHAPTER TWENTY FIVE

Emily was busy working behind the desk of the B&B as numerous couples milled in and out of the dining room, living room, bar, and grounds. Emily had seen an influx of couples booking the B&B for the weeks either side of Valentine's Day— probably thanks to Colin describing it as a "perfect romantic getaway" in his piece in the travel magazine—and it was now fully booked. The speakeasy was a huge hit, Matthew's new brunch menu was going down a storm, and Tracey's yoga sessions (rebranded Gentle Yoga for the Loving Couple) were proving incredibly popular as well. Emily couldn't have been happier with the increased traffic since she was the sole breadwinner during Daniel recuperation.

Just then, Serena waltzed in for her shift, slinging her leather satchel onto the reception desk with a thud.

"You are not going to believe this," she said to Emily, grinning widely, a glint in her eye. "Owen finally asked me out!"

She looked happier than Emily had ever seen her.

"That's amazing," Emily gushed. "I'm so glad." Then she let out a breath. "Took him long enough!"

"I know," Serena replied. "Better late than never. I suppose he just needed the Valentine's Day prompt." She picked absent-mindedly at the petals of the red and pink bouquet Raj had delivered that morning. "We're driving out of town. He's taking me to a restaurant."

"But you're both supposed to be working tonight," Emily said. There was no way Lois could handle all these guests on her own, and she'd booked Owen to play a romantic movie soundtrack over dinner!

"Don't worry. I've got cover," Serena said. "Marnie will do the desk. And Alec said he'd help out too." She gave a little shrug. "I thought Owen just played for free, when he felt like it. It's not like you pay him."

Emily let out an exhalation. She wished Serena hadn't taken it upon herself to reorganize the shift pattern. And Marnie was a housekeeper, not a hostess! It should be Emily's decision whether she changed roles or not. It made Emily realize then that the inn was starting to become bigger than she'd anticipated. No longer was it a case of her friends chipping in to help her out. Serena's priorities were changing, especially as she was soon heading into the final year of her studies. She'd been neglecting her work with Rico for Emily's benefit. Maybe it was time to look for new staff.

"What about you and Daniel?" Serena asked, jolting Emily out of her thoughts. "Are you two celebrating Valentine's?"

As though on cue, Daniel came down the stairs. Other than his cast—which was scrawled in Chantelle's doodles and well wishes, not to mention some choice sparkly stickers—he was looking healthy and well put together. Emily felt a spark of fire alight inside of her.

Once he'd reached the bottom step, she sidled up to him and wrapped an arm around his shoulder. Daniel tightened her against him.

"We're off for a cliff walk," she said. "It would have been a bike ride but someone wrecked his bike." She gave Daniel a look of light-hearted disapproval.

"Then we're spending some family time together in the evening," Daniel added.

Neither had wanted to hit the town, to spend the evening out, favoring instead to spend some time as a family. Chantelle's request was to bake heart-shaped cookies and decorate them with sprinkles, so that was the plan. The cliff walk was for Emily and Daniel's private enjoyment while Chantelle was at school.

"Well, enjoy yourselves," Serena said, waving them off.

Emily and Daniel left the inn together and got into Emily's car. During his recuperation, she'd taken over all the driving duties and the pickup truck had sat idle in the garage.

Emily drove them up the hills—which would take them at least a third of the way up the cliffs—then parked in one of the designated bays. The hike would take a few hours and though the wind was brisk, with winter still biting in the air, the first signs of spring were evident, from the lighter evenings to the daffodils just starting to germinate.

They climbed the cliffside path arm in arm, hand in hand, maintaining physical contact with one another the whole time. The beautiful ocean views opened up beside them, the empty harbor looking more like a toy town from this distance.

"It's almost time for the boats," Emily said, remembering with excitement how much fun they'd had together sailing and fishing in the warmer months.

"Knowing me, I'll probably sink it right away," Daniel replied, more than a hint of self-derision in his voice. Then he looked at her earnestly. "I'm so sorry about screwing everything up."

"Wow, talk about an opener!" Emily joked. She stopped walking and took Daniel's hands in hers. "And what exactly did you think you screwed up?" she asked gently.

"The wedding plans," Daniel said with a sigh. "Recklessly taking my bike out like that. Dealing with my upset by riding too fast. Breaking my arm. Taking sick leave from work. The added financial burden. I mean how much longer does the list need to be? I was acting like a moron and I'm so sorry."

"Well, I'd have to agree with the moron part," Emily gently ribbed. "But it's forgiven, okay? Stop beating yourself up about it. The important thing is that we're here, together, still going strong."

Daniel pulled her closely into him, tightening his arms around her. "I love you, Emily," he said. "Sometimes I don't think I deserve you."

Emily snuggled against his chest, smelling his fresh, air-kissed scent, feeling the roughness of his stubbled chin resting against the crown of her head. "I love you too," she said. "More than words can say."

Daniel released her from his embrace. "I think we should speed things up a bit," he said.

"What do you mean?"

"I want us to get married right away."

"On this clifftop?" Emily laughed, gesturing her arms widely to indicate the sparseness of their surroundings.

Daniel shook his head. "How about the first day of spring?" he said.

Emily gasped with shock. "March twentieth?"

It was so soon. Barely even a month away. It was the first time a date had even been uttered aloud. Emily felt suddenly elated.

"Okay," she said, feeling herself getting swept up in the moment, in the excitement, the pleasure. "Let's do it!"

Daniel picked her up and spun her round. In spite of his injury, he was still strong enough to pick her up. Emily squealed as they twirled. Then he set her gently back down.

"March twentieth," he said, taking her hand in his, entwining their fingers together.

She smiled and nodded her agreement. "March twentieth."

Daniel grinned, looking like the cat that caught the cream. They continued their ascent along the clifftops, swinging their hands between them. Emily didn't realize such happiness could exist.

"Now we have a date," Daniel said. "We can think about booking the honeymoon. Wanna hear my shortlist of locations?"

"Of course!" Emily replied, laughing, delighted that Daniel had already put thought into their honeymoon.

He grinned. "Paris for the romance. Thailand for the excitement. New Zealand for the adventure."

"All excellent suggestions," Emily replied. But then a small bit of reality crept back in. "It sounds expensive," she sighed. "We'd never be able to afford flights to the other side of the world."

Daniel looked deflated too. They'd both gotten wrapped up in the moment but now they'd both remembered the practicalities. "You're right. Maybe we should defer the honeymoon until I'm earning again? I mean we saw how expensive the wedding could get when we met with Adrianna."

"Or..." Emily said. She had a sudden idea, one that would save them a considerable amount of money, and one that had been playing on her mind ever since Daniel had proposed. "I know a way we could save a ton of money on the wedding. Then we could use whatever we have for the vacation. But I'm not sure you'll like it."

She looked at him with wondering eyes, worried the suggestion might offend him. He matched her with an expectant expression that urged her to go on.

"We could have the wedding in the ballroom," she said finally.

Daniel looked at her, stunned. "Our ballroom? At the inn?"

"I know it's not the glitziest idea in the world," Emily said hurriedly. "And also maybe a little bit copycat since that's what Amy was planning. And it's not just about saving money." Her words were tumbling out of her in her haste to explain herself clearly. "I think it would be kind of perfect. The inn is what brought us together in the first place. It makes sense that we celebrate that by holding it there."

She stopped and gave him a coy smile.

"Do you know what?" Daniel said after a moment. "I have a confession. I *always* wanted it to be in the ballroom."

Emily gasped. "You did?"

Daniel nodded. "I didn't want to say because I thought you might think I was being cheap or that I wasn't prepared to give you your dream wedding. And then Amy got involved so quickly with all her questions and grand ideas, I thought that was what you wanted. I didn't know how to say otherwise."

Speechless, Emily shook her head, completely thrilled and stunned. Finally she found her tongue. "So we're getting married in the inn? On March twentieth?"

Suddenly it all felt so real. And for the first time since Daniel had proposed, Emily could picture the unique and beautiful wedding they deserved, the one that represented their relationship perfectly.

Daniel nodded eagerly. "We'd better send out the invites. There's hardly any time to prepare!"

They grabbed each other's hands and hurried down the cliffside, both eager to get back home and start organizing.

They were still buzzing with excitement as they picked Chantelle up from school.

"What's wrong with you two?" Chantelle asked when she saw their twin grins.

Emily looked from windshield to Daniel beside her, her hands gripping the steering wheel. "Do you want to tell her or should I?"

"You do it," Daniel grinned back.

"Someone tell me!" Chantelle cried, growing impatient.

Emily looked at her in the rearview mirror. "We're getting married at the inn. March twentieth."

Chantelle's eyes practically popped out of her head as she absorbed the news. "Really? Does that mean no more horrible wedding venue visits?"

Emily laughed. "I guess they have all been rather unpleasant."

They reached the inn, all three chatting with excitement as they entered through the main doors. Serena was still on shift at the reception desk and Emily noticed that she was crying.

"Oh no," Emily said, rushing over to her friend and scooping an arm around her shoulder. "Did Owen stand you up?"

"It's not that," Serena managed through her tears. "It's Trevor."

At the sound of his name, Emily became cold all over.

"What about Trevor?" she stammered.

But she already knew.

"Dr. Patel is over there right now," Serena said quietly. "He hasn't got long left. I think you should go."

Emily didn't need to be told twice. She rushed immediately out of the inn and ran full pelt across the lawn. All happy thoughts of weddings and honeymoons evacuated her mind as she ran. Her focus was now solely on Trevor and what she would find when she burst through his door.

CHAPTER TWENTY SIX

Emily rushed into Trevor's house and straight into his bedroom. Sunita glanced up from a chair beside his bed as she entered, a mournful expression on her face. She stood from her seat and paced toward Emily.

"He's been asking for you," she said.

Emily couldn't help but feel guilty for having been out celebrating with Daniel, living with such carefree abandonment when Trevor was in his lonely home, knowing he was dying.

"Is he—is it—" Emily couldn't get the words out.

Sunita nodded. "He's in his final hours." She looked over her shoulder at where Trevor slept, tucked up in his enormous bed. Every breath he took made his chest rattle. "I'm sure he understands that this is the end." She squeezed Emily's arm. "I think he'd prefer it if it was you with him when he goes. Do you think you can do that?"

Emily didn't even need a second to consider it. Of course she would be with Trevor when he took his last breath, no doubt about it. She'd been out of contact all day, hadn't been with him when he needed her, and she vowed to make up for it now, to stay with him until the end.

But she was scared. Scared to see the moment when Trevor's soul left his body, when the light went out from his eyes. Emily had only ever seen one dead person before—Charlotte, floating face down in the swimming pool—and the memory had been so traumatic she'd blocked it out for close to thirty years. But she was stronger now. She'd learned so much, become more confident, braver. She could do this.

"I'll be just outside," Sunita said as she pulled up the chair next to Trevor's bed. "Call me if you need me."

Emily nodded. Sunita left the room and Emily stepped cautiously up to Trevor's bedside. He was in a very bad way, his skin looking pale and rubbery. Never had he appeared so small, so fragile. The pillows seemed to engulf him.

Emily sunk to her knees beside the bed, trying her best to hold it together. But as she rested her head against the bedspread, silent tears began to fall.

"Emily?" Trevor suddenly murmured.

She sat up and wiped the tears away hurriedly. She reached out for his hand. "I'm here," she said, giving him a reassuring squeeze.

Trevor's eyes were open now, but he was barely able to focus on her.

"Don't die like me," he whispered in a raspy, barely audible voice. "Alone."

"You're not alone, Trevor," Emily implored. "I'm here."

A small, wry smile flitted across Trevor's lips. "*Now* you are." It was clearly a lot of effort for him to speak. He paused between each word to catch his breath. "But I wasted so much time fighting you."

"That's all in the past," Emily told him with a choked up whisper. "Forget about it."

She hated the idea of Trevor dying filled with regret.

"Just because of money!" Trevor continued. His eyes seemed to find hers for a moment, and there was a flash of lucidity behind them. "Money doesn't matter. People. People are what matter." He turned his head, allowing it flop to the side now that the muscles of his neck were too weak to hold it up. "I had to find a way to say thank you. I hope it was enough."

Emily wondered whether he was fully there, fully conscious or whether he'd started his journey to the other side already. She frowned, no longer understanding his words, no longer sure whether he understood them either.

"There's a letter," he said, each syllable he uttered quieter than the last, more strained, like he was having to punch each word out of his chest. His eyes were hardly focusing anymore. "For you."

"What do you mean?"

Trevor's eyes rolled up. He took another deep, wheezing breath. Emily was expecting it to be followed by another, but it was not. Instead of another wheezing breath, Emily heard a sudden, suffocating silence, almost deafening in the absence of sound.

Trevor's whole body slackened against the bed. He was dead.

For a brief moment there was nothing, no thoughts, no sounds. It was like someone had paused the universe. Then Emily's mind caught up and she gasped, feeling tears forcing their way up her gullet.

She sat back, her tailbone clunking against the hard floorboards. But the pain didn't even register. She buried her face in her hands and tears wracked her body, making her gasp, making her wail. The emotion tore out of her chest like some kind of wild beast.

Suddenly someone was behind her. She flinched at their touch, thinking at first it was Trevor back from the dead. But it was Dr. Patel, taking her by the shoulders and drawing her into a hug. Emily held on to her friend, sobbing like a child.

"You were a good friend to him," Sunita said soothingly. "In his time of need, you came through for him. I believe he learned an important lesson about forgiveness thanks to you, even if it did take him sixty-odd years to learn it."

Somewhat comforted, Emily nodded against her shoulder. She took control of her crying and was finally able to remove herself from Sunita's embrace. Like a distraught child, she allowed Sunita to lead her from the room.

"What now?" Emily asked when they were on the other side of the door.

"There's nothing for you to do at all," Dr. Patel said. "I'll declare the death and arrange for the undertakers to pick him up."

Emily was relieved. She didn't think she could handle any official conversations of a morbid nature. She wasn't quite ready to refer to Trevor as a corpse, as a body.

"There's one thing, though," Sunita added. "Trevor wasn't making that much sense toward the end but during one of his more lucid moments he mentioned that he'd like the wake to be held at the inn. He didn't seem to think his house would be an appropriate venue."

"Oh," Emily said, taken aback. Just earlier today she and Daniel had decided to hold their wedding at the inn. Now she was planning on holding a funeral there too. "Of course. I want to honor his final wish."

Sunita patted her hand. "There's no obligation, Emily. It's just something to think about. He may have been confusing things. Most people prefer the wake to be in their own home if it's not at a funeral home."

"I'll plan something," Emily said with confidence and finality.

She was suddenly exhausted and craving affection from Daniel. The thought of breaking the news to Chantelle filled her with dread.

"There's one more thing, Emily," Dr. Patel said as they went to part ways at the door to Trevor's home.

Emily looked down and saw an envelope in Dr Patel's hands. "It's from Trevor. He gave it to me during one of our consultations, the one where his prognosis was reduced. He actually wrote it there and then during his appointment. He told me to give it to you once he'd gone."

Emily read the front of the envelope. Instead of her name, it said *To be opened once the funeral is over.* It had been sealed shut.

Was this the letter he'd whispered about on his deathbed? Emily wondered whether Trevor had written it in order to add a little mystery to her life, to help chip away at some of her grief by giving her something to focus on. A small smile flickered across her lips as she realized Trevor wasn't gone quite yet. There was still a little piece of him inside this envelope, some words he'd composed for her, knowing, she presumed, he may not get the chance to say them.

As she walked out of Trevor's home, Emily held the letter to her chest like it was a precious gem, a security blanket. Things in Sunset Harbor would never be the same again.

CHAPTER TWENTY SEVEN

The door to the inn stood open. On this day, it would be open for all.

Chantelle's handmade signs and balloons informed everyone who ventured near the street that there was a funeral taking place, and thanks to Emily's appeal to the townsfolk, it was clear that many were coming to pay their respects.

After Trevor's passing, Emily had told them all of his illness, and the general attitude toward him had softened.

Karen was the first to arrive, hugging Emily closely at the door. Karen had always been the closest to Trevor, working on the zoning board with him, and had never let the old man rile her. Mayor Hansen, also, arrived early, his aide Marcella in an outfit identical to the one she always wore save for one small detail—it was black.

Derek Hansen shook Emily's hand, which he held tightly in his own in a gentle, paternal kind of way.

"A damn shame," he said, patting her hand over and over. "He left us before his time."

Emily nodded somberly. She felt comforted in Mayor Hansen presence, with his jolly Santa Claus face. She fought the urge to throw herself into a bear hug.

"Please, head on through to the ballroom," she managed, keeping her poise. "Father Duncan is already there."

Derek and Marcella headed off down the corridor, and then the Patels arrived. Emily watched Raj's van creep up the driveway, wondering why they hadn't come in Sunita's flashy black car. But when he hopped out and opened up the back doors, Emily instantly understood why. He'd brought several huge bouquets with him.

Emily hurried down the steps toward the van.

"Raj, you didn't have to do this," Emily began.

But Raj was shaking his head. "Sunita explained everything to me," he told her. "Now I understand why you got him such a thoughtful gift with those fruit trees. I can help you plant them on his plot whenever you're ready."

"Thank you," Emily said softly, though she couldn't yet envisage a time when she'd feel able to do so.

She helped Raj unload the van, and then she, Raj, and Sunita returned to the inn, their arms laden with flowers. Parker hurried to help, taking an enormous bunch from Emily.

"Are these all for the ballroom?" he asked, his face obscured by the incredible arrangement.

"Yes," she said. "I'll follow you in. I need to be with Chantelle."

She turned to Lois and the rest of the inn's staff who had volunteered to be on ushering duty and they nodded in affirmation. Emily was so grateful for them, for everyone in the town. Their support was getting her through a very tough time.

Inside the ballroom, rows of chairs had been placed facing Trevor's coffin at the front. Chantelle sat in the front row as though guarding over Trevor. She looked too grown up in her black smock. Emily wished she could have protected her from this pain.

Daniel sat beside Chantelle, wearing a suit that rarely saw the light of day. Jack Cooper was a few rows behind them, here to support Daniel but also keeping a respectful distance.

Emily went up to Daniel and sat beside him. "Look what Raj brought," she said.

Daniel glanced behind and saw the bouquets that were being positioned around the room. He looked as touched by the gesture as Emily felt, and gave Raj a nod of gratitude.

"How is she?" Emily added in a whisper, looking at Chantelle, with her serious, drawn expression, chin tipped upward as though saving face.

"She's okay," Daniel replied. "She's coping."

Just from his inflection, Emily could hear the sorrow in his voice, and the same desire to protect Chantelle from any more harm that she shared. Seeing their daughter grieve was a new pain for them both.

Emily settled into her seat. More and more townsfolk streamed into the ballroom, from Tracey to Jason, Cynthia to Alec; even Richard Goldsmith came along to show his respects. It warmed Emily's heart to know so many of them would go out of their way for Trevor, even when he had shown them little in the way of friendship during his life.

Father Duncan's ceremony was comforting. Emily could sense that Chantelle in particular was soothed by it and hoped it would go at least some way in comforting the child. Then the congregation moved to the dining room for snacks and the sharing of commiserations.

It was only after the last guest had trickled away that Emily found herself with enough time to open Trevor's letter. She went up to her father's study, a place where she always felt supported, and sat down at his desk. Then she opened the envelope, unfolded the letter, and began to read.

Emily my dear,

I have had plenty of time to think things through over the last few months. There is nothing quite like the knowledge of one's own impending demise to motivate a thorough spring cleaning of personal affairs! To cut to the chase, I met with my attorney shortly after my diagnosis, to get things in order with my estate. Emily, I am leaving it all to you. The house. The grounds. Everything. You may do with it what you wish.

You have been a true friend to me, Emily. I hope my house goes some way in helping you live the life you deserve.

Trevor

Emily was stunned. She'd managed to hold it together throughout the entirety of Trevor's funeral, throughout the small talk and well-wishers, even through the times when she'd had to comfort Chantelle. But now she could hold it together no longer.

Her tears began to fall, splashing onto the letter, smudging the ink of Trevor's writing. She folded it away quickly, not wanting to damage the last correspondence with Trevor she would ever have. But even once it was tucked out of sight in her pocket, the words she'd read were still burned onto her retina.

Trevor had left her the house? She could hardly believe it. The tables had truly turned, the wheel had turned full circle. It made her head spin to think of how much her life had changed, how completely, how a man she had once deemed an enemy had become a friend. Once, he'd tried to ruin her life; now, he had changed it irrevocably.

She stood and went to find Daniel, her heart hammering as it began to sink in what this truly meant for them. She found him in the living room, the fireplace roaring, a slumbering Chantelle resting against him with the dogs snuggled up to her. It was a snapshot of a perfect family, only it was tinged with sadness.

Daniel looked up at her as she came in. "Where have you been?"

"Daniel, I have news," she said seriously. There was no point beating about the bush. "Trevor left us his house."

Daniel's eyes widened with surprise. "Are you sure?"

"One hundred percent sure," Emily said, handing the letter to Daniel. "He says we can do whatever we want with it. Sell it or keep it. There are no conditions."

Daniel sat up, straight-backed, scanning the words of the short letter. Then he looked back up at Emily. "How will we decide what to do?"

Emily felt her whole body begin to tremble. With every passing minute, it became clearer and clearer to her what an incredible gift Trevor had given her, had given them all.

"I don't know," she said.

She stood, her body agitated, excited, and went over to the window. She looked over, and just through the hole in the hedgerow she could see Trevor's house, now shrouded in darkness.

"We don't need two houses," Daniel continued. "And he kept it immaculately clean so it won't be hard to sell. Although, we could move in there, couldn't we? Then turn this completely into the inn." He started talking very quickly. "Or we could make the new house an extension of the inn? Oh my goodness, there are so many options. Should we go and look at it?"

But Emily remained silent, her gaze fixed on the house that Trevor had given her.

"Not yet," she said softly. "It's too soon. I am not ready yet. One day soon, but not today."

CHAPTER TWENTY EIGHT

It was March thirteenth. Spring sunshine warmed Emily's skin as she sat out on the balcony for the first time this year, her cell phone wedged between shoulder and chin, chatting with Amy. It was a bright, beautiful day, made brighter by the sight of the first crocuses of spring blooming in the lawn below her. Spring was coming to Maine and Emily for one was welcoming it.

"I can't believe it's only one week until your wedding!" Amy said on the other end of the line.

Emily smiled to herself, recalling the flurry of wedding preparations she'd made over the last few weeks. Everything from the style of tables (two long banquet tables for either side of the ballroom) to the food (local Maine lobster) to the color scheme (white and rose gold). "I can't believe you and Jayne will be here this evening. And that you're staying for a whole week!"

"I can't wait to see you."

"Me neither," Emily replied. And she really meant it. The last few months had been turbulent. She wanted her friends with her so much.

After she and Amy ended the call, Emily swiveled on the stool to discover that Chantelle was standing in the doorway. The little girl was grinning widely.

"One week," she said in a sing-song voice, coming into the room and hopping onto Emily's bed.

Thanks to Chantelle, there was quite a buzz in the air. Although it wasn't just the little girl's enthusiasm causing it. All of the staff members seemed light-footed and breezy as they went about their duties. Perhaps it was the feeling that spring was almost coming to Maine that had lightened everyone's spirits, or perhaps they really were all that excited for the upcoming nuptials.

"I've been practicing," Chantelle said.

"Practicing what?" Emily asked.

"My flower girl duties." She leapt off the bed and began to walk slowly across the floor, miming tossing petals from one side to the next with a theatrical flourish.

Emily laughed. "Very good," she said.

"And," Chantelle said, swiveling on the spot to face Emily, "Owen has been practicing too."

Emily could hear the sound of piano music in the background, something she'd become quite accustomed to. But something about these particular pieces was somehow even more beautiful, more evocative. Emily couldn't imagine how Owen's playing could be even more magical but he had somehow managed it. She wondered if it had something to do with the fact that he and Serena were attending the wedding as each other's plus one.

"Emily!" Daniel called up from the hallway. "Liquor delivery! You need to sign!"

Emily held Chantelle's hand and they went downstairs together. The liquor delivery was three times the usual size, because this time it had to stock the speakeasy, the inn, *and* the wedding.

"Wow," Emily gasped, looking at the stacks of boxes that awaited her. "If I was worried about us getting a reputation before…"

She scribbled her signature onto the paper and the deliverers began bringing the boxes inside. As they did, Emily and Daniel saw another van pull up.

"Banquet tables!" Daniel said. He seemed thrilled about this, more enthusiastic than Emily had ever seen him. "I can't wait to see these."

"Oh, shoot," Emily said. "There's a yoga lesson taking place in the ballroom. We'll have to store these in the outbuilding for now."

She went outside and trotted down the porch steps to the deliverers. It was a warm day for this time of year in Maine and she felt the sunshine kiss her skin.

After signing off on the delivery—her signature little more than an excited scrawl—Emily led them round the side of the house to the outbuilding that was mostly watertight. It would only be for a few hours, she reasoned, then she'd get Daniel and Parker to move them back to the ballroom once Tracey's "Mature Ladies" class was over.

Once they were in place, Emily walked back outside into the warm day. The warmth made Emily smile, and gave everything a dreamlike quality. Another winter was over, and though it had been tough—with Trevor's passing, Chantelle's meltdown, and her and Daniel's terrible fight—there had been some wonderful moments also. Chantelle singing at choir. The discovery of the speakeasy. The fabulous parties. There were so many things to be grateful for.

Emily went to skip up the porch steps and was surprised to see the back of a man standing at the door. She wondered if there was another delivery but the man had nothing with him. Perhaps it was a guest who'd left their key and needed to be let into the inn.

"Can I help you?" Emily said, as she grasped the banister to the porch steps and swung herself up the first few steps.

The man turned and Emily stopped in her tracks, stunned. She stepped back once, twice, until her feet found solid ground again and there was nowhere left to go.

She had felt like she was dreaming but she knew she couldn't be. Because the face now staring at her was one she'd seen a thousand times in her dreams. Only in her dreams, his face was the same as the last day she had ever seen it. But this face had been aged by time, by the twenty years that had passed since she'd last set eyes on it.

Emily's heart raced as she stared at the man. Then a small, single word escaped her lips.

"Dad?"

COMING SOON!

FOREVER AND A DAY
(The Inn at Sunset Harbor—Book 5)

"Sophie Love's ability to impart magic to her readers is exquisitely wrought in powerfully evocative phrases and descriptions….This is the perfect romance or beach read, with a difference: its enthusiasm and beautiful descriptions offer an unexpected attention to the complexity of not just evolving love, but evolving psyches. It's a delightful recommendation for romance readers looking for a touch more complexity from their romance reads."

--*Midwest Book Review* (Diane Donovan re *For Now and Forever*)

FOREVER AND A DAY is book #5 in the bestselling romance series The Inn at Sunset Harbor, which begins with book #1, For Now and Forever—a free download!

35 year old Emily Mitchell has fled her job, apartment and ex-boyfriend in New York City for her father's historic, abandoned home on the coast of Maine, needing a change in her life and determined to make it work as a B&B. She had never expected, though, that her relationship with its caretaker, Daniel, would turn her life on its head.

In FOREVER AND A DAY, Emily is stunned to finally, after 20 years, meet her missing father—just a week before her wedding. Their reunion changes both of their lives, and unlocks the key to the house's many secrets, and to Emily's missing memories.

Spring has finally arrived at Sunset Harbor, and with just a week to go until the big wedding date, the wedding preparations are busier than ever, including Daniel's surprise talk of a honeymoon. Will Emily and Daniel have their dream wedding? Or will someone appear to tear it apart?

Meanwhile, Chantelle's custody battle comes to a pitch, and as Memorial Day looms, they must figure out what to do with Trevor's house. Yet amidst all of this, another issue weighs most heavily on Emily's mind: will she herself ever be pregnant?

FOREVER AND A DAY is book #5 in a dazzling new romance series that will make you laugh, cry, keep you turning pages late into the night—and make you fall in love with romance all over again.

Book #6 will be available soon.

"A very well written novel, describing the struggle of a woman (Emily) to find her true identity. The author did an amazing job with the creation of the characters and her description of the environment. The romance is there, but not overdosed. Kudos to the author for this amazing start of a series that promises to be very entertaining."

--*Books and Movies Reviews*, Roberto Mattos (re *For Now and Forever*)

Sophie Love

A lifelong fan of the romance genre, Sophie Love is thrilled to release her debut romance series, which begins with FOR NOW AND FOREVER (THE INN AT SUNSET HARBOR—BOOK 1)

Sophie would love to hear from you, so please visit www.sophieloveauthor.com to email her, to join the mailing list, to receive free ebooks, to hear the latest news, and to stay in touch!

BOOKS BY SOPHIE LOVE

THE INN AT SUNSET HARBOR
FOR NOW AND FOREVER (Book #1)
FOREVER AND FOR ALWAYS (Book #2)
FOREVER, WITH YOU (Book #3)
IF ONLY FOREVER (Book #4)
FOREVER AND A DAY (Book #5)

Printed in Great Britain
by Amazon